I got out of the car and, without thinking, slammed the door.

A voice called out. It was just one word—one syllable—that might have been ''Help!'' or might have been a name. It was off to my right, toward the fading sunset.

Well, they knew I was out here by now, so I tore off into the brush while trying to imitate the Seventh Cavalry. It was rough going . . . I stumbled half a dozen times, but kept going, not knowing if it was the right direction or not, until I found I was heading up a slope.

Then I heard another noise . . . an engine being started. It wasn't a car engine, but something smaller, more rackety. It dopplered away from me as I scrambled up the slope toward it.

I went right over the edge. . . .

Getting up, I saw a dry wash below me. I had fallen halfway down the slope. The other side was odd—it rippled, light, dark, light, like aurora borealis.

I can't say I was thinking clearly. I pushed forward, then slipped and slid down the slope and hit the bed of the wash. It was all gravel and sand, very flat. Very dry. Nothing moved. I could no longer hear even faint desert noises. And, looking up, I could have sworn that Venus was gone—or moved. I must have hit my head. I headed toward the middle of the wash. Suddenly a wall of water hit me, and I was swimming.

And somehow it had become midmorning, because the sun was shining and I could see clearly the other side of the creek I was in. So I swam toward it. . . .

Edited by Michael Cassutt

Sacred Visions (with Andrew M. Greeley)

MICHAEL · CASSUTT

DRAGON SEASON

TOR
fantasy

A TOM DOHERTY ASSOCIATES BOOK
NEW YORK

This is a work of fiction. All the characters and events portrayed in this book are fictitious, and any resemblance to real people or events is purely coincidental.

DRAGON SEASON

Copyright © 1991 by Michael Cassutt

A Tor Book
Published by Tom Doherty Associates, Inc.
49 West 24th Street
New York, N.Y. 10010

Cover art by Alan Gutierrez

ISBN: 0-812-50392-9

First edition: December 1991

Printed in the United States of America

0 9 8 7 6 5 4 3 2 1

For Cynthia

"Before there were nukes, there were dragons."

1

I had this TWA flight from Guam via Honolulu and Phoenix, which put me into Tucson at eleven on Sunday night, August 24, which was noon of Monday the 25th, as far as I was concerned. By the time I walked off the plane I had read two paperbacks (one Ludlum and, like every third person on the plane, the new Tom Clancy), the *Air Force Times*, and *TWA Inflight*; consumed three meals of airline "chicken," a dozen cups of coffee or Coke; and (occasionally) managed to sleep next to, successively, one oversized clothing retailer from Sherman Oaks, California; one nineteen-year-old jarhead; and one twenty-seven-year-old refugee from a religious commune.

I felt like ten miles of bad road. And Maia wasn't there. I had worried about that.

We hadn't seen each other in eight months. Twice my unit was placed on alert just when I was supposed to go on leave. First it was something to do with rumors of a new series of Soviet missile tests, then Seventh Fleet maneuvers in the Sea of Okhotsk. Then a guy named Barry Owings, my relief, gave himself a compound fracture of the right anterior tibia in a softball game between Det 422 and some overly enthusiastic boys from the 432d Tactical Fighter Wing at Misawa, earning himself an extra month on Honshu and costing me an extra month on Guam. All of this meant that, through no one's fault, I had spent eight straight months, from January through August, on Okinawa, Guam, or Honshu. No USA. No Maia.

We had not parted on the best of terms. In fact, just days before I shipped out we'd had our first, last, and only major fight. But by late March, after two months of silence, I had broken down and phoned her . . . and two days later received a postcard she had mailed before the call.

Since April we had written a lot. And I personally spent over $260 on phone calls. But, still, we had not seen each other since the end of last year . . . and that is a situation guaranteed to take the heat out of the best relationship. So here I came off the plane in my rumpled blues, half expecting to find no one waiting.

The plane was a 767 and it had been about two-thirds full, so by the time I managed to disembark (I'd been seated about row 50), the arrival area was completely jammed. I searched for Maia's face. There was a baby crying somewhere.

After a few minutes of this I cornered the ticket agent, a no-nonsense woman in her fifties. "Did a woman named Maia Chios leave a message with you?"

The agent raised a finger, effectively putting me on hold. I doubted she heard me at all, since that baby was really yelling now. Everyone else was starting to notice. "Excuse me, but first let me check on that baby. I'll be right back."

I leaned on the counter, thinking, okay, so Maia hadn't shown up. There could be all sorts of perfectly good excuses. The ever-popular car trouble. A sudden change in work hours, though the university library wasn't open this late in summer.

If only that baby would shut up!

It also occurred to me that this might just be an unusually creative version of the classic Dear John letter. After all, we had only known each other for a year, total—much of that spent apart. We had not pledged undying love . . . Maybe it was time to head up to the second-floor servicemen's club and beg a ride to Davis-Monthan.

"Lieutenant?" It was the TWA ticket agent. "Were you asking about a Maia Chios?" She pronounced it right: *MY-ah kee-OHZ.* I guess she *had* been listening.

I nodded. The agent dragged me over to a row of seats, where a Continental agent was calming a very unhappy infant. One of those massive yuppie strollers was here; next to it was an overturned baby bag that had spilled Pampers and formula bottles all over one of the chairs. My TWA agent—Hazel was the name on her badge—handed me a wallet.

"This wallet, and by implication, this child, belong to a Maia Chios, 1221 East Ninth."

Continental cooed and held the baby close. I looked at the driver's license. It was Maia's, all right. "That's her address, but I don't know anything about any child. Uh, she's not even married." Well, I didn't *think* she was married. Twelve hours in an airplane, remember?

"Poor little thing," Hazel said, patting the baby. "A little boy?" Continental nodded. "How old, do you suppose?"

"Less than a month," the other agent said.

"Good heavens."

"Maybe she went to the ladies' room," I suggested.

The Continental agent, a very thin young woman with a bad complexion, looked at me sadly and sighed. "*I* wouldn't . . . but I suppose you never know." She handed the baby to Hazel and sprinted off.

"I haven't held one this small in thirty years," Hazel said. She looked me over. "Are you the daddy?"

"Just a friend."

"He seems to have your eyes."

I had about three seconds to fit my head around that idea before Continental came back. "Nobody in there named Maia."

"It's time to call security," Hazel said.

"Name," the man in the brown herringbone jacket said.

"Richard Earl Walsh."

He was writing this down. Hazel was holding the baby, who, after a diaper change, a bit of formula, and some gentle rocking, had fallen asleep.

"And you are a first lieutenant, U.S. Air Force," the man said with a hint of satisfaction. Well, a lot of people can't read military rank. Like everyone else I'd met in the airport, this guy had a plastic badge clipped to his coat pocket. Vic Roelke was the name. "Your cooperation is appreciated."

"I'll do what I can."

"Stationed at D-M?"

"Officially, though, I'm TDY at Guam at the moment. Andersen Air Base."

"So you have no local address."

"I was, ah, planning to spend some time here with Miss Chios. I'm awaiting orders for my next PCS. Permanent change of station."

"And you know nothing about this child?"

"No."

"And nothing about Miss Chios's whereabouts?"

"No. I mean, she was supposed to meet me when I got off the plane."

Vic frowned and began looking through Maia's belongings, which were piled on his desk. There was the baby bag, her wallet (she never carried a purse), and a set of familiar car and house keys (she drove an old Mazda). The bag turned out to have Maia's name and address on it.

And there was the baby. The baby boy.

He had a full head of dark hair and was wearing some kind of fuzzy white sleeper. He seemed healthy and, for the moment, happy in Hazel's arms.

It was clear that he belonged to Maia . . . but did he also belong to me?

"In case you're wondering," Vic said, "his name is Gus." He had found a prescription bottle in the bag. He went through the wallet.

"Vic," Hazel said quietly, "are you going to call the police?"

"What choice do I have?" He turned to me. "Is Miss Chios the sort of person to walk off and leave an infant in an airport?"

"No."

"Didn't think so." He sighed and looked unhappy. "Son, you do know what this looks like, don't you?"

"I'm trying to figure it out."

"I don't know any other way to put it, but we've seen situations like this a couple of times before. Hazel, remember the Steiner girl?"

Hazel didn't answer. I said, "What happened to the Steiner girl?"

"It was ten years ago, I think. Laurie Steiner was this young woman, maybe twenty-three, here to meet her husband, who was coming back from overseas. He came off the plane and she was gone. She just disappeared. Her car was found in the parking lot."

"Where was she?"

Vic didn't answer. Finally Hazel said, "About five months after she disappeared, they found a body in the desert."

5

Something like that had been percolating in the back of my caffeine- and fatigue-racked brain. The thought that something awful had happened to Maia. You never want to start thinking it . . . as if acceptance of the possibility makes it more likely. But Maia would *never* have left her baby alone in the airport.

"Jesus."

"Now," Roelke said, "there's no reason to get upset. We've got no evidence of any foul play. The little guy is reason enough to call the police." It was a nice try, but I was not reassured. "Uh, you're probably going to have to keep yourself available to answer some questions, Lieutenant."

"I wasn't planning to leave town." I realized I was on my feet.

"Where are you staying?" Hazel asked quietly.

I hadn't given it much thought. "I suppose I can get into the VOQ at the base . . ."

Hazel was giving Roelke some kind of look, enough to make him drop his ballpoint. "Hazel, it's late. What are you trying to tell me?"

"What do we do with Baby Gus?"

He stared at her. "What do you think? The police'll come, I'll fill out a pile of paperwork, they'll take the kid, do some more paperwork, and he'll wind up with some social worker. And, yes, it's a terrible idea, but what else am I supposed to do? *I* can't keep him."

She nodded in my direction. "But couldn't *he*?"

Me?

Hazel pressed her case. "Vic, it's almost midnight. By the time the police get here it'll be one. This child won't be settled somewhere until the middle of the night, and then it'll be with some unhappy stranger. Ordinarily I'd be forced to agree with you, but this situation is different. Here's this fine, upstanding young gentleman who's a friend of Miss Chios's. He's supposed to stay at her place. That's where this child belongs.''

Roelke closed his eyes. I knew the feeling. I was getting a headache, too. Then he opened them. "Lieutenant, would you excuse us for a moment?"

Hazel promptly handed the baby to me and ushered me out the door. Little Gus was surprisingly light. He smelled good . . . fresh, somehow, even after all he'd been through. Like new life. Tiny, tiny hands. He merely yawned and opened his mouth a couple of times when Hazel made the switch, then burrowed into my neck.

Most bachelors and a lot of fathers panic when an infant is placed in their arms, but I've held babies before. My older sister Kate has a three-year-old. When Molly was born, we were all living in Omaha, so I was a frequent visitor and part-time baby-sitter. I can change a diaper, warm a bottle, and rock a baby to sleep. When they're a certain age, babies don't require much more maintenance than that. As we say in my line of work, I was operationally capable of handling Baby Gus for a little while.

But the question was a political one.

Hazel hadn't closed the door all the way, so I heard key portions of their discussion. Roelke kept coming back to words like "liability" and "responsibility" and "lawsuit" while Hazel countered with "common sense" and "Make up your own mind!" and "How would you like to have your new grandson handed over to strangers?"

Just as suddenly, it was over. The door opened; Hazel appeared carrying the baby bag and Maia's house keys, and just like that the three of us were heading down the hall.

"What did you tell him?"

"Nothing! He talked himself into it."

I'm sure. "Hazel, if I'm ever court-martialed, I want you defending me."

A hint of a smile crossed her face as she traded me the

bag and the keys for Gus. "You're very sweet, Lieutenant, and I suspect you actually *could* be trusted with this little boy . . . but I'd be out of my mind to turn this baby completely over to you. The idea is to keep Gus out of the clutches of 'social workers' long enough for some relative to come for him. That takes two of us. So we're in it together. Come on."

I hadn't been in Tucson in eight months, but even in that time you could see the signs of new construction all along the airport access road. What had been nothing more than scrub desert—beige ground covered with the occasional stunted plant—was turning into scrub development—beige ground covered with rows of stunted buildings. I guess there's some law that says high-tech operations have to look like Bekins self-storage units.

I'm originally from the Midwest, which is not, as you might expect, Utah or Colorado—the middle of the West—but Minnesota, Wisconsin, and Iowa. Green places, by and large. Stepping off the plane in Tucson a year ago on a hot August afternoon, having lived in green places all my life, I thought I had been sentenced to a lingering death in a brown hellhole. Everywhere you looked, things shimmered in the heat. They say the angular size of the sun is about that of a quarter held at arm's length, but this one was more like a blinding white basketball stuffed in your face. Nothing moved. The only notable odor in the air was that of diesel fuel. On the ride to D-M all I saw were squat little adobe cottages on patches of arid ground. Cars on blocks in the front yards. Graffiti in a language that was not English and probably not even Spanish. And nothing moved.

At night, though, especially in late summer, the place is blessed with a monsoon that sneaks up from the Gulf of Mexico and bumps into the Santa Catalinas, where it lets loose an hour-long barrage of lightning and heavy rain which washes away the heat and dust. The hundred-plus temperatures give way to those in the seventies. You don't see the dirt and the scrub, only the lights. It's very comfortable—even invigorating. Had I not been on such a sad mission, I would have begun to feel great.

I waited with Gus at Maia's Mazda, which was in short-term parking, while Hazel picked up my one bag and her own car, a new Beretta. The two of us got Gus strapped into his baby seat—it faced backward in the front passenger position—and traded keys. I took Hazel's car and led the way while she followed with Gus in the Mazda.

We headed out of the airport, west on Valencia, north on Park, through South Tucson and close to the old city center, all the way to Ninth, where we turned right. Since Maia worked at the university, she needed to be close— easy commuting is not one of Tucson's amenities—and her apartment was just a few blocks south of the campus.

In the daytime it was a depressing-looking place, a one-story brick building with a front yard made of gravel and a backyard—well, five feet from the back door there was a culvert. At night it merely looked lonely. I carried my bag and Hazel carried Gus.

There had been some changes inside. What was the living room had become Maia's bedroom. The sole bedroom had been turned into a nursery. A little animal border ran around the walls where they joined the ceiling. A crib had replaced the bed; a changing table stood next to the dresser.

Oh yeah: across one wall of the living room stretched a big printout banner saying, "Welcome home, Rick!"

"Well, I guess we can put *some* of those suspicions to rest, can't we?" said Hazel as she lay the oblivious Gus in the crib. He was a cute kid, allowing for his age, meaning he bore no resemblance at all to Winston Churchill. If he was mine as well as Maia's, an idea I was not allowing

9

myself to consider seriously, I had every right to be pleased.

But at that moment all I felt was equal parts fatigue and fury.

Hazel must have seen this. As we tiptoed out and gently closed the door, leaving it open only a crack, she nodded toward the kitchen. "I can think of two people who need a drink, how about you?"

"What kind of blue suiter are you, Lieutenant?"

We were sharing what was left of a bottle of white wine. I don't know what kind; if the bottle doesn't have a screw cap, it's generally all right by me. "Call me Rick," I said. "Unless you want me calling you Mrs. Hazel."

She laughed. "It's officially Mrs. Swensen, but Hazel will do, thank you."

"Won't Mr. Swensen be wondering where you are?"

"Mr. Swensen is deceased."

"I'm sorry."

"And even if he were alive, he would know that I'm working at the airport until three."

I glanced at my watch. "Well, you're in big trouble. My watch says it's almost eight. And God knows whether that's A.M. or P.M."

"You came in from the Far East, didn't you? In Guam or Hawaii, that's P.M." She looked me over. "You're not rated and you don't have a service ribbon. Since, allowing for fatigue, you look reasonably bright and responsible, I'd say you were in spook work. Or nuclear weapons. Those are the only people I know who are stationed at D-M but working on an island in the Pacific."

This is one of the dangers of being a military officer in a military town. When you go out in your blues, whether you like it or not, you tell some people a whole lot about yourself. "Close," I said. "It's actually a little bit of both. I'm with MAC—"

10

"Military Airlift Command. A weather officer!" She beamed. "My late husband was in the Air Force, too."

No kidding. "A master sergeant?"

She half smiled. "A lieutenant colonel. Thirty years."

"Even worse. Anyway, I did weather predictions for missile tests in the Pacific. Dummy nuclear warheads, SDI. A little spook stuff."

We were wandering around the apartment, from the kitchen to the dining area, to the "living room" and back. The biggest window in the place looked out on the fence along the culvert; great view. Hazel stopped at Maia's desk.

On it was a Polaroid in a plastic frame: Maia and Gus. It couldn't have been taken more than a week or two ago.

Hazel picked it up. "That's a surprise," she said.

"What?"

"I was beginning to picture Maia as a blonde."

Hazel had glanced over Maia's identification at the airport, but, as you might expect, the driver's license photo looked more like a Rorschach print than a person.

But the Polaroid was a nice picture. Maia was a big, brown-haired woman, green-eyed and conventionally pretty, but not beautiful. It was her presence that was so unusual . . . and that only now I was beginning to miss. The sort of presence that encouraged strangers to talk to her—and may have gotten her killed.

Hazel put the picture down and deftly—so smoothly that you couldn't possibly object—began to go through the desk. "What brings you back to D-M?"

"R and R, for the moment. I'm supposed to pick up new orders any day."

"You don't sound like an Academy type."

"I'm not. University of Wisconsin, Platteville. You've never heard of it."

We were both beginning to run out of the nervous energy that fueled the small talk and allowed us to postpone

11

the inevitable. "Hazel, what do you think happened to Maia?"

She looked right at me. "You have to prepare yourself, Rick. She's probably dead."

"Intellectually I know that, but I'm not prepared to deal with it."

"We never are. But he"—she inclined her head toward the bedroom—"needs you to deal with it."

"And what am I supposed to do with him? Or with you?"

She sighed. "My arrangement with Mr. Roelke was that he would delay making a police report long enough for us to take Gus home. You're going to have to deal with them. Now, what is this?"

She held up a quarter sheet of yellow paper, torn at the top.

"It looks like a receipt." She handed it to me, and I read:

REQUEST FOR BIRTH CERTIFICATE RECORD
UNIVERSITY HOSPITAL
TUCSON AZ 85720

CHILD: Chios, August Richard (M) **BORN:** August 4
MOTHER: Chios, Maia
FATHER: Walsh, Richard Earl

"I told you he had your eyes."

My ears were roaring. *My* son? I didn't know whether to jump for joy or scream. "How could she do something like this!"

Hazel frowned. "Is that what people say these days instead of 'It's a boy'?"

"You know what I mean. Maia never mentioned a word of this. How would *you* like to find out you're a parent under these circumstances?"

"Fair enough. Congratulations, anyway. He looks like a fine boy."

"Thank you." I sat down and stared at the paper.

"Rick," Hazel said, "do you know anyone you can call for help? What about Maia's family?"

"She never mentioned them. It wasn't that sort of relationship. At least, not yet."

I was waiting for the first hint of disapproval, but if that's what Hazel felt, she hid it well.

"Well, what about your family?"

"I've got a sister in Omaha who's expecting her second in three months. I couldn't ask her to jump on a plane and come out here."

"Absolutely not." She thought. "Who do you know locally?"

All I could do was spread my hands. "Hazel . . . I was transferred here from SAC last August to work on a doctorate. After one semester they yanked me out of school and shipped me to the Far East. I think Maia was the only friend I had here."

"Well, then." She smiled. "I guess it's up to you and me."

Ten minutes later I had her home phone number, a list of instructions ("Not that you really need them, but just in case"), and a promise that she would come by early in the morning, preferably before the Tucson P.D. arrived. Then she left.

It struck me about then that the worst thing about this worst day of my life was that it was now thirty-six hours long.

I opened the hideaway and collapsed.

2

If I dreamed, I don't remember it. I woke to the sound of a baby crying and thought, for a moment, that I was still on that 767. Then I recognized the room; Maia's clock radio said it was 5:15. The sun comes up early in Tucson in late summer, but even so the sky was just growing light. It was pleasantly cool, meaning it would be unpleasantly hot by noon.

Gus was lying on his back without his blanket, Hazel's three-step papoose wrap having come unraveled during the night, freeing Gus's arms and making it easier for him to wake up. Of course, he was also hungry and wet, but when they're that age, that's usually the case. His crying was halfhearted, more of a pout than anything else. I picked him up and he quieted down.

Making that first diaper change was a real challenge. I could see where everything was—here you've got your Pampers, here you've got your baby wipes—but the whole process was complicated by the fact that Gus had wet not only the diaper but his sleeper. So I got him half un-dressed, then had to pick him up again while I scrounged for a fresh sleeper, which I found. Laid him down again and got some real squalling for my trouble. Slipped on the new diaper, snapped up the fresh sleeper, picked him up again, and headed for the kitchen.

Hazel the Fairy Godmother had left a pot on the stove. I got the burner lit and dug a bottle of Similac out of the refrigerator while I waited for the water to get warm, not hot. Gus was being a pretty good sport throughout all this. He whimpered a couple of times, but I could understand that: I was whimpering myself.

Eventually, after what seemed like hours, I got a bottle warm, turned off the stove, and went back into the bed-room, where we sat on the rocking chair and Gus chowed down. My niece Molly never took a bottle and would as soon have belted you with it as drink from it; Gus was different. He let me pop the bottle in his mouth and started sucking away.

It felt nice.

For the first time since entering U.S. airspace, I saw something I wanted to laugh at: on a shelf next to the bedroom door, something you'd have to turn around to see, was a Sony portable TV. The orange power light was on. On the floor beside the rocking chair was a remote unit. I stabbed at it with a toe and was rewarded with a blast of MTV. I managed to press the mute button before upsetting Gus.

The only way to watch the TV was to sit in that chair. Maia. When we'd first met, she was the only person in the United States who didn't own a Walkman, so I had helped her join the video revolution, picking out a TV and a cheap VCR. Maia must have grown to really *love* MTV.

This particular video was about a band and a girl, and the band was in one place—some bombed-out building which was supposed to suggest Hiroshima, I think—and

15

the girl was just getting out of bed and into her clothes in another place, and as the song went on, she came to where the band was. That was it. It occurred to me that this is what's in *every* video, except for the part about Hiroshima, and before I could come up with a specific exception I noticed that Gus was snoring.

I set the bottle down, then draped Gus across my shoulder and patted his back. After a few moments he spit, which added nothing to the already-negligible appeal of my T-shirt, and snuggled in for a nap. That was exactly what I had in mind, so I edged over to the crib and tried to lay him down.

He wailed.

This is an old baby trick and a good one, because there's nothing you can do about it except pick him back up. I didn't really mind: I was just getting to know him. So we walked around a little.

Whether she hadn't been living in the apartment long enough—though I know she had had the place for at least a year—or for some other reason, Maia had put almost nothing on the walls. It had never struck me before, but I noticed it now. People usually put up family pictures or Ansel Adams prints or college diplomas. My roommate on Guam had an *Aviation Week* cover of an E-3 Orion over his bed rather than, say, Miss April, which is what you'd expect. (When I asked him about this he said he was going to be spending a bit more time inside the airplane . . .)

But here in the Tanque Verde Apartments, everything was just a faded and cracked white—except for the Polaroid on the desk. On the floor beside the desk was a Motorola VHS video camera. Cradling Gus, I bent to look it over: there was a tape in the camera, some of it used.

Well, well, the student had surpassed the teacher. Maia had obviously gotten the camera because of Gus, but I just knew she had found someone to get footage of her. But I couldn't see any cable. The TV was in the corner of Gus's

16

room. So viewing the tape would have to wait. It was hard: at that point I could have told you about every moment I'd spent with Maia till then, because there'd been so few of them.

I had come to Arizona from Offutt Air Force Base, the headquarters of the Strategic Air Command, south of Omaha, because I was being bribed, nicely, to stay in the service. My four-year ROTC commitment was up; the Air Force promised to send me to school for a doctorate in atmospheric physics (promoting me to captain) if I would sign on for four more years. I was stalling; maybe I was negotiating. Let's face it: even with all these rumored reductions in manpower, you don't have to have any other qualification than a body temperature of 98.6 to make captain these days. A guy with a degree in engineering, which is what I had, and familiarity with Air Force systems, can walk into Northrop or TRW and double his salary. And not have to wear blue suits. I had convinced myself that *they* needed *me*—which would prompt them to offer me not only schooling but some fun job, like building spy satellites or working at the Pentagon . . . not making weather forecasts in Alaska.

But this makes the process sound much more systematic than it was. Hell, the only reason I was *in* the Air Force was that it was the only ROTC program available at P-ville. I suppose I wouldn't have needed even *that* if Mom and Dad hadn't split up so angrily, and Mom hadn't died. And I wound up in the Air Weather Service because I wanted to be based near my sister Kate, who lived in Omaha, and Offutt had a big AWS detachment there.

I found I liked weather work and did a good enough job that the Air Force wanted to keep me—not me personally, you understand, but one (1) O–3 Weather Officer, Air Force Global Weather Central, Offutt AFB—and was willing to send me to one of three schools to make me either an Aerial Reconnaissance Weather Officer or an Advanced

Weather Officer. Since the other two schools had the, to me, great disadvantage of being located in places even colder than Omaha, I chose Arizona.

It had been a crucifyingly hot day—105 at least—with the lowest humidity this side of the Antarctic, and I was on my way from the Space Sciences Building on the northeast quadrant of the campus to the Military Affairs Office in the southwest quadrant when I found myself ducking into the new Science Library. You've heard of sirens luring sailors to their doom? Circe had nothing on those cool, darkened windows with their promise of air-conditioning.

Since at that point I thought I would be spending a lot of the next nine months in that building, I decided to take a look around while allowing my body to rehydrate. I got as far as the reference desk and promptly forgot about that idea.

Some fast-talking grad student was at the reserve-book window there complaining about not being allowed to leave with what was apparently the sole existing copy of Bayer's *Uranometria*, which was a heavy, coffee-table-type book. The librarian on duty, a bearded guy with glasses who looked as though he would shatter at the sound of a voice raised in anger, was holding his own, but in libraries as in real estate, possession is what matters: the grad student had the book in his hands and was clearly contemplating a mad rush for the door. Trapped as he was behind the counter, the librarian would never catch him.

Now, for roughly the past twenty years, social rules have required that we allow others to do whatever they want . . . especially if it's illegal. I mean, God forbid you should grab a litterer by the collar and force him to pick up his discarded beer can. You'd probably be charged with assault. Maybe I'm old-fashioned. Maybe I'd spent too much time being ordered from one line to another for one day. I reached back into the Ur-memory, where I keep my basic training, and said to the grad student, "Son, do you have a problem?" This in spite of the fact that he was probably older than I was.

If nothing else I short-circuited the argument. The grad student looked at me and snapped, "I don't think this is any of your business."

"Sure it is. I'm a book lover."

The librarian laughed. While he and I were appreciating my wit, the grad student, seeing he was outnumbered, hefted Bayer and bolted out of the reserve-book room, vaulting the gate.

"Stop him!" the librarian hollered.

I took off after him, but got hung up on the gate, which was a bit too high to be vaulted by a guy in long pants. I had to swing under it. By then the book thief was almost at the front door. The only barrier to escape from the building, into the crowds flooding the quad, was the student who usually sat there politely checking the odd briefcase for stolen materials.

The checker on duty was a woman in her early twenties, who seemed to be paying no attention to the approaching thief. She merely got up from her chair—so calmly that I was afraid she was about to hold open the door—then, just as our grad student reached her, smiled—

—And tripped him.

Bayer must have been important to this clown: he kept it in a death grip as he hit the pavement. His book bag went flying. The woman simply loomed over him and, perfectly pleasantly, said, "I don't think you checked this out." She had a trace of an accent—European, I thought. And removed the volume from his hands. She gave it to the librarian, who was standing there with me, witness to this, then picked up the book thief's bag and delivered it with some velocity to his midsection—close enough to his crotch that he flinched.

Then, without a word, without a glance, she went back to her work.

As we took Bayer back to his rightful place, I asked the librarian where they got the Glamorous Lady of Wrestling. "She's new here," he said. "Her name's Maia something. Maia Chios."

Exactly a week later, at almost exactly the same time, I made a point of visiting the library again. I had given this some thought—more thought than usual. On leaving Omaha I not only said goodbye to my sister's family and the other charms of the Cornhusker State, I also extricated myself from a mutually abeneficial personal relationship. Now, I had asked Sarah to come with me to Arizona, but she had a practice in the city and wasn't about to give it up to chase off into some potential happy-ever-after land. Which I certainly understood.

What probably tore it was that I didn't act depressed *enough* when she told me she was staying. So I had sort of promised myself to engage in cheap (in the emotional sense) safe sex while waiting for the rest of my life to make itself clearer.

At this point the prosecution points out that, nevertheless, the defendant approached Miss Chios on his own initiative, knowing full well that it could lead to a commitment. All I can say is that it seemed like a good idea at the time. After all, I come from pioneer stock.

"Hi," I said.

She looked up. "Hi. I remember you." Now, this could have been a tired response from a pretty woman who gets asked out by strangers once a day. But from her tone you'd think I was the first one ever. It wasn't my looks: I have my days, but I don't get an automatic second glance in your average singles bar.

"I was just going to say, 'You probably don't remember me, but—' *Now* what am I supposed to do?"

"You could ask me out for coffee."

"Okay. Would you like to have coffee?"

"No, it's too hot. But you can buy me some lemonade." She consulted a little notebook on the desk, then nodded toward the Student Union across the quad. "I'll see you in Louie's in twenty minutes." And she smiled.

"That was easy," I said.

"It gets harder."

I was waiting at a table in the corner of Louie's Lower Level counting the obvious cases of PSS around me. (Parental separation syndrome, commonly found in college freshmen their first week away from home and indicated by heavy sighs, excessive intake of chocolate, and extreme disgust at all university paperwork, especially drop-add slips, which were being shredded all around me.) I sympathized; I'd suffered the same thing twice, once when Dad moved out and all over again when I moved to Platteville.

I had counted thirteen cases when suddenly all of Louie's seemed to cheer up somehow. Three athletes—two of them black guys and one white—who were leaning against a nearby wall like a nine-hundred-pound Oreo cookie, suddenly straightened up and smiled. "Check this one out," the white guy said. Freshmen boys caught the buzz and, turning around, failed to see what was going on. Two women students next to me deigned to raise their eyes, no doubt expecting to see the typical college homecoming queen package of tan legs, high heels, Guess miniskirt, blond hair, and halter top. What we all saw was a woman with wavy dark hair wearing a peasant blouse and flowing yellow skirt with sandals. Without heels she was almost as tall as the football players. Even across the room you could see the green of her eyes. And her smile. And the fact that she carried no purse. She seemed to have a word for everyone, eye contact at the very least, as she swept

21

through the place, hands in the pockets of her skirt, radiant and regal—

—And sat down next to me. I didn't even have the presence of mind to stand up.

"How do you do that?" I asked, as out of the corner of my eye I saw the two women students at the next table. One turned to the other and gave a combination shrug and side-to-side shake of the head that means, *That one is playing in a different league.* "I think everyone here wants to be your best friend."

The very first thing I learned about Maia was that she had no false modesty. "Everyone here is very nice. I could make worse friends."

"What's the secret? Is it that after-shave you're wearing?" It was a joke, but it struck me as the words left my mouth that Maia's fragrance was . . . memorable. She reminded me of the first girl I ever kissed. Make that *every* girl I've ever kissed.

"I suppose I just pay attention. I've seen most of them before and I recognize them now."

"Oh, you come here often."

"Every day since I moved here." Well, that was some explanation. Back at Offutt there was a secretary who worked in Global Vectors admin who was so pretty and so nice that after two years it was hard to find anyone who hadn't had at least one crush on her.

"When was that?"

She thought for a moment. "July."

The front door was opening and my left arm was asleep. Eventually I realized that I'd fallen asleep in the chair while rocking Gus, who was happily snoozing away. It would have been cute except for the fact that I felt paralyzed. I was struggling to get up when Hazel appeared at the bedroom door.

"That's very conscientious of you, but he *will* sleep in

22

the bed," she whispered, smiling indulgently. "Good morning."

"What time is it?"

"Almost eight."

She took Gus and he began to wake up. I gave her a Gus status report, which she accepted, and said, "Let me feed him and get him dressed for the day. You might want to take a shower."

"Can I sleep in there?" I'm twenty-six and in fairly good shape, but at that moment I felt like eighty. The left arm was still numb, my eyes felt as though I'd dumped one of those sand-based body rubs in them, and someone seemed to be sitting on my chest.

"You can try. But the police are going to be pulling up any moment." She gave me a good-natured nudge down the hall. "Welcome to parenthood."

When I came out of the shower the police were there. Two of them, a detective in plain clothes and a woman in uniform. Hazel had made them coffee. Gus was reclining in his car seat while everyone made a fuss over him.

The plainclothes guy was named Sanchez and he asked the questions, writing down the answers in a little notebook. He was as pleasant as you can be under the circumstances, and these were grim circumstances. "We've had disappearances like this one for something like thirteen years. Young woman at the airport, usually with kids, just vanishes. Never seen again."

"Do you find bodies?"

"We've found some . . . but only in about three out of ten cases."

"Who does things like this?" That was Hazel.

Sanchez shrugged. "Tucson's got a lot of drug traffic, a lot of it amateur drug traffic, which is even worse. It could just be robbery. Take the woman, take her money, get rid of her. Or . . ." He cleared his throat. "My theory is that the disappearances aren't due to some maniac, they're kidnappings. Somebody grabs young women and tries to get money for them."

"Has that happened?" I said. "I mean, you'd have ransom demands, wouldn't you?"

He shook his head. "I don't think the kidnappers sell them back to their families."

"We aren't talking about white slave trade, are we?" I rather hoped we were: that way there was *some* chance Maia was still alive.

Sanchez wasn't any older than me, but at that moment he reminded me of my father. "Maybe." He sighed and tried to smile. "Just a theory."

"What else do you need from me?"

"A local contact . . . just in case."

"You can reach me here, or, in a couple of days, through the D-M locator."

He glanced at the phone on the table. "Is that the number?" I nodded. "Now," he said, glad to change the subject, "what about the baby?"

I hadn't given much thought to the uniformed officer at that point. The name on her badge was Price and she was about twenty-four. She'd stayed in the background while Sanchez did the talking . . . but I realized now why she was here.

She was supposed to take Gus away.

I'll be honest. For a nanosecond it occurred to me that my life would be a lot simpler from this point on if I let them take Gus. Becoming a father overnight was a major adjustment for someone who had, at that moment, no home, and whose total possessions would fit in the back of a station wagon. I couldn't get used to the idea that I was going to have live-in company, one way or another, for the next eighteen years. And I thought of people like the Migdens back on Guam, a married couple who were anxious to adopt and couldn't find a child; Gus was the perfect age and, though I hate to say it, the perfect color to qualify for quick adoption. He would find a home in a few days. Given that he currently had a short-term memory of about ten seconds, he would never miss old Dad. He would probably never remember Maia . . .

And that's what bothered me. I didn't much like the idea of my son growing up without me, and it was unthinkable that he would never have a chance to remember his mother. "Gus is no problem," I found myself saying. "I'll keep him right here."

The cops exchanged glances. "Lieutenant Walsh," Sanchez said, "you really don't have a choice . . ." Hazel was shoving a piece of yellow paper under his nose. The request for a birth certificate. "Oh!" Sanchez said. "We didn't know you were the father."

"Well . . . there was a lot of confusion last night."

Sanchez and Price looked relieved. They got up. "We'll be in touch if anything develops." He handed me his card. "Just in case Maia turns up . . . or, you know, if you want to talk."

"Thanks," I said, and showed them out.

Then I turned to Hazel and Gus. "Now what do I do?"

3

This is what we agreed to do: Hazel said she could take some half days off work or otherwise rearrange her schedule so she could baby-sit from about 10:00 A.M. to 6:00 P.M. through the week. I would be on duty the rest of the time, which would allow me to visit Davis-Monthan and straighten out my increasingly confused affairs. By Sunday other arrangements would have to be made . . . though we both pretended that by then this nonsense would be over, and Maia would be back where she belonged.

"And I hope you aren't going to insult me by offering to pay me for this," she said, just as I was doing some pessimistic mental calculations concerning cash in hand versus cash I would have to lay out.

"Okay." She reminded me of Mom on one of her few good days.

For the past couple of minutes Hazel had been scribbling some words on a piece of paper. It was a list. Pampers, formula, garbage bags, baby wipes. "Save your money for these items. With infants you have to shop every other day and this is probably the day Maia was going out." She took a look in the refrigerator, too, then added more items and handed the list to me with a smile. "And anything *you'd* like to eat, of course."

I threw on a clean—well, my cleanest—set of summer blues and got in Maia's car. I had let Matt Mitchell buy mine while I was gone. It was already hot, which made me think of my money problems.

I was carrying about $200 in advance travel pay. The orders sending me back to Tucson hadn't left me a lot of time to tie up loose ends on Guam. My checks were going straight to the Bank of America there and I had planned to take an hour about Friday this week to write them a letter closing the account and transferring it to a new bank, which I would have found in Tucson in the meantime, figuring that I would be able to survive on the $200 for that long. I would either have been staying with Maia, rent-free, or at the visiting officers' quarters on base, also rent-free for a month. I had a Visa card with a $1,000 limit and only about $35 charged on it which I planned to use for extraordinary expenses such as car rental.

Well, as they told me in Squadron Officers' School, no battle plan survives first contact with the enemy. Now I had a household to support. I was looking at a grocery list worth forty bucks at least, unless I could find a store that took Visa, which was unlikely or, at best, impractical. The real money drain was going to be the car.

Maia's Mazda was gray with a gray interior, which might as well have been black. I had teased her about this: having a car with a gray interior in Tucson in the summer is an invitation to heatstroke. Leave it unshaded for fifteen minutes and you not only can't touch the steering wheel, you'll literally blister the skin on your legs (especially if, like everyone else in Tucson, you happen to wear shorts in summer). The temperature inside can reach 140 degrees. But you can't function in Arizona in the summer without air-conditioning . . . and the first thing I noticed as I turned onto Broadway for the drive out to D-M was that nothing but warm air was coming out of the vent.

Okay . . . stipulate that I could survive, for a few days, without air-conditioning. I still couldn't subject Gus to that. So now I had to find a place to get that fixed. There was forty or a hundred bucks out the window before I bought any groceries.

And I had to put gas in the car. Another ten bucks gone. If I wasn't careful, half my money would be gone by noon. I could be careful . . . but only for so long. So to my growing list of stops I had to add a bank.

An hour later I'd drunk a Classic Coke and eaten a donut and was sitting at an empty desk in the Consolidated Base Personnel Office, happily filling out inprocessing forms. The wad of paper needed to move a junior officer from one base to another is impressive: pay records, PCS orders, passport, forms for inbound personal property, and a few other items I either carried or acquired. It makes me glad I never have to plan an invasion.

But a big base like D-M has several thousand people moving in and out of it over the course of a year. They're prepared for any contingency. And my papers showed that I had a sponsor, a Captain G. G. Alquist, whoever that was, of the 868th Tactical Missile Training Group, whom I was supposed to contact immediately upon departing the CBPO.

My assignment was to Detachment 13, 25th Weather Squadron, filling in for some other guy who was on extended temporary duty, but the 868th would be one of my customers. This was good news, at the moment, since that unit trains people to launch cruise missiles. Its instructors are more interested in teaching operational basics than in proving that you can get a Tomahawk to target in a hurricane or something. Tucson has about 350 sunny days a year—which is why the training unit got based there in the first place—so my comprehensive "customer briefing" would be the equivalent of your local TV weather report: it's going to be sunny and warm. Remember, I was on hold awaiting new PCS orders; there was no point in giving me a job that would require a lot of time or training.

I expected to find those new orders in the stack of in-processing paperwork, but they weren't there. Personnel said they'd put a tracer on them. So I filled in what I could, submitted to a badging photo session, then trotted around to VOQ and told them I had quarters for the moment, which was good, because they didn't have a vacancy, then to "resource management," aka finance, where I managed to sweet-talk a sergeant into promising me an advance on my next set of checks ($694.64 salary, $295 housing allowance, and $112 subsistence), which turned out not to be an immediate impossibility, unless I wanted it in cash—which almost was. I explained that I didn't have a bank yet. She told me to get one, or I'd be waiting until next week for the money. I grumbled and said I'd be back in the morning with an account number . . . somewhere.

All I had to do now was go through the formality of making a flyby at Base Ops to check in with Larry Devine, my boss in Det 13, then deal with this sponsor person and get on with my real work.

In a shameless bit of gamesmanship I had planned to drop in on Devine when he was sure to be at lunch, thus earning points for making the effort while avoiding the inevitable chat—and work. I figured I could show my face to his orderly and be done with it. I figured wrong.

I usually get along with people, I really do. But during my first tour at D-M I had problems with a master sergeant named Escobar who, I suspect, had little liking for smart asses of any kind and smart-assed lieutenants in particular.

29

Part of the problem was that he had a nonregulation droopy mustache and a swarthy complexion (he was part American Indian), which prompted me, in a weak moment, to dub him "Ming the Merciless." I didn't say this to Escobar's face; I just let it slip to another smart-assed lieutenant, who let it get to Ming . . . who made my life living hell.

He was Devine's assistant, and he wasn't about to let me get away. "I'm sorry, Lieutenant," he said, all sneering formality. "Major Devine said I was to put you right to work. With Lieutenant Teller gone, the entire observing section consists of you."

Observing section—that was a joke. You step outside and look at the sky once an hour. The work was usually handled by a couple of enlisted men. I was in no condition, mentally, physically, or financially, to commence this nonsense. I put on my friendliest smile and told Ming, "There must be some mistake, Sergeant. I'm still traveling. I'm not required to check in at all until tomorrow morning."

He spread his hands. "The major was very insistent."

I could feel my carefully planned schedule of stops blowing away in the wind. "Okay. Where do I go?"

"*This* way, Lieutenant," said a strangely familiar voice. I turned around and saw Greg Alquist, a guy I'd served with in Omaha. Then he had been a first lieutenant; now he wore captain's bars. To Ming he said: "I'm Lieutenant Walsh's sponsor, Sergeant. Tell Big D that I'll be needing him this afternoon." And he managed to steer me out of the office before he broke up. "Asshole. That's why you're supposed to see your sponsor *first*."

"Hey, I didn't know any 'Captain Alquist.' Last time I looked, you were a crummy little lieutenant, like me." I nodded at the captain's bars. "Congratulations. A year deep?"

"Yeah."

"Signed up for four more years?"

"Why not? They sent me to school in Utah. But now I'm here. Welcome back, stud. We're going to have some fun."

Fun. At various times in my life, fun has been playing baseball, drinking two entire cans of Schlitz malt liquor, or getting my hand under Jennifer Nosseck's blouse. Right now fun would be getting a lot more sleep. Or a little more sleep. Anything but bouncing along Picacho Street at sixty-five miles an hour in the front seat of Alquist's 280Z.

"After I finished grad school I got assigned to the Technology Center at Kirtland, but they've had me hanging around here since June." He accelerated to pass a truck. "What were you doing on Guam?"

"Missile tests, recon work. Spook stuff." This was more or less true. If nothing else, it was a good way to deflect conversation.

"Did you get your orders?"

"They haven't shown up."

That surprised him. "Well," he said, smiling confidentially, "I think you've got a surprise coming."

"Christ, they're not sending me to Shemya, are they?" There are at least a dozen places the Air Force can send you that you'd rather not be sent, and Shemya, which is a rock about the size of a football field in the Aleutians, is at least three of them.

"I can't say. I'm not supposed to know at all. But I have the feeling it's a great gig."

"Do you have something to do with it?"

"Hey, I'm just your sponsor. We're going to be working together."

"What on?"

"Project called Puff the Magic Dragon." He sang the title.

"Never heard of it."

31

"If you had, I'd have to shoot you. It's a black project—a cruise missile that's completely stealthed." *Puff*. No doubt named by the same humorist in the Pentagon who dubbed the B-2 bomber *Harvey*, like the invisible rabbit. "We're gonna handle the first tests."

"Who's we?"

"My unit, which includes you."

"I'm a weather officer."

"Look, the test area includes the whole western U.S. And we're kind of under the gun. Our goddamn contractor can't make the guidance work, so the prototypes are in pieces right now while the brains are back in the factory. When they show up, we've got to move. We won't have time to clear and brief fourteen hundred support people. Putting you in the loop *now* saves me that step. You haven't been integrated into the usual base ops, so they won't miss you. And you're going to be out of here in a few weeks, so you won't be getting any nosy questions. Here we are."

We had arrived at admin building for the Aerospace Maintenance and Regeneration Center, the boneyard for abandoned airplanes. They had hundreds of them sitting out there on the far eastern section of D-M. B-29s, B-36s. A forest of tail sections. "You're working out of this place?" I asked.

"I told you this was a black program."

"You should have said ultraviolet."

We went around back to a trailer, the kind you see at construction sites. Alquist kept chattering. "Puff's spread all over—Kirtland, DARPA, Florida. This is just one of the test sites. But what a cutie: imagine a cruiser that's got artificial intelligence *and* smart weapons guided by three different kinds of radar and terrain-following avionics. It can hunt out a target without being detected and decide on its own whether or not to hit it. Either way, it can loiter in the area and pop the target again, or look for a second-ary.''

''Sounds like a dream.'' By now we were inside. It was about twenty degrees cooler and I was feeling the heat.

He stopped. ''Are you all right? You look tired.''

Alquist and I weren't what you'd call close. He'd been one of my customers when I was working in Global Weather Central at Offutt. He was an Academy type whose eyes had knocked him out of flight school. Typical ''RAF,'' Real Air Force. He was still hoping to wind up as chief of staff someday, though losing the pilot or navigator rating probably spiked that. He had the other quali-fications, though: the Academy ring, the promotion to captain a year ahead of schedule, the premature hair loss (there are a disproportionate number of bald guys at the top of the Air Force; check it out sometime). And, best of all, deep and abiding dislike of civilians, especially pol-iticians. He even hated contractors. And though he loved secrets—he thought black programs were the best part of the Air Force—he wasn't someone you confided in.

But he was all I had. So I told him what was going on. When I finished he stared at me for a good five seconds. ''Sounds crazy, doesn't it?'' I prompted.

''What are you gonna do?''

''I'm open to suggestions.''

''There's no way in hell you can take care of a kid.'' He thought things over. ''Are you in love with the girl?''

I could have said yes. Two days ago I might have. What I said was, ''I *like* her a lot.''

He smirked. ''People *like* their cars, Walsh. You *like* Whitney Houston. You don't turn your life inside out for that.''

''I don't remember doing this on purpose.''

''Who ever does?'' He shook his head and smiled to himself as he rewound his memory. ''You get hurry-up orders to leave Guam, come walking off a plane in the middle of the night expecting to see your girlfriend, who's been kidnapped and left behind a baby, and you're the father. Right at the time you're supposed to be deciding whether to stay in the Air Force or become a filthy civilian. Someone up there has it in for you."

"Hey, I've got my health."

"Have you looked in a mirror lately? Never mind. It looks like you've got a lot on your mind at the moment. I can cover for you for a couple of days. Devine's not a micromanager, so if I tell him you're here and doing what I want, he won't bust my ass about it. Should give you a couple of days to figure out what the hell you're going to do. I'll be damned if I could." What a fine leader of men he was going to be.

On the other hand, before I left he did lend me thirty dollars. Maybe he wouldn't be so bad after all.

On the third hand, I was feeling shitty for having gone into the Judas Mode. I loved Maia. Why had I been afraid to admit it?

After that first memorable encounter in Louie's Lower Level I badly wanted to see Maia again. And badly is how I went about arranging it. To begin with, she wasn't listed in the phone book. And she didn't bother to visit Louie's at any time during the hours I spent there. Finally I took to hanging around the library, hoping to find her working. Not only did this have a positive influence on my grades, it worked.

"Hi! Still remember me?" I said.

"We don't have *that* many foiled robberies around here."

"Would you like to go out to dinner?"

I didn't get an immediate answer, as a couple of students chose that moment to have their book bags searched. Then Maia frowned. "You mean, go on a date?"

"Yeah."

"Why?"

That was a new one. I mean, I've been told "Sure" and I've been told to "Get lost!" and I even recall being laughed at, but—"Why?"

I suppressed the obvious response—"Why not?"—and found myself saying, "Because I think I like you. And you might even like me. Ten years from now we'll both hate ourselves if we don't take the chance."

She was thinking it over. Another student went through the gate. He gave me a dirty look.

I said, "Is this what you tell all the guys who ask you out?"

She straightened up and gave me a Mona Lisa smile. "No other guys have asked me out."

"Then you'll *really* hate yourself if you don't give it a try."

"I wouldn't want that."

So that night we went to see a movie called *The Graduate* at the New Loft, the revival house near campus.

As dates go, it was about a six on a scale of ten. Maia had a lot of questions about the movie, which was supposed to be some kind of classic. I'd never seen it and it originally came out when I was about five, so I was hardly able to tell her what the big deal was.

In the course of the debate over Dustin Hoffman's suitability as a mate, I did manage to learn that when Maia wasn't working in the library she was a part-time student at the university in something called General Studies, whatever that meant. "I've been to school for many years already," she said. Great, I thought: I'm falling in love with a perpetual graduate student.

But an interesting one. It was fun to watch her watch things . . . in the same way that it had been interesting to watch my niece Molly discovering the world around her at age two. Maia liked my car. She liked sitting in the

35

dark and eating popcorn. She liked everything she saw in the movie—the jokes, the wedding. As if it were all new.

If you think I enjoyed playing Mr. Answer Man for this very attractive woman, you'd be right. But I also began to wonder. When I asked her where she was from—hardly a challenging question, right?—she said, "Ninth Street," in a tone that encouraged me to drop the subject.

Well, there are people in the world who've never seen a movie. Who have never been asked out on a date. There are even such people in the U.S., and many of those speak, as Maia did, with a vaguely European accent. The Amish.

I don't know much about the Amish beyond that Harrison Ford movie I saw a couple of years ago, but I had the clear impression that you didn't just resign from the community, not unless you had some real problems with it, or vice versa. So, okay, she was a fugitive from a repressive religious community.

How much do we ever know for sure about other people, anyway? It wasn't until I was sixteen—four years after my parents split up—that I learned that my father had been involved with a woman other than my mother for a decade. I had hardly recovered from that news when my mother told me that she, too, had had an affair. It was impossible for me to reconcile the mental picture I had of Mom and Dad driving Kate and me to Chicago one summer, sniping at each other all the way, with this mismated pair who were in love, at various times, with other people, meeting secretly, I presumed, for hand-holding and little gifts and great sex.

By the time I dropped Maia off at her place on Ninth Street, I was about half convinced I wouldn't see her again. But before she got out of the car, she leaned over and gave me a significant kiss. "Thank you for a wonderful evening," she said. "I have a question for you."

"Please ask."

"Do you want to see me again?"

I was still reacting to the kiss, but, nevertheless, I found that unusual. Refreshingly frank, as they say, but still unusual.

Suddenly it was very important that I see Maia again. "Yes," I said. "Very much."

"It's important: you must be very serious about this."

"I am."

She sighed, but not unhappily. A trace of a smile was on her lips. "Call me tomorrow between two and three." It was an order, not a request.

"I promise."

How much do we ever know about ourselves?

I got back to Maia's place about five. I was seventy-six dollars poorer, but in its place I had accumulated two bags of groceries, one (1) copy of Dr. Spock's *Baby and Child Care*, and a tank of gas, and I had recharged the Mazda's air conditioner. I'd also spent ninety minutes at the South Craycroft branch of the First Interstate Bank trying to prove I was who I said I was. I'd made progress there. All in all, I was feeling pretty smug. I didn't have the faintest idea how I was going to get through an evening alone with Gus, but unskilled laborers have managed it before me.

Hazel was sitting on the couch watching Oprah when I came in. "Is Gus sleeping?" I whispered.

She shook her head. That was odd. "Where is he?"

"Right here."

I looked up. A tall woman about forty-five years old and infinitely weary—she had the look of a society widow—had stepped out of the kitchen holding Gus. I looked at Hazel. "Who's this?"

"My name is Jayan," the new woman said.

Hazel said, "Rick, I'd like you to meet Maia's mother."

37

4

I carried the grocery bags to the table, then stuck out my hand and introduced myself. Half a dozen questions popped into my mind at the same time, but all I could manage to say was, "I wasn't expecting you."

Jayan ignored my hand and looked at me with real suspicion. "What are you doing here?"

I pointed to Gus. "That's my son."

Her eyes flicked from me to Gus to me. Maybe she saw the resemblance, because she went right from suspicion to submission. "Please forgive me."

"It's okay," I said gently. "I guess Maia didn't tell you . . ." That sort of trailed off. If I thought long enough I could come up with a couple of reasons why Maia hadn't bothered to tell me I was Gus's father, one of which being the tremendous argument we'd had the day I shipped out.

Why she wouldn't be more honest with her mother, I had no idea. I was feeling more and more stupid with every passing second.

"Where is Maia?" Jayan said.

Hazel came to the rescue again. "Rick, Jayan just knocked on the door about fifteen minutes ago," she said. Her voice was so sweet that I knew they had had a difficult encounter. "I think she's a bit surprised by everything."

Which meant that she didn't know Maia was missing. Well, why would she? As far as the police were concerned, *I* was technically next of kin. There hadn't been a newspaper report that I knew of. The whole thing had happened less than twenty hours ago.

So this must be a scheduled visit, from wherever Jayan lived. (Amish country? She had the same accent that Maia did.) I saw a bag on the floor—not your basic American Tourister, either, but some canvas thing with a foreign logo on it, a winged dragon with what looked like an eagle's head. It was so beat-up it had to be something expensive. No airline tag, though. I hadn't noticed a car out front, either.

"Mrs. Chios," I said, "I think you'd better sit down."

"I think this young man needs a change," Hazel said, snatching Gus from Jayan's arms and disappearing into the bedroom.

Jayan sat down. "What did you call me?"

"Mrs. Chios."

She absorbed this. Then, making some internal connection, she nodded and said, "Just call me Jayan."

"Fine. Look," I said, "I don't know what Maia told you about me—about us." I cleared my throat. "When was the last time you saw Maia?"

She looked puzzled. "A long time."

"You didn't know she was pregnant?"

She actually blushed. "No."

Oh boy. "If I start apologizing, it could take all night, so please just hear me out." I nodded toward the bedroom. "That little boy is your grandson. Please!" She had started to get up, but she sat back down.

"Maia and I got involved about a year ago, before I was shipped overseas. I returned last night and she was supposed to be waiting for me. Instead, the baby was there, and Maia was gone."

I could see the alarms going off. "Gone?"

"Vanished. Her car and her baby bag and the baby were still there. It looks as though she was abducted." Jayan was tough. She waited for me to go on. "The police are investigating and that's literally all I know. Hazel and I are taking care of Gus for the time being."

She thought it over for maybe four seconds. "Then I should help, too." And with that she got up from the couch and went into the bedroom.

"She's never seen Pampers before," Hazel told me later. We were standing out in the driveway and she was getting ready to go to work. Thunder was rumbling all around as the monsoon rolled up against the mountains.

"You're kidding."

"I don't mean she's never *used* them before. Until last night I'd never used them, either. She doesn't seem to know what they *are*. She asked me where the diapers were, even though the box was right in front of her."

"Hazel, should I be getting worried?"

"I don't think there's anything to worry about—yet. Jayan is strange but nice. She was handling Gus very well. It was just an observation."

Rain began to fall. Heavy stuff, too, driving us, after a moment's hesitation, inside Hazel's car. The windows began to steam up as I told her my theory about Maia's origins. "That would explain things, I suppose." She frowned. "Jayan doesn't look Amish, if you ask me. There's a certain . . . face that you wear when you live apart from the real world, don't you think? I've seen it, and Jayan doesn't have it."

"Well, where do you suppose they're from?"

"Why don't you ask Jayan?"

"Oh, I'm going to."

"Then you can tell me."

"Hazel . . . you aren't going to leave me alone at a time like this, are you?" I was pretty dependent on this woman, but I owed her a chance to free herself. Caring for a motherless child and a shiftless man is not the sort of commitment one accepts casually. There are people in the world who will do things like this; about six. But I was shameless: if Hazel was going to do the smart thing—that is, go home and read about Maia's fate in the *Arizona Daily Star*—I wanted her to tell me face-to-face.

"Of course not. I'll be back tomorrow morning at ten."

I got out and she drove off through the rain.

That turned out to be one of the weirder evenings in my life, though by this point I was noticing a disturbing trend toward weird evenings. I made dinner—salad and turkey sandwiches—under Jayan's intense scrutiny, and we ate, all of this in almost total silence. No talking, no music, no television. When the rain stopped after an hour, I opened up the place and let the breeze in. I put a blanket on the floor and let Gus wave his arms and legs there while Jayan and I hovered over him.

Only then did we begin to communicate, though it was more like two nannies in the park than in-laws. Strictly baby business. "Look at those eyes. He's following your finger." "He's trying to coo!" "I think he's just burping." When it was clear, about eight o'clock, that the little guy was starting to tire, I simply scooped him up and headed for the bedroom.

This time Jayan looked at me as if I were a crazy man. "What are you doing?"

"Putting him to bed."

"Do you know how?"

"Sure," I lied. Well, I had put him to sleep earlier in

the day . . . and I'd managed to put my niece to bed a couple of times. "What's the problem?"

She started to explain, then obviously thought better of it. She kissed Gus and whispered something that sounded like *"Manna leaf."* And let me take him into the bedroom.

Forty minutes later I emerged, triumphant. My sister once told me there's no feeling of accomplishment in the world quite like putting a baby to sleep.

Jayan was standing by the window, looking out at the culvert, apparently waiting for me.

"Would you like me to bring the TV in here?" I asked. I was starting to think about the logistics of sharing quarters with Jayan—there was one bed, for example.

"No."

"Is there anything I can get you?"

"No."

I couldn't help it. "Would you like me to leave?"

She shook her head. "No. I'm sorry. This is all so strange for me."

"Let's sit down," I said. "We have to talk."

We sat down on the couch. "This is going to be difficult for both of us. You have lost a daughter and acquired two . . . boys you knew nothing about." She didn't challenge that. "I have a missing girlfriend and a son I knew nothing about. I'm not going to criticize Maia, but I'll tell you honestly that one of the reasons I hope she's alive is so that she can explain this to both of us.

"But until we know for sure what's happened, we're stuck with each other. I can't take care of Gus myself. Hazel can help, but not indefinitely. She's got a life of her own. So you and I are going to have to work together. You're welcome to stay here, if that's what you'd like, but I need to know now so I can find a cot or a sleeping bag or something, because I'm not ready to sleep on a hard-wood floor. And if you want to help with Gus—"

"Show me," she said suddenly. Before I could react, she was off the couch and headed for the kitchen. I followed.

"What don't you know?"

"I don't know how you do that." She pointed at the bottle of formula sitting in its pot on the stove.

I touched the dial. "You don't know how to turn on the stove?"

"No."

"Then we'd better get started. We've got a *lot* to cover."

By about ten o'clock I was feeling much better. Jayan was a quick study. She had the stove, the formula, the Pampers, the baby thermometer, the Dr. Spock, and the schedule all in their proper places. At one point I dropped a pan on the counter and cringed visibly, horrified at the unnecessarily loud noise it made. With Jayan watching me, I waited probably twenty seconds, worried that I'd woken up Gus. I hadn't. Jayan laughed and said, "We have a saying at home. 'The prince is sleeping.' "

"Yeah," I said, "and you don't dare wake him."

I took this as an invitation. "Speaking of home, where did you say it was?"

"Will knowing that help you teach me?"

"I've already taught you everything I know."

"I'll let Maia tell you." She did give me a little smile. "I can see why she liked you."

Okay, I'm easily satisfied. I didn't press the issue. I was too tired.

I doubled a couple of blankets on the floor and gave Jayan the bed. At one-thirty or so Gus woke up crying and I went in to feed him. I held off Jayan by reminding her that she would have Gus all to herself all day.

After the bottle Gus decided to be a bit fussy, so I sat

down to rock him again. I kick-started the TV and spent ten minutes watching CNN Headline News before remembering that I had wanted to look at Maia's tape.

I suppose I was a little out of my mind with fatigue by then, because with Gus resting on my shoulder, I tiptoed out to the living room and popped the tape out of the camera. Jayan stirred, but didn't wake up, so I sneaked back into the bedroom and, feeling as though I had the nuclear codes in hand, loaded the VCR.

I could have chosen a more convenient time for viewing, but I wanted to see Maia, even if it was only her video ghost. And I didn't necessarily want to share her with Jayan yet.

The first thing on the tape was Gus just home from the hospital. He was sleeping in his car seat, which was propped on the kitchen table as Maia zoomed in on him. "This is August Richard Walsh and he's two days old," Maia was saying.

The picture wobbled, then steadied. Maia walked into the shot with Gus and sat down with him. She looked pretty good for someone who had just come home from the hospital. A little heavier than I had ever seen her, and more pale, but happy. "Say hi to Daddy." But Gus, wisely, just snoozed on.

"He was delivered at seven pounds three ounces. It was a fairly easy labor, I understand, though I didn't believe it at the time—"

I stopped the tape, shaken, again, by the knowledge that Maia had had to go through this whole thing alone. Who was her partner in Lamaze classes? Who gave her foot rubs? Who drove her to the hospital? And whose fault was it? Mine.

I rewound, and found a shot of Maia, pregnant, sitting on the couch. "The doctor says I'm due yesterday, and since I haven't had a twinge all afternoon, I'd say it's going to be a while yet. It's very hot and I'm trying not to move.

"Rick, I hope I have a chance to sit down and watch this tape with you. It's funny to talk like this because there's so much you don't know about me. I mean, not including the fact that I'm pregnant, which I wanted to tell you a long time ago. I just didn't see how I could then. There hasn't been another 'right' time since, I guess.

"I'm glad you're coming back. I believe you when you say you want to, that you want to see me. I'm also a little afraid that you won't, once you find out what's been going on. But don't ever get the idea that I can't take care of myself."

A lot of anger there. It almost made me flinch. Then she softened: "You never really knew much about me. And I didn't know much about you. And so this is where I start to be honest—" At that point, on the tape, there was a knock at the door. Not wanting to be interrupted, Maia hesitated. I heard an off-camera voice: "Maia, it's Carolyn." Carolyn was a woman who rented the apartment next door. I had met her once or twice.

"Coming," Maia said, struggling to elevate herself off the couch. I was thinking how nice it was that she'd kept her sense of humor, until she leaned into the lens and said, "This is all your fault, Walsh," just as she shut off the camera.

I waited for more, but after a few glitches, found myself looking at new baby Gus once more. So I rewound again, going further back this time, and found a moderately pregnant Maia sitting at her desk, writing. She was obviously pissed off; she didn't even look at the camera, and every sentence cost her some effort: "I'm not going to waste time complaining about the past, Rick. Let's just say I misjudged you. I thought you were more . . . serious than you were. I know a little better now. Maybe you aren't capable of being honest. No one else in this place seems to be—"

It was about two in the morning. Maybe I didn't want

to be beaten up at the moment. I went back to Gus and Maia. "Say hi to Daddy."

That was better. Then I went all the way back on the tape, and I did find something unusual. It was shot outside—Sabino Canyon, maybe—and Maia didn't look very pregnant, so it must have been months old. In fact, from the way she was handling the camera, it was probably the first time she had tried to operate it herself.

She aimed it at a cactus. "This is what my people call *britch*," she said. A mesquite branch. *"Marsh."* A flower. *"Rock you."* A moment of bumping and thumping, and I was looking at Maia. She was wearing billowy shorts and a white cotton blouse that clung to her in the gentle breeze. She brushed back her hair, looking positively golden. "And I am Maia Chios, daughter of Reth and Jayan, granddaughter of Chios Himself." She added some words in her other language, which I didn't catch. Then she laughed: "Oh God, I can't believe I'm doing this." Shaking her head, she walked toward the camera and shut it off.

I was too tired to mess with the tape any more. Gus was sound asleep on my chest. It was easier to keep rocking. Trying to figure out who this Chios was and where Maia was from and what difference it made would be a lot easier come morning. I dozed.

About three the phone rang. It was Lieutenant Sanchez and he was calling from the east side of town. He was sorry to bother me, but they'd found a body and wanted me to look at it.

5

An hour later—it was maybe four by now—I was turning off Old Spanish Trail onto Houghton. Sanchez had given me directions to a Circle K a few miles south of the intersection.

Even though I first arrived in Tucson not much more than a year ago, I could see the changes out here on the east side. The city just kept growing and growing; it would grow until it ran smack up against the boundary of the Saguaro National Monument, which included most of the Rincon Mountains. It wasn't orderly growth—I suppose it never is. A developer would pick up some chunk of land, blade it bare, and slap a few dozen houses on it. On the corners other developers would plant their mini-malls, each of which contained a donut place, a convenience store, a laundry, and a video outlet. No matter how they tried blending the malls into the landscape, the beige-colored Circle K still had a bright white sign above it, like a lighthouse on a dark shore. You couldn't miss it. At four in the morning, on my way to identify the body of my dead girl-friend, I sort of welcomed it.

By the time my relationship with Maia was one week old I was already curious about her previous life. She knew as much about cars as I do about no-load mutual funds, which is to say she had a certain amount of interest—no pun intended—but no real feel for them. She operated on cash, and seemed to have enough of it. (I knew there was an Arizona Bank account because I saw a savings pass-book lying on her desk, and though I'll snoop to the extent that I'll notice something like that, I won't stoop low enough to open it.) She couldn't have watched ten minutes of television in her life, either. References to *Leave It to Beaver* and David Letterman and *Wheel of Fortune* went right by her.

She didn't know who the Beatles were.

She'd never heard of Lee Harvey Oswald. The World Series. *Star Trek.* The Constitution of the United States. Or even the U.S. Air Force—you should have heard me trying to explain that one day. (Though she was quite pleased when she realized I was a "warrior." And you wouldn't have tried to disillusion her, either.)

I hope you don't get the impression that I was quizzing her like the M.C. of some game show from hell. These are just things I noticed, by and by . . . and Maia knew about it. "Do you think I'm terribly ignorant?" she said once.

Well, how do you tell someone she's ignorant because she doesn't know who Vanna White is?

Besides, Maia seemed to possess a body of knowledge entirely different from mine. She was extremely charming. She had a rare ability to laugh at her own mistakes and learn from them. (No sooner had I begun to tease her about her unfamiliarity with automobiles than she was tak-ing driving lessons. And then one day she turned up with a license and the Mazda.) She knew to an almost frightening degree just how people worked, as if she could read a diagram of your inner being just by looking at you. This is what helped her stay so charming.

Once I was waiting for her to get off work at the library. I was sitting around the corner where I usually met her, reading in the shade, when some tortured freshman boy flopped down on the grass nearby. Maybe he was lonely; maybe he'd just flunked an important quiz, I don't know. But he sat there in his misery, sinking lower and lower, as Maia came up the sidewalk behind him.

You couldn't hear this kid. It wasn't as though he was sobbing aloud, anyway. He had just given one of those momentarily audible groans that are unique to eighteen-year-olds, I think. I saw Maia glance at him, the way she or anyone would glance at someone that close to your route.

Then she stopped. She was still several steps behind him. I don't think he saw her. I was about to call out to her, but, for some reason, didn't right then. She cocked her head and looked at the kid, then went up to him, leaned down, and whispered something to him.

The kid almost jumped . . . it was a bit of a surprise, after all . . . then he laughed. He laughed and shook his head and you could tell that what had been a universal tragedy moments ago was now just one of those things.

Maia came right around the corner, saw me, and gave me a hug. "Who's your friend?" I asked, nodding toward the kid.

"I don't know him," she said.

"You said something to him."

"Oh, he was unhappy. It was just some words my mother taught me."

"Tell me."

"I'll show you." And she kissed me.

Maybe this is all New Age garbage, but Maia had a

talent. If nothing else, like her mother, she certainly knew how to change a subject.

Sanchez was sitting alone in an unmarked car and drinking coffee when I drove up. He was properly businesslike and somber. "Sorry to do this to you," he said.

"*You* didn't do it to me."

I got in his car and we headed back on Houghton a few blocks, then west on a new road that quickly ran out of pavement. Up ahead I could see headlights shining in the darkness.

As we got out and began walking, Sanchez said, "This whole area's supposed to be a fifty-year floodplain, but every time there's a good rain, it just swamps it." He nodded toward the new houses a hundred yards to the east. "When we really get a big rain, it's going to relocate most of those people to Sonora."

I wasn't really paying attention to him. I was trying to recall Maia's face from happier times . . . the chestnut bangs above the brows that took on a truly fierce slant when she frowned . . . the delicately narrow lips . . . the way she would brush her hair back behind her ear . . . I fried to etch it into my memory so permanently that whatever horror I was about to see wouldn't wash it away to Sonora. It didn't work.

"A guy named Henderson, lives over there, had his dog out for a late walk and the dog found the body. We think she was buried north of here. I've got a guy backtracking up the wash, but I don't think he's going to find the place."

"Which means you've got no evidence so far."

He didn't look happy. "No."

The body had been swept along by the sudden flood and snagged in some ocotillo. Apparently it was still clothed; there were pieces of fabric in the cactus. And now it lay under a rubber tarp.

"Can you handle this?" Sanchez said quietly.

"Will it make any difference if I say no?"

He lifted the tarp.

I've never been a cop or a mortician or in combat, so I have no more experience with the dead than your maiden aunt. I have heard stories about the smell, about the bloating, about the color, but the desert is forgiving in these matters. The body was blessedly normal . . . clearly that of a dead woman. The arms and legs were twisted—almost wrapped around her—and the head lolled to one side, eyes open and staring. The lips were parted in what could have been a final scream—or just gravity doing its work. She was wearing the remains of a T-shirt and jeans, though she was covered with so much matted sand and mud it was hard to tell what color her clothes were. What color her hair was. In fact, the only color was from a single gold front tooth. She'd obviously been beaten—the face was swollen and bruised.

"That's not Maia," I said.

"You're sure?"

"Absolutely. Jesus."

Sanchez grabbed a clipboard from one of the uniforms who was firing Polaroids of the site. He looked from the driver's license portrait of Maia to the body and back again. The picture was a clean black-and-white print that had been blown up; it didn't show Maia at her best, but it did show her smiling, and in that smile there was no gold tooth.

"No recent dental work?"

I shrugged. I was starting to feel relieved, which allowed me to appreciate the horror of the situation. "I haven't seen her in months, but it wouldn't change anything. Maia's taller and thinner than this, and she never wore jeans."

"Well, that's hardly unimpeachable evidence," Sanchez said, "but it works for me. Looks like you dodged a bullet."

"Yeah. And twenty minutes from now, some other poor son of a bitch is going to get a phone call to come out here."

The sky was brightening behind me as I got back to Ninth Street. It was going to be another hot-but-otherwise-perfect day, not the kind of day to leave you quaking in fear.

But I was going to do my best.

When he'd taken me back to my car Sanchez told me that the rate of disappearances here in Pima County was much higher than he'd said. It wasn't just a dozen over as many years . . . it was more like one every other *week*.

"I don't want to sound ungrateful," I told him, "but that's a significant difference."

"Your girlfriend is one of a dozen airport kidnappings over that span of time. When it comes to bodies in the desert, there are lots of other sources."

"Oh."

He went on to say that there were certainly dozens of other disappearances that were never reported. In fact, the Jane Doe out on the east side matched the description of no other woman but Maia. Yet she was lying dead in the desert. Whoever she was, she was probably one of those who had slipped through the cracks.

"Who's doing this?"

"I don't know. This town's got a lot of drug traffic, professional and amateur, and some of these women get into it. They're coyotes carrying a couple of bags in their luggage from one place to the next. Pretty girls have ways of getting wherever they want to go without necessarily being checked. The downside, of course, is they attract a lot of attention from your everyday psycho killer.

"And then you've got your hookers who get picked up by the wrong guy, and your everyday woman who gets grabbed off the street by a rapist. Christ, if you're a woman you just can't go out of the house after dark—not alone, anyway."

"Maia wasn't grabbed off the street, she was in a goddamn airport surrounded by people! She wasn't a hooker. She wasn't running drugs. She just disappeared into thin air. I don't expect you to know what happened to her, Lieutenant, but please don't try to bullshit me."

Sanchez just looked down at the steering wheel. "Look, you're in the service—you've heard of the phrase 'need to know.' You don't need to know what we think about these disappearances. Not yet, anyway; if you're lucky, maybe never."

"Don't hand me that need-to-know crap. I get enough of that in the Air Force. If you people were *really* interested in solving your mystery, you'd be looking for help from anyone who'd talk to you." I was getting a bit too angry for the circumstances, but I couldn't shut up. "Besides, if anyone has a need to know, it's me."

He blinked. "Okay. There's one thread, one trait that a lot of the women being grabbed around Tucson share. They're all doing religious work. One of them was a nun, a couple of others were Mormon gals, most of them are volunteers from one damn church or another—all of them known as religious activists."

"And all of them gone."

"About a dozen of them, yeah." He sighed. "Don't lose sleep over it. We'll probably never figure it out."

As if what I'd just seen hadn't been enough, now I was getting chilled. What's worse than your basic random psycho killers? Organized psycho killers? Psycho killers from Mars? Agents of the Devil?

It occurred to me that Sanchez hadn't said *murders*; he said *disappearances*.

Every time I start thinking I've grown up enough to understand how the world works, something comes along to make me feel as though I'm four years old again. Presidents have affairs with show girls who also have affairs with "retired businessmen." Baseball players bet on games. TV evangelists not only steal from the video faithful, they lie to their own families. People in the Middle East who claim to be fighting for personal freedom always turn out to be eager to put bullets into the skulls of other human beings.

I was trained to be a scientist, of sorts. I like the part of science that says that identical procedures lead to identical results. I like the security of that. The predictability. The sense that the world works according to rules I can understand. I don't understand voodoo or crystals or the Mob or holy wars: they don't follow the rules.

And neither did this.

I was about to pull into the parking lot at the apartment when I noticed something else that violated the rules.

A couple of houses east of the apartment, at a place I passed driving west, there was a car. A big gray Oldsmobile, fairly new. That was unusual in itself: the area south of campus was home to lower-middle-class people or students, meaning you found older American cars or fairly new imports. No Mercedes or Jaguars and very few new Oldsmobiles.

What struck me about the car was that there were four men inside, all of them sitting very still, staring straight ahead, as if they were hoping not to be noticed. I tried not to notice them; I didn't slow down.

Four strange men in a strange car sitting in front of a tacky little Tucson bungalow—a bungalow which had a lawn of gravel painted green—at five in the morning. I wish I had had the presence of mind to notice the plates, but I was trying so hard to be casual that I failed.

Maybe Sanchez had shaken me up. Or maybe I was just too damned tired.

I mean, why should these guys scare me?

I wasn't surprised to find Jayan waiting up for me. I had considered calling her from the Circle K, but I suppose you have to find yourself in a similar situation—no change in your pockets and no wallet—to understand why I thought it would be less trouble to come straight home. I told her that the police had found somebody who wasn't Maia and that as far as we were concerned, she was still alive . . . somewhere. I asked how Gus was and she said he was fine, and then I collapsed on the bed.

6

I awoke to the sound of voices and found Hazel and Jayan chatting over Baby Gus at the kitchen table. I looked at the clock and saw that it was after noon. I must have groaned.

"Are we getting too loud?" Hazel asked.

"I'm getting too late," I said. "I'm supposed to be at D-M."

"We didn't even think of waking you up. I'm not sure we could have."

I sprinted for the shower as best I could, feeling as though I'd been in a coma. When I came out of the shower and dressed, Jayan had some coffee and toast waiting, and I felt better than I'd felt in days. Jayan and Hazel insisted that they would handle Gus together today; I carried him around for a couple of minutes just for the fun of it, then turned him over and headed for the car again.

The sun was shining and the only clouds in the sky were some wispy altocumuli over the Catalinas. It was already eighty, but the humidity I judged—in my professional opinion—to be in the low twenties. Given what I'd been going through, it felt like spring.

But I still couldn't lose that seed of fear I'd picked up the night before. I actually did a walk-around of the Mazda before I got in it, looking for what I don't know: wires, I suppose. No one seemed to have planted a bomb in it, so I started it up. But I orbited the block once looking for that Oldsmobile—which wasn't there—before I peeled off and headed for the base.

Ming the Merciless wasn't on duty when I walked into Base Ops, meaning I saved myself minutes of pointless sparring. I signed myself out to AMARC, where I found Alquist already at work with his favorite reading material, a red folder stamped "Special Project 14: Classified." The Diebold safe behind him was open. "Morning," he said, and slid the file toward me.

"What's this SP-14?"

"Project Puff," he said proudly.

"Should I even be looking at this? When I get my orders, I'm gone."

"Hey, you never know. Besides, it never hurts to learn what you can when you can." He grinned. "I spent a couple of weeks in administration at Offutt and used the time to leaf through as many Form 490s as I could." Those were the officer performance reports; in the Air Force, your Form 490 was your life. "Fascinating."

"So that's how you made captain so quickly." It was a joke, but it came out with too much edge. Alquist picked up the Puff file with his thumb and forefinger and took it back.

"Greg," I said, "I'm sorry, I've been acting like a dick. You've been trying to help me, and I'm grateful. I've just got too much on my mind to be civil." But he'd locked the file away.

"Another day," he said. "You probably want this, anyway."

He tossed a business-sized white envelope on my desk. The return address was Department of the Air Force, Personnel, Randolph AFB, San Antonio. These were my orders.

I stared at them.

"Aren't you going to open them?"

I ripped it open and took out the paper. It was a permanent change of station—PCS—form and it was stamped August 22:

REPLY TO ATTN PB

SUBJECT: Permanent Change of Station

TO: 1LT Richard E. Walsh, Jr.,
AWS/SYP Davis-Monthan AFB

1. Report to AFSC, Space Systems Division, Los Angeles, AFB, as systems project support officer, Project SP-14.

2. Enroll at University of Southern California for completion of Ph.D. in atmospheric physics.

3. Accept by or on 03 September. [This had been inked in.]

4. Acceptance entails a four-year active-duty service commitment and carries selection for rank of captain.

"Not bad, is it?" Alquist said. I was still staring at the piece of paper.

Not bad didn't describe it. There's a great danger in the Weather Service of being stationed wherever there's bad weather. Greenland. Iceland. Alaska. Montana. I had lucked out so far in drawing service in Nebraska and the Far East. Being assigned to Southern California was nevertheless like winning the lottery. And most of the natives spoke English.

To make things even more enticing, they were offering to send me to USC to finish up my doctorate while I got familiar with the same Project Puff that my good friend Captain Alquist had been pushing so hard.

"You knew all about this," I said.

"I only knew that you were going to be working on the same project," he said smugly. "I inferred that you would be stationed here or in New Mexico or in California, because that's where the project is." He looked at the orders. "L.A., too. I was wrong. Someone up there *likes* you."

Based on my recent experiences, I could easily have challenged the statement, but I let it pass. I just folded up the form and stuck it back in its envelope.

Alquist watched that with amusement. "I know. You don't want to appear *too* eager. Stiff upper lip and all that." He did a passable British accent. "We'll miss you 'round the place."

"I haven't accepted . . . yet."

"You will. You'd be an idiot not to."

"I've got a lot of things to straighten out before September third."

Now he stared at me. He was still doing his accent. "I do believe you're *serious*."

I nodded toward the safe. "Greg, what kind of a career move is Puffster, anyway? So we work on a stealthed cruise missile, so what? No matter how good it is, it can't really be deployed anywhere. We could be wasting our time."

Alquist's accent was gone. "You're not thinking this through, Walsh. It's a good project working for good people. What else do you need?" Well, when you got right down to it, he was absolutely right. On a better day I'd have dived on the offer. I just wasn't ready to think about a new job, in a new state, with Maia missing.

Suppose she was never found. What would I do with

Gus while I was trying to be a grad student *and* an Air Force engineer?

"Don't worry, I'll do the right thing." Whatever that would be. "Greg, you follow all this spook stuff. If you wanted to look into some long-term police investigation, how would you do it?"

"What kind of investigation? Drugs? Fraud?" He lowered his voice. "This about your girlfriend?"

"Yeah. Missing persons."

He thought for a moment. He loved this kind of thing. "The FBI always has jurisdiction for missing persons, though there's some cross talk between FBI and CIA if it involves foreign nationals. Actually the FBI interfaces with every agency you can think of, and some you've never heard of, when it has to, but it always has the lead. Otherwise they wind up in front of Congress."

"I couldn't just call the local FBI and start asking questions."

"Probably not. Besides, an interagency operation would be run by some special task force and the local office might not know anything about it."

This didn't sound promising. Alquist could sense my frustration. "Look, this must be tough. I know a few people who know a few people. AFI interfaces with the FBI, too." AFI was Air Force Intelligence. "You want me to make a couple of calls?"

"That would be great . . . but I don't have anything to give you beyond a vague suspicion that some large-scale investigation is going on, and Maia's disappearance might be part of it."

He was determined now. "I'll make some calls. Maybe we can get some of this shit straightened out so you can take these fine orders and go surfing."

I spent the next couple of hours chasing after my luggage, which should have arrived via transport, and found it was probably sitting at Beale Air Force Base near Sacramento waiting for its C-135 to get fixed.

The good news was that admin had freed up my money; since I had a contact at the First Interstate Bank branch just outside the main gate, I was able to set up an account and get some walking-around cash without driving around half the city.

Once I got the money situation straight I hopped in the car and took off for the first shopping center I could find. I grabbed a hot dog, then poked around in a K Mart and Radio Shack for a while, picking up a lot of doodads, including a small mirror, some brackets, screws, and tools, a small hot plate, a rheostat, wire, and, after a visit to a thrift store recommended by the guy at Radio Shack, the foot pedal assembly from an old Singer sewing machine.

Gus's bedroom was not designed for efficient use. There was no way to tell when the little guy had his eyes closed when you were trying to walk him to sleep, for one thing. At least, not without racking him around (and waking him up in the process). So I wanted to install a small mirror at eye level near the door.

The hot plate was an experiment in physics. Those baby wipes were always cold and damp, even in Tucson's weather. I could only imagine how they felt on a tender bottom, so I wondered if warming the carton would bring them closer to body temperature . . . without cooking the things.

And the foot pedal I was going to hook up to the rheostat—light dimmer—and the remote unit for the TV. If I was going to do a lot of baby rocking at weird hours, I saw no reason not to watch a little TV. And why should you have to get out of the chair to turn the light on and off?

When I got back to base I stopped in admin again, don't ask me why. If I declined the assignment to Los Angeles

I was effectively quitting the Air Force. But it isn't as
though I had to give two weeks' notice. I could stay in the
service until next February, what with accumulated leave,
sick pay, etc. My interrupted enrollment at the university
had been prepaid for one whole school year and so far I'd
only used one semester.

It seemed that in the unlikely event I decided to leave
the service, I could stay in uniform and complete my doctorate in Tucson, and be assured of money for rent and
groceries—and Pampers and day care—for at least six
months. It was something to think about.

But as Alquist said, I'd be an idiot not to take the assignment.

I called home and got no answer. Maia didn't believe
in answering machines, anyway. I was worried for several
seconds, but assumed that Jayan and Hazel and Gus had
gone for a walk. I just hoped they kept him out of the sun.

As a concession to the taxpayers, I thought it would be
nice if I made at least a token appearance at AMARC
before heading home. On my way in I almost collided with
Alquist, who was on his way out.

"Hey, did you find out anything about any special task
forces?"

He just shook his head. "Struck out. Looks like you're
dealing with a routine disappearance."

"It's hardly routine to me, Greg."

He swallowed, having realized his error. "Of course
not. Sorry. I just didn't find anything helpful."

"Thanks for trying." He clapped me on the shoulder
and took off.

It was starting to get to me. I wondered if Sanchez had
been able to make a positive identification of the body out
on Houghton Road; if nothing else, it might be a good
way to get him to tell me more about who and what I
"needed to know."

The only phone in our little office sat on Alquist's desk. I dug Sanchez's business card out of my wallet while I sat down. "Lieutenant David Sanchez," it said. No department given, no title, just the name and a phone number: 885-7736. I dialed.

"7736," a woman answered. For some reason that struck me as odd. Shouldn't she have said, "Tucson Police"?

"I'm trying to reach Lieutenant Sanchez."

There was a pause. "He's not available at the moment. Do you have a message?"

I really didn't. I suppose I only wanted to chat. "Ah, no," I said, "I'll call later." Before she could hang up, I added, "Excuse me. What department is this?"

Another pause. "This is a Tucson police number."

"I know, but is this homicide or traffic—"

"I'm not authorized to discuss that, I'm sorry."

"No problem." I hung up.

Well, agencies always like to keep their little secrets. I wouldn't have thought any more about it if I hadn't glanced down right then at the notepad on Alquist's desk. (He was very meticulous, the kind of person whose handwriting is legible.)

STG? 885-7736

STG. Special Task Group? Maybe. Why would he have Sanchez's number?

I began to think that I was showing signs of mental fatigue again. STG could be Systems Test Group or any of a hundred military offices. There must be a dozen different 885-7736 numbers in the United States, too, with all the area codes.

I got another inspiration, found the Mountain Bell phone book, and looked up the Tucson Police number: 792-1000. That was also odd: a 1000 number implies that it's part of a rotary calling system in which most, if not all, direct-dial numbers would be between 1000 and 2000. You'd think the homicide desk of the Tucson P.D. would be a number like that, wouldn't you?

Unless the office I was calling—the 7736—was located elsewhere. That wouldn't fit homicide at all.

In any case, I was feeling better. I had all my goodies in the car, the air conditioner was working, and all I had to do was be careful not to run into somebody on my way home. (Because of the way the streets are laid out in Tucson, driving west at sunset is a special challenge.)

As I walked across the gravel to the apartment, I noticed that the front door was hanging open—a silly thing to do on such a hot afternoon. Then I saw that the top hinge was broken and the screening pulled back.

And I ran.

7

The apartment had been turned inside out. Someone had swept an arm across the desk, spraying envelopes and pencils and the rest all over the dining area. The table had been moved. The cushions were off the hideaway. I picked them up and tossed them back where they belonged. The place was as quiet as I've ever heard it. The only noise, in fact, was the ever-present drone of Maia's air conditioner.

I checked in the bedroom. Fewer signs of a struggle, but still untidy. The rack holding the Pampers and baby wipes on the side of the changing table was gone. The side of the crib was up and the blankets were unruffled. Gus hadn't been there lately.

I found Hazel in the bathroom, lying next to the tub, out cold. There was a bluish lump the diameter of a baseball on the side of her face. She had either hit her head on the tub when falling, or been clubbed.

But she was still breathing.

I picked her up off the floor and carried her into the living room, where I laid her on the couch. I grabbed the phone—surprised that it still had a dial tone—and called 911. As I was giving the dispatcher the address, I happened to glance toward the back door leading from the kitchen to the culvert.

It was still swinging.

I thanked the dispatcher, begged her to hurry, and hung up—at least I hope that was the order—and skidded through the kitchen. Between the door and the fence which bordered the culvert was a clearance of about four feet, and in that clearance the apartment builders, in their wisdom, had planted water pipes, gas meters, and electrical connections, leaving just enough room for the occasional meter reader to struggle through.

I saw immediately that no one had gone to the left. The branches of a black olive tree that grew in the culvert had taken over that approach, leaving barely enough room for a cat to sneak through.

If you went to the right, you went toward Mountain, the side street which intersected Ninth. I got there as quickly as I could, through the obstacle course of pipes and vines, and looked toward the front of the apartment.

A car just about ran me over. I suppose that was the idea. It came barreling around the corner from behind me, across the culvert, and, clipping me, made a right onto Ninth.

I jumped when I caught the motion in my peripheral vision, and that probably saved me from a broken leg or torn knee, since all the glancing impact did was spin me around and dump me in the gutter. I scraped my hands and knees, but I still managed to see the car.

It didn't have a license plate. I didn't need one by then, since I recognized the car as that gray Oldsmobile that I'd seen parked out front the day before. I ran to the corner in time to see it making a fast left down Santa Rita, the next cross street. A few blocks away was Broadway.

There were several people in the car. Two in the backseat were struggling. I convinced myself that one of them was Jayan.

I ran around the front and into the apartment. Hazel was still out cold. Her breathing sounded funny, giving me one more thing to worry about.

Jayan and (presumably) Gus were getting further out of reach with every passing second. What choice did I have? I grabbed one of the hideaway blankets—it was on the floor—and covered Hazel the best I could. Then I grabbed my keys and headed for the Mazda.

As I shot across Ninth to make the turn onto Santa Rita, I heard a siren. Further down Ninth a rescue vehicle was on its way. So I consoled myself that Hazel would have professional care in a few moments . . . and that I hadn't *really* abandoned her.

Tucson's rush hour was already in progress and Broadway was starting to resemble a parking lot . . . at least the three eastbound lanes leading out of downtown. I didn't have any idea where the Oldsmobile was headed, but it couldn't have gotten far going that way. I took a moment and scanned the traffic. I saw a car or two that might have been the one I wanted . . . but they seemed to have solo drivers. The kidnappers must have taken a right, and so did I, veering uncomfortably close to some guy who had the bad luck to be in my way. He and I shared a moment of what a friend of mine calls Corvette's syndrome—the automotive equivalent of Tourette's syndrome—which is the automatic and uncontrollable vocalization of frustration suffered by big-city drivers. It's notable for the recurring use of one four-letter word in particular, as well as several others of varying lengths. You've had it, too. Listen to yourself the next time you find out the hard way that the Department of Water and Power has torn up that street you use on your way home from work, backing up traffic for miles.

As is usually the case, these pleasantries only took a moment.

I had the window down as I headed toward the railroad tracks which forever prevented downtown Tucson from growing, so I noticed that the air was suddenly getting cool. In the rearview mirror I could see the thunderheads building over the Catalinas.

Great; I needed to chase these people through a monsoon.

The Mazda had a lot of engine for its size—more than a late-model Oldsmobile carrying four adults, at any rate—so I was pretty sure I'd be able to catch them. What I'd do with them when I did was another matter.

But I hit downtown, veering onto Congress at the Greyhound depot (Broadway became one-way against me at that point), and fairly flew past City Hall and La Placita without spotting them.

I hit outbound traffic and a light just past I-10. Just as I was about to curse myself for acting like an idiot in a TV show, I spotted the Olds up ahead at another red light. Both of us were stuck.

So I *became* an idiot in a TV show. I gunned the car onto what I choose to call the shoulder (this was a two-lane street, not a highway, but the dividing line between pavement and dirt was fairly indeterminate) and ran the light. I only had to hit the brakes once to avoid cross-traffic.

The first drops hit my windshield. Tucson's monsoon is tropical. When the drops come, the deluge isn't far behind. I switched on the wipers and saw that the light up ahead was green, and the Olds was gone. There it was: to my left, heading south on Grande toward the base of "A" Mountain.

Somewhere below "A" Mountain, Grande became

Mission. By either name the road was a washboard, so neither car was setting any world land-speed records. It gave me time to wonder who these guys were, and where they were going. This Sanchez business had me confused. Was this a drug investigation or spy stuff or mail fraud? Maybe immigration—Tucson is the sanctuary headquarters of the U.S. It's a place where a lot of refugees from El Salvador and Panama come for help.

Where they heading to San Xavier? I tried to remember whether the old mission had been designated a sanctuary, but who pays attention to news like that if it doesn't affect him?

Just as we were about to emerge from the shadow of the mountain, the rains came with a roar, shutting out the sunset as quickly as if you drew a shade. I had to slow down. I guess the Olds did; by then I could barely see the front of my car, much less taillights a hundred yards ahead.

I did see them take a right at Ajo Way, which shot the hell out of my old mission-sanctuary theory right there, and left us heading due west. Ajo briefly became a four-lane road, but believe me, to no great effect. Off to our right was some park which you'd have a hard time differentiating from wild desert, and here and there were new housing developments—I'd heard the area described as "the poor man's foothills" once—all an illusion. We were heading out of town, right into the heart of the Papago Indian Reservation.

All I knew about the Papago was that they were dirt-poor, even by wretched Indian standards, and that their name meant "bean eater" in Spanish. (It was derogatory; like every other group in the world, their name for themselves translated as "people.") They did some farming using the flash flood method—wait until there's a flash flood, move your home there, and plant your crops; when you harvest them a few months later, look for another flood—which was hardly the sign of a formerly great civilization. The Hohokam a few miles north of Tucson once had observatories; the poor Papago had rocks.

It must have been ten miles out of town that the rain suddenly stopped. Back in Tucson, of course, it was still drenching the foothills and the city . . . but I'd crossed into the low desert. The setting sun peeked through the clouds.

And on the clear stretch of road ahead of me there was no Oldsmobile.

I drove on for a few hundred yards until I reached a high place, then pulled off. There was little traffic of any kind—battered pickup trucks, mostly. The air was cool and charged with ozone. The only sound was the wind, and the distant thunder from what was now the other side of the mountains.

I found a map in the glove compartment. It wasn't much help, since it showed no major roads of any kind between the fork which branched off to Old Tucson, something I'd passed long ago, and Robles Junction, still several miles away.

Well, this part of the low desert was anything but track-less. You could pull off the road at almost any point and strike out across the land in either direction. They must have done that. I got back in the car and turned it around.

Less than two miles back I came to a series of curves so sharp that had they been on a hillside you'd call them switchbacks. I'd had to slow down coming through the first time . . . and I slowed down again, only now I was looking.

Sure enough, at one curve there was a dirt road leading straight into the desert, just like the escape chute at a raceway. The rain had reached here and the surface was still wet, and when I got out to look I saw fresh, deep tire tracks. A clot of mud fell even as I watched. Not that it was easy to see: the sun was down by now, and the clouds that still covered half the sky made it all the darker.

But someone had just made a high-speed turn through here.

Even though it was dark I kept the lights off. The road ran fairly straight and was wide enough that I wouldn't have to worry about losing it just yet. The Mazda ran very quietly, too, so I figured I might be able to sneak up on these people. Stealth, in fact, was all I could count on. The kidnappers probably had guns.

You can make a cruise missile or a bomber "invisible," but what about someone in my situation? That was one of my thoughts as I played Great White Tracker. It was as close as I got to remembering that I was an Air Force officer with a lot of decisions to make.

Then I saw the Oldsmobile.

Mud-spattered but otherwise unchanged, it sat in the road. There had been no attempt to move it to one side. I stopped a few yards back and turned off the engine to listen. All I heard were the sounds of the desert at night. Rustles and distant birdcalls. Something that might have been the roar of a jet going into the airport. Presently I got out of the car.

It was cool enough that I wished for a sweater—perhaps that was just the tension. I looked both ways and behind me as I walked toward the Olds, fearful that somebody would jump me . . . but I reached the car unmolested.

Figures. It was empty.

The tag in the window said the car had been registered less than a week ago. A decal on the bumper said it was from Budget. All the doors were unlocked; there was no key in the ignition. I left the door open so I had light from the dome bulb. I searched the front seat and found nothing; there was no rental agreement in the glove compartment, either. The thing looked swept, but I took a moment to crawl into the backseat.

An object made of rubber and white plastic had fallen under the front seat. Gus's pacifier. Well, I'd assumed he was with Jayan, but it still hurt. I remember thinking that the little guy was *really* unhappy now. And that if they did anything to him I would kill them all.

I got out of the car and, without thinking, slammed the door. So much for my stealthy pursuit.

Then a voice called out. It was just one word—one syllable—that might have been "Help!" or might have been a name. And it could have come from Jayan. It was off to my right, toward the fading sunset.

Well, they knew I was out here by now, so I tore off into the brush while trying to imitate the 7th Cavalry. It was rough going. What little light I had was in my face, which was great for showing me mesquite branches six feet off the ground, but made me blind as far as knowing where my feet were landing. I stumbled half a dozen times, but kept going, not knowing if it was the right direction or not, going on, until I found that I was heading up a slope.

Then I heard another noise . . . an engine being started. It wasn't a car engine, but something smaller, more rackety, like a chain saw (horrid thought) or a lawn mower. It dopplered away from me as I scrambled up the slope.

I went right over the edge.

It wasn't a great fall, thank God; it was more of a slide, which left me on my back staring up at Venus. It was curiously comfortable and for several moments I was tempted to stay there. After a bit the feeling came back and I realized I was lying on a bed of rocks. Getting up, I saw a dry wash below me. I had fallen halfway down the slope. The other side was odd—it rippled, light, dark, light, like aurora borealis.

I can't say I was thinking clearly. I'd heard some sort of machine start up, but what? An all-terrain vehicle? That sounded likely. You could drive it up one of these washes with relative ease. You could also track it in the dark . . . maybe.

To hell with stealth. "Jayan!" I shouted. "Gus! Maia!" There wasn't even an echo. I guess I was starting to panic. I pushed forward, then slipped and slid down the slope and hit the bed of the wash. It was all gravel and sand, very flat. Very dry.

Nothing moved. I could no longer hear even faint desert noises. And, looking up, I could have sworn that Venus was gone—or moved. I must have hit my head.

I headed toward the middle of the wash, looking for tracks. Suddenly a wall of water hit me, and I was swimming.

At first I thought I'd wandered into a flash flood. I gulped air, hoping I would be swept toward one of the banks. Then I realized that the water wasn't roaring down the wash, it was just *there*. Like a creek. And somehow I'd fallen in it.

And somehow it had become midmorning, because the sun was shining and I could see the other side clearly. So I swam toward it.

8

When your life is threatened, thirty seconds can take forever . . . or so they say. Life-threatening situations are generally not in my job description. My only experience with this purported time expansion was sitting in the garage trying to work up the courage to go in the house and face Mom, knowing I had just run her Pontiac into another car, causing something like a thousand dollars' worth of damage to both. This was three weeks after I got my driver's license.

Trying to swim to shore took too much energy. All I knew was that something weird had happened in the middle of that wash. Period. And that within seconds, minutes, whatever, I was scraping my hands and knees on the far shore and coughing creek water out my mouth and nose.

For a few moments I could easily have been convinced that I had drowned and was now in a post-death situation. Fine. I'm open-minded about life after death. I mean, what's not to like? But presently I noticed that my shoes were waterlogged and my feet were bothering me. As I sat down to make adjustments, I noticed that what I remembered as the evening of a desert monsoon now resembled a day in early spring. Therefore Saint Peter was not expected to make an appearance; even if heaven exists, it's not likely to be a place where your primary activity is wringing out socks and stretching loafers. (Isn't there some old song that deals with the problem of heavenly footwear for all God's children?) The sun was high; the air was cool. Obviously I had been knocked silly in the creek and fetched up someplace downstream, some hours later.

It took me ten seconds to question that theory: even if I'd been walking around in a daze, my shoes would have dried by now. My Timex said it was just after eight o'clock; A.M. or P.M.? At least thirteen or fourteen hours should have passed.

Well, I could have walked back into the water, right? Who knew? All I remembered was hitting the water in darkness and climbing out in sunlight.

Whatever. I felt just miserable enough to still be alive. I'd figure out the rest later.

Although the air was cool, it was warm in the sun, and I stripped off my shirt and pants to let them dry. It gave me a few moments—not that I was in a hurry to go anywhere—to look around.

How do I explain this? It no longer felt like southern Arizona to me. Certainly I was no longer in the low desert, but in a much greener place. The vegetation around me suggested pines and juniper, which are trees that grow in the higher elevations or in colder climates. The opposite shore, now that I had a chance to look at it, was wooded and free of the cliff-like structure I'd discovered the hard way, though it was still steep and kept me from seeing very far.

All around me were wooded hills and beyond those—

close enough that I could see individual rocks and trees—
were several mountain peaks. Had I been chasing around
northeast of Tucson instead of southwest, I could have
convinced myself I was near Mount Lemmon in the Catalinas . . . but that would mean I had wandered, delirious,
some fifty miles. Uphill, too. Across a major freeway. Not
very likely.

What really struck me as odd was the sky. It was blue,
all right, that beautiful clear blue you see these days only
on mountaintops, or (so they tell me) in Alaska. The sun
was up there shining away at about ten o'clock.

But something was wrong with the clouds. There is a
high layer of very thin cirrocumulus that exists above
20,000 feet, high enough that it won't spoil your "clear"
blue sky. You probably don't notice it unless you fly in
747s or DC-10s, which punch through the layer on their
way to transcontinental cruising altitudes of 34,000 or
35,000 feet. Nevertheless, the layer exists, and it can in-
dicate where the jet stream is . . . that high, cold movement of air that starts in the Arctic and races around the
world at speeds upwards of 150 miles an hour.

It was there . . . but it was weird. Instead of looking
like a few spidery wisps running from northwest to south-
east, it looked like the ripples from a pool. The structures
were circular and immense. Picture a gigantic bull's-eye
made of wispy cloud up in the sky and you'll get the idea.

I'd seen circular cloud formations before, but never like
that.

I would have blamed it all on the blow to my head, but
I couldn't feel a lump anywhere. So all I had were mys-
teries and questions. Where was I? Was this where Gus
and Jayan and Maia had been taken? And by whom? And
why?

People make jokes about clothes made of synthetic
blends, and I confess to having made a few myself, but

when I saw my shirt and pants returning to a usable state, I promised never to do that again. I didn't much relish the thought of hiking cross-country dressed in my Jockey shorts.

Even the shoes were okay, though for several hours to come they would squish when I stepped. I wouldn't have passed an inspection, but I wouldn't draw stares.

Once I was dressed I turned my attention to the river. It flowed gently, spilling around some good-sized rocks, and not too deeply. I could probably have waded across. But what was on the other side? The river wasn't that wide— forty yards tops—so I tried an experiment. I picked up a rock and heaved it toward the other side, half expecting it to disappear in a blast of lightning. For some reason I felt disappointed when it just splashed into the water a couple of yards from the other shore.

The splash disturbed a flock of birds, who scattered into the woods before I could get a good look at them. They had long wings and necks. Maybe they were vultures (I did bacteria instead of birds in freshman biology) but if so, they had been fed. No creatures seemed to be lurking about, waiting for my imminent demise.

It had occurred to me by that time that, for a couple of days, at least, I might very well be forced into some Robinson Crusoe existence, building Boy Scout traps in the slim hope that I could snare a rabbit, sharpening reeds or branches and spearing fish, building fires out of a rock and an old joke to cook all this hypothetical game. Well, unfortunately my Boy Scout career topped out at First Class Scout, meaning I had stuck around just long enough to be promoted from Tenderfoot. Where I grew up camping meant sleeping in a "park" equipped with barbecue pits, showers, and precut paths through the woods. I managed to qualify for one of my very few merit badges— Forest Management—by spending one of those "camporees" collecting beer cans from those woods. I don't blame

the Scouts; if I'd stuck around and persisted, I might have
learned to skin and cook a rabbit. Who could have pre-
dicted that someday I'd find myself wandering dazed in a
wilderness far from room service?

A realistic assessment of the situation forced me to
overrule my own instincts, which were to stay right where
I was. The best I could do by staying put was eventually
starve to death or, more likely, break my neck climbing a
tree. At worst something evil—like the people who took
Gus and Jayan—would come back here and find me, probably asleep, certainly weakened.

I decided to attack. "Die trying" is the precise technical term.

Sticking to what I called "my" side of the river, I
headed north, the sun warm on my back.

Had I thought her strange? Too strange for a white boy
from the Midwest? Several times in those first three weeks.
She had this accent and she was uncomfortable around
cars and, in spite of her charm or radiance or whatever
you want to call it . . . she was always alone. She offered
no information about her family, if any, or hometown.
When I thought about it—and I did wonder about it from
time to time—I developed a pleasant fantasy which super-
seded my original suspicion that Maia was Amish. In the
revised version Maia was a rich woman from a country
like Venezuela or, better yet, Monaco, where she learned
English as a second language at a young age, where they
didn't have cars or, at least, not many of them, and her
wealth meant she was surrounded by servants all her life.

And since we had not only not slept together, we had
hardly even kissed, she'd obviously come out of a convent
school. The Virgin Maia.

As I sat in classes in which orographic lifting and in-
tertropical fronts and anticyclogenesis were the hot topics
of conversation, I began to wonder if this apparently ca-

sual friendship was going anywhere . . . and, if so, whether it ought to.

I think it happened the last weekend in September. Had we been the sort of cute couple inclined to such things, we would have been celebrating the one-month anniversary of our cute meeting. We had had three formal dates and a couple of encounters.

This was strictly a date-of-opportunity. I had been in a lab class that ran late and was passing the Science Library about five-fifteen on my way to my car when I saw Maia coming out. She wasn't supposed to have worked that day, but someone else had called in sick. She seemed unusually subdued, even distracted. One thing I had learned about Maia was that she was organized. In that little black book she had her day organized to the quarter hour. Any disruption tended to throw her. I asked her if school was going all right. (She continued to be damned vague about what she was studying, and why.) And did she want to get something to eat with me?

I don't remember if she answered the question or even said yes. She just took my arm and we kept walking until we reached a little Italian restaurant called V-J's on Sixth Street, just to the south of the campus. It was one of those six-tables, no-waiting places, and on a quiet Wednesday night at five-thirty, we had it all to ourselves.

We talked about food. We talked about her work. We talked about *my* work. Unlike many people I met then— or any I would meet now—Maia wasn't immediately horrified when I told her that I worked with delivery systems for nuclear weapons. In fact, she never showed any horror or disdain at all. It was the first time I'd actually talked about it, though. Being up all night reading DMSP satellite weather reports and charting forecasts for B-1 and B-52 crews. Or looking at the daytime weather over Moscow or Drovyanaya or Pervomaysk or any of a dozen target environments. (You'd be amazed at what a thunderstorm

79

could do to a trio of warheads, not to mention a low-flying bomber.) How it was unreal and yet all too real.

We finished, I paid, and we were out on Sixth Street when a car drove by. I never got a good look at it—it was just some old yellow beater carrying three or four teen-aged boys. They yelled, and Maia, shocked, turned to-ward them—

—And got hit in the face with a salvo of water balloons.

I was standing behind her and managed to duck. She took all of it, and the car squealed off down Sixth. Like an idiot, I took off after them, running a good half a block, calling them choice names from my official basic-training vocabulary, until they were out of sight. When I turned back I guess I expected to find Maia in tears or stamping her foot in anger, but she was *laughing* . . .

"Do I look that funny when I run?"

"My hero," she said. Then, as if she'd been doing it all her life, she kissed me.

While I recovered, she deftly removed a handkerchief from my pocket and wiped off her face. She pushed back her hair and took my arm again, and we walked the three blocks to her apartment.

This time when we said, "Good night," I followed it with, "Aren't you going to invite me in?"

Maia frowned and smiled slightly at the same time. "Don't say it unless you mean it," she said.

"I mean it," I said. And, heart pounding, I followed her inside.

Sometime about midnight I discarded the idea that Maia was a sheltered rich girl from Monaco. Rich, maybe; but she had *not* come straight from a convent.

By the time the sun was roughly overhead I had covered a little more than a straight-line mile. I can't say the going was hard, but since I did most of my walking on man-

sized rocks that clogged the river passage, I probably
walked two zigzag miles for the single straight one.

The rocks did give me a way across the river, though.
I took off my shoes and socks and, clutching them for the
valuable possessions they were, jumped and splashed my
way to the other side at the first opportunity. The water
was cool—something I knew already, of course—but not
mountain cold, which meant that the water must be coming from some sort of spring. If that was true, I couldn't
be far from civilization: this was late summer in Arizona.
There just aren't that many sources of water. The Rillito
River that ran through the north side of Tucson was so dry
it was used as a track for all-terrain vehicles.

Once on the other side I put my shoes back on and
pulled myself up the considerable slope. At the top I found
a bit of a view, which only confused me further: There
were mountains to the west and south, and wooded hills
in front of me. Far off to the northeast I could make out
dark shapes which might have been the Catalinas, and
might not.

In any case, that was where I was headed.

I was getting hungry, but a drink from the stream helped
me forget about it for a while. I passed several bushes
which held rosy berries, but decided not to chance them
until it became absolutely necessary. I saw far-off birds
shooting across the sky and heard the odd rustle of invisible creatures nearby. It gave me the strange feeling that I
was in some prehistoric or uninhabited world . . . Ridic-
ulous.

But I saw no signs of air travel, and there aren't many
places in the U.S. where that's true. Even in the deepest
Rockies you can see jet contrails. Tucson had the Air Force
base and an international airport as well as several general
aviation centers. On most working days the sky has more
lines on it than a ghetto sidewalk and there's always some

piece of machinery breathing overhead. Yet in two hours I'd heard not a single engine of any kind.

Before I had time to get depressed about that, I found a bottle in my path.

I was never so happy to see a piece of litter, but it didn't tell me much. It was just a dirty glass cylinder about five inches in length, tapered at the top, and maybe three inches in diameter. I crumbled some of its dirt covering and found not a Coca-Cola or Dr Pepper logo, but some funny-looking beast: a winged lion. Well, *someone* had dropped it there. Meaning I couldn't be that far from civilization.

Maybe that's why I didn't faint dead away when fifteen minutes later I stumbled out of the woods and onto a paved road.

It wasn't wide (maybe a lane and a half) and it wasn't new (the various concrete-like slabs which formed it were cracked and, at the edge, crumbling) but I had no complaints. Roads have beginnings and ends. I would have been happy with either.

The road ran perpendicular to my line of travel, sloping downhill to the right, so that was the way I went. It would have been a pleasant walk under most circumstances.

Within a half hour I had walked down out of the hills and come to land that had obviously been cleared and cultivated. Some things don't change: now there was a fence running along the road. I dug into it with a finger-nail. Weathered wood, no paint. And, on closer inspection, incredibly ancient. It had been put together so long ago that I couldn't find discrete crossbeams and supports . . . it was all of a piece.

Fences exist to keep animals in or unwanted visitors out. Since this fence consisted of three widely spaced rails, the top one about chest height, I judged it to be one of the former—even though I saw no animals. I reminded myself that it was midday and actually quite warm. Cattle or sheep would be off in the shade somewhere.

I hoped for a bit of breeze. The road had been carved out of a hollow that ran back into the mountains and should have provided a fine path for cool air, but air didn't seem to move much in this green world.

Before too long I spotted a break in the fence, which, on closer examination, turned out to be a dirt road running at right angles toward, presumably, a farmhouse. Should I keep going, or should I find that house and ask for help?

I was about to make the turn when I heard a shout behind me.

I jumped out of the road just as a truck bore down on me. The driver was a man of about forty dressed in a brownish shirt and full-brim hat, and I did what any serviceman down on his luck would do: I stuck out my thumb.

The truck slowed to a stop.

Then I almost screamed: the truck wasn't a truck. It was some kind of *animal*.

9

You know how you take a glance at the front end of a car and sometimes it looks like a face with the headlights where eyes would be, and a chrome bumper for a smile? This was something like that . . . only it wasn't chrome and glass, it was flesh and probably blood, too. A blocky gray creature the size of a Nissan pickup. Its eyes glowed red. There was a sheen of sweat on its sides. It snorted.

But it looked like a truck! There were even two wheel-like appendages in the rear to go with a pair of track-like "feet" up front. The creature's "back" was flat with bony ridges all around making a "bed," and in the bed were bundles of what looked to me like produce of some kind.

In front of the bed was a "cab," one open seat, in which sat a man who looked at me with my mouth hanging open as if I were the village idiot.

Okay, it was a farmer on his way to market.

"Slowmo weapon?" the farmer said, or something like it, which I took to mean, how far was I going?

I hadn't had much to eat. I had almost certainly been knocked on the head. I mean, that was as close as I've ever come to fainting. It wasn't the sight of the amazing truck monster, it was everything up to and including that.

I wasn't dead. But I wasn't in Kansas, either, Toto.

No, as I stood there in the cool sunshine of what seemed like a beautiful day in spring, I began to suspect that what had happened to me was the stuff of *In Search of Ancient Astronauts* or *Arthur C. Clarke's Mysterious World*. I had slipped through the cracks into some other Where, probably one in which the South won the Civil War or Nazis ruled America.

A world which was not on Mountain standard time.

A world called . . . the Twilight Zone. I half expected Rod Serling to step out from behind the nearest rock.

"Downtown," I said with a hopeful smile, pointing straight ahead.

The farmer looked at me. He had shaved this morning and bathed in recent memory. He had obviously been out in the sun a few times in his life. His eyes narrowed; he was being polite. *"Hockey?"* Or, I didn't quite catch that . . .

I spread my hands and pointed to my mouth and his mouth and said, "Don't speak the language."

He looked at me again. He looked at my semi-rumpled blues. I was still wearing my little blue name badge. Then he made a face that I translated as "what the hell" and nodded toward the area next to him.

I hesitated. Impatiently he gestured for me to walk around the "truck." As I did, he barked a whole series of sounds, and damned if a "seat" didn't take shape right next to him.

What else could I do? I climbed aboard.

The farmer was pointing to himself. *"Hissam Varney,"* he said, or the equivalent. He held out his hand.

"Rick Walsh," I said hopefully, and shook.

"Wick Wash," he repeated, more or less, and added a few other syllables for his own benefit. Then he chuckled. Maybe he made a little joke. I smiled the way you do when some street person accosts you with gibberish about vegetarianism.

Then he did a strange thing. With one hand on the "wheel"—actually, it was a cross between a wheel and a tiller, more of a wing with handles at the tips—he took off his hat and bowed his head. I didn't have a hat, but I did likewise. He uttered a few words to himself and shouted, *"Python picador!"* at our vehicle. Which started to move.

He raised his head and put his hat on.

All I could think of was a song from *Dumbo*. "I seen a vegetable stand and I seen a horse fly."

I seen a meat truck?

The seat felt like leather—no surprise there. There was no windshield, but as we got going about thirty miles an hour, the meat truck's ears deployed sufficiently to keep the bugs out of our mouths. If there were bugs. The ears were almost transparent, too.

I'll say this for the goofy-looking thing: considering the road, it had a suspension as good as any small pickup I'd been in, and it made less noise than a squeaky door.

The Walshes were never regular churchgoers, even when we managed to fool people into thinking we were a nuclear family, though after the divorce Mom turned Kate and me into Presbyterians for a while. It was the church all her friends attended. So my religious education was informal; I never got my fair share of Catholic or Jewish guilt.

Nevertheless, swaying in the front seat of the meat truck next to Mr. Varney, I began to acquire religion in a hurry. The guilt part, anyway. Because this was all my fault.

Between our first night together, which was in late September, and the second week in February, Maia and I had spent only three days apart—when I flew back to Omaha to spend Christmas with Kate and her family. It had been unusually cold, and though I was happy to see Molly again, I was miserable the whole time. (I was also nervous about being on Sarah's turf; I hadn't told her I was going to be in town and dreaded an accidental meeting.) I realized that I missed Maia. I wasn't even able to call her on Christmas, because she had told me she wouldn't "be around," whatever that meant.

Someday I'll look back on the first weeks after my return as some of the happiest in my life. I was on leave or light duty—remember, my Air Force job at the time was getting a doctoral degree, and this was semester break. We had the whole town to ourselves, it seemed, since thirty thousand of Maia's immediate neighbors were out of town, and the snowbirds that flock to Tucson in the winter don't arrive until mid-January or later.

We went to the Fourth Avenue Street Fair. We saw all the new movies. We hiked from downtown all the way to "A" Mountain and back. We made love every day. We even took Lambada lessons.

Then it all came crashing down.

On Friday afternoon, January 14, Big D told me to stop by his office. It was rainy and cold, miserable weather. My sinuses were killing me. And Ming the Merciless made sure I waited before announcing me.

"I need you to go to Guam," Big D told me, once I'd managed to get in to see him.

He could just as easily have said I need you to go to Mars. My response would have been the same. "It's kind of early for April Fools', isn't it?"

"I'm not kidding."

"When?"

"This weekend."

"I'm in the middle of a semester—"

"We all know that. It's a numbers game. Third Air's

being reorganized yesterday and they've come up short in a few areas, weather being one of them. You were actually about fifth on the list of barely suitable candidates, but I guess everyone else managed to come up with a better excuse than 'I'm in the middle of a semester.' Sorry.'' He smiled. ''It's only for four months. Then you can come back here and pick up where you left off.''

With school, maybe. But what about Maia?

By that time I was basically living at her place. I had my own apartment, but basically used it as a mail drop and storage. So the first thing I did after getting out of Devine's office and signing a bunch of outprocessing paperwork was head for Ninth Street.

I got there about four-thirty, about half an hour after Maia usually got home from class. No Maia. I let myself in and waited. And waited. I was supposed to be back at the D-M clinic by six to get my shots; everyone was going to be pissed off if I got there after closing. But I had thought it more important to tell Maia what was going on.

She finally showed up about five forty-five. ''Where have you been?'' I met her at the door and I wasn't happy.

She looked startled. ''I didn't know you were coming over.''

''Maia, I'm *always* over here after work.''

''I had an appointment.'' She brushed past me and went straight into the bathroom. I heard water running.

''I have some important news,'' I said to the door.

''I'll be right out.''

Well, she wasn't right out. She took ten minutes. I timed it. When she finally appeared she looked odd. Her face had been scrubbed, but her eyes were red. ''I'm sorry,'' she said, and then the phone rang.

She answered it while I fumed. ''Yes . . . No, I'm not . . . I suppose . . . Can't Leslie—?'' Maia looked at me and closed her eyes. Then, into the phone, she said quietly, ''I'll be there in fifteen minutes.''

"Be where?" I demanded as soon as she hung up. She sat down in a chair. I'd never seen her looking so tired and unhappy.

"Jeff's sick. They need me to work tonight."

"Oh."

She tried to smile. "What's your news?"

"I have to go to Guam." I reran my conversation with Devine and didn't even give her a chance to interrupt. When I was through, Maia merely got up from the chair and went into the bedroom.

"Is that all you've got to say?" I followed her. She was changing for work . . . quickly, precisely, obsessively. Trying to change the subject. "Damn it, Maia . . ."

She turned toward me. I'd never seen her like this—her face wore a mixture of pain and sadness and anger, and strength, too. "What should I say, Rick?"

I was being an ass. "How about, 'So long, soldier'?"

"If that's what you want. So long, soldier."

Well, how many relationships end pleasantly? "Don't be late for work." And I turned around and walked out.

Before I left, I threw the keys against the wall.

As soon as I'd belted myself into my car, I had second thoughts. Go back, sit down, to hell with the shots and getting to work. Talk this out.

But I didn't. And three days later I was packed and gone.

The arithmetic was easy, later: Maia had just come from an appointment with her doctor. She had just found out she was pregnant.

Hissam and I rode in relative silence for a while. I did see a couple of structures which might have been farmhouses, though both were so well hidden from the road— and fortified—that they could just as easily have been Club Meds.

The meat truck did a consistent thirty to forty miles an

hour, I judged, and fairly flew—all in that strange silence—through farmland. After a while Hissam turned to me and said, *"Neo macho excess apollo?"* and pointed behind his seat. There I found a bottle a little like one of those two-liter things your neighborhood 7-Eleven sells, half empty (before the events of the past few days I would have said half full). The fluid contained in it was amber and carbonated. I was thirsty and hungry, so I wasn't inclined to be picky. After a momentary struggle, I popped it open and held it out to Hissam, who shook his head. He gestured for me to take a drink. I raised the bottle.

Hissam grabbed it and gave me a dirty look. *"Peanuts brute!"*

I'm afraid I just stared. I had screwed up here, but how? Was I about to be pitched out of the truck on my head?

Hissam just stared back for a moment, then, with a shake of his head, said tiredly, *"Overcast structure . . ."* He took off his hat again and bowed, and mumbled words I couldn't make out. Finally he raised his head, put his hat on again, and motioned to me, as you would to a two-year-old, *"Apollo."*

So I *apolloed*. It was some kind of fruit drink, maybe a little alcoholic, and not bad at all. I was considering another swig when a . . . a shape swooped by overhead.

I almost dropped the bottle. I looked up, and there, heading south of us and moving fast, was the biggest bird I have ever seen in my life. It must have had a wingspan of a hundred feet.

Then I took a closer look. It wasn't a bird. It was some kind of creature with scales. A reptile. There were markings on the side which made no sense to me and I realized the air was thick with a smell like ozone crossed with diesel.

A *dragon*?

Hissam could have cared less. Maybe this was the approach pattern to Dungeon Central and he saw it every day. But it shook me up, I tell you.

Dragons.

I thought about Maia and Baby Gus and Hazel and even Jayan, and felt like crying. It was just too much.

Then a hillside appeared in front of us, and in it, a tunnel. We drove through it and emerged into the sunlight, and saw before us a huge city stretching to distant mountains.

"Tucson?" I said, more out of reflex than anything else.

Clearly annoyed, Hissam merely squinted at me. *"Chios,"* said he.

10

"Chios," of course, was Maia's family name. When I got over the shock of hearing it, I realized it was the first familiar thing I'd heard or seen yet.

Somehow I didn't find that particularly comforting, not after the meat truck and the dragon and the impossible sky. I was still vaguely suspicious that this was all a long, unpleasant dream. And I couldn't wake up.

We weren't actually close to the city proper yet. We had emerged from the tunnel heading downhill toward the flatland of Tucson/Chios, but there were quite a few smaller hills to negotiate. The farms here were more modest. I suspected that some of them were simply homes for the rich—assuming, of course, that in this world rich people *wanted* land around them.

Before long we hit our first intersection and Hissam stopped the truck. This other road was wider, but free of traffic, and there were no stop signs—no markings of any kind. Yet he stopped, bowing his head for an instant, then nudged us across.

The hesitation gave me a moment to glance around. Off to my right, on the limb of the road heading back into the hills, there was a cluster of buildings surrounded by a serious-looking fence. It struck me as a great place for a Circle K or even a truck stop, but the look suggested only one thing: a guard shack. I could even see a barrier across the road. Then we started up again.

Well, that might explain why Hissam was so nervous about crossing the road. Military traffic, whether in the form of vehicles like this one or dragons the size of B-52s, would have priority. You wouldn't even want to argue the point.

A couple of other meat trucks passed us going the other way. They looked enough like Hissam's to be cousins, I suppose. Maybe they were from the same litter. And they passed us on our left. So in both worlds people drove on the right side of the road, and we both had rich people and military bases. I wish I could say that it was beginning to feel like home.

Maybe it was just too neat. No billboards. No beer cans on the shoulder. No *shoulder*.

The hills had given way to land as rugged as the average tabletop. The only thing preventing me from seeing downtown Chios was the dust in the air—or what might have been smog. It obviously couldn't come from trucks like Hissam's: you can't see methane, assuming that was the "by-product" of the meat trucks, and buses and cars, if they existed. The thought of all that methane made me wish we were headed away from Chios. But I didn't have any choice, and might have been worried unnecessarily: automobile engines aren't the only sources of smog. Industry and even farming (everything around me looked dry) will ruin your sky very nicely.

Then I saw my first billboard.

It was a big thing about the size of those yellow Stuckey's signs that blot out the landscape throughout much of the Midwest, sitting off to our left and, in some strange way, commanding our attention. There were letters all over it, and a picture of some winged animal—not a dragon this time, more like a lion with an eagle's head—that could have been painted by the same people who used to do Lenin for the Soviet May Day parades. There were others as well, all of them bearing the winged lion. I don't know, maybe they sold Winged Lion shaving cream or reminded us that our Winged Lion Meat Truck Stop was just a few hundred yards ahead. I sort of hoped it was the latter: I was hungry.

We finally hit some inbound traffic. Many of the vehicles were the now-familiar Hissam meat trucks. The others could have been vans, station wagons, even compact cars in function. In fact they were meat things, too: fast-moving "compacts" that moved like ponies, bigger "vehicles" that were cousins to turtles, but not quite. They were all too big. Their colors were garish greens and yellows and oranges that would never be found on creatures that had to survive in a jungle, much less on a product out of Seoul or Detroit. All of them had passengers of some sort perched on their backs, and all of them seemed quite comfortable.

The only change I noticed was that the road now had a slit trench right down the middle of each lane. I guess that made sense.

I was so stunned by this visual feast that my conversational skills had not come into play. No matter; Hissam had been singing to himself since we entered the tunnel. Now, in what seemed like mid-song, he stopped and began to pay a lot of attention to the traffic. A couple of one-syllable words came out of his mouth and it was clear he wasn't happy.

Suddenly a kid appeared among the slow-moving meat

cars. I put his age at thirteen or fourteen. He was pimply-faced and quick on his feet. He had to be: a couple of the catmobiles took swipes at him.

He was hustling something. He had a sheaf of papers in hand and moved from one "vehicle" to another, offering them, largely, in vain. When he popped up in Hissam's face, the farmer grabbed him and asked him a question. The kid shrugged. Hissam sighed and took one of the papers, handing over a coin. The kid smiled and answered Hissam's question, whatever it had been. Hissam started cursing (I think he had a touch of Corvette's syndrome, too) and the kid took that as a hint to move on to the next customer.

Hissam crumpled the paper he'd just bought and tossed it aside, spurring the meat truck into a lurch forward. The paper wound up in my lap. I offered it to Hissam, who ignored me. Uncrumpled, the paper turned out to be nothing more than a line of tiny, handwritten marks. A single sentence, maybe. I stuck it in my pocket.

When we found ourselves at a complete stop, Hissam actually stood on his seat for a better look. He sat down promptly and looked at me . . . and cursed again. This time he was angry at himself. He sighed and said, *"Macho society underwear. Macho reverend enthusiast."* And, shaking his head at either me or the universe, edged the meat truck off the road.

There were some buildings on either side of us now which *had* to be stores. They even had mall-like parking lots around them and a few "customers" wandering in and out. At the moment, most of them were lollygagging around, watching the developing traffic jam.

The truck wobbled to the right of the meat things ahead of us until it reached the mall, then zipped behind one of the buildings, where Hissam parked. His manner made it clear that he wanted me out, now.

I'd like to think it was more in sorrow than in anger.

Hissam was certainly agitated. I said, "Thanks for the lift, see you around," and got out. He made some squiggly sign in the air as if he wanted me to "Go in peace" or "Live long and prosper," then he wheeled the truck around, headed through the other side of the mall, and joined another line of traffic stacked up at the intersection.

There was something about the whole change in Hissam's attitude that made me curious, and at the same time, cautious. I took a look around the same corner of the building we'd just passed. A few folks were out front, their attention focused on the intersection maybe a hundred yards away and not on a stranger in a rumpled blue suit behind them.

No wonder. Somebody was running a real professional roadblock at that intersection, stopping every east- and northbound vehicle for inspection. They weren't taking people off the road and ripping the insides out, which would, I imagine, have been fatal to the vehicle in question, but they surrounded every meat truck or car and gave it—or the occupants—a good stare.

I wanted to think this was a routine operation, the sort of screening that keeps fruit flies out of California, but there were too many people standing around with their mouths open for that. This was a much bigger deal. And if you think that I immediately wondered if these guys were looking for me, you're right. After all, they were checking vehicles that had come from the hills . . . like me.

While I tried to decide whether I was being paranoid or merely cautious, I backed up, coming close enough to one of the buildings to get a good look at it. It wasn't built; it looked like something that *grew*.

The lines were straight enough that I had been fooled from a distance. These places were basically block-like, but that was the end of the similarity to anything in my experience. The sides were mottled and rough rather than smooth, like the bark of a tree. At the roofline the material simply grew at an angle—not protractor sharp, but notice-able—and roughened further.

The building I was examining was big, too, probably three thousand square feet, though it was only one story. I wondered what kind of supports "grew" inside and whether you could grow enough of them to make, say, a ten-story office tower. There was something in the feel of the place that made me think of bonsai trees I'd seen in Japan.

I concluded that they probably used Jack and the Bean-stalk magic beans. Toss one out the window, and presto! Next morning you've got a department store.

The area behind the "store" was taken up by a loading dock—well, a big "door" covered with an unsecured flap, and a shelf of some kind—and a couple of large pits that must have been used for the burning of refuse. I guess no one here had yet managed to invent—I mean, breed—a dumpster. If I'd been in position to take a few hours to sort through garbage, hoping to learn more about this world, I'd have been kind of disappointed. But I was past those pits and into the rough country beyond in thirty seconds.

I didn't have a plan, other than not getting caught. All my instincts told me to get away from the intersection and I had no problem following them, even though my only choice was to head back to the hills. The same instincts didn't think much of that idea.

Nevertheless, as I tore through scrub brush that finally reminded me of the terrain around Tucson, I figured I could split the difference between the two impulses: get away from the intersection while not actually going back into the hills. After all, I was hungry and soon to be cold (it was midafternoon by now) and with every step I was getting further away from food and shelter.

I stuck to this plan right up to the time I came up across one of those serious fences—some kind of electrified vine, of course. I was getting the idea, thank you. I consoled myself, briefly, with the thought that I'd clearly outfoxed my

pursuers by heading *right toward their base*, as I backed off
and worked my way to the right, away from the city.

I was walking along, minding my own business, when
a winged thing flew by overhead. This wasn't a dragon.
This was an aerostat, for want of a better word—a vehicle-
creature with stubby wings and a crew cabin beneath a
rigid, jellyfish-like gasbag—and it carried men in uniform.

They were polite enough to wait for me as I walked up
to them.

I guess I haven't traveled enough. True, I spent eight
months in Asia, but most of that time was on an American
military base on an American-dominated island. I'd have
gotten more culture shock on a visit to Miami. I got to
Misawa AFB on Honshu twice for about three days each
time, during which I managed to once catch a ride on a
bullet train. What little I saw of Japan was at night, when
all unfamiliar places look equally strange.

So the moment I was arrested by these men in green I
couldn't help feeling as though I'd been picked up by a
county sheriff for a crime I naturally didn't commit, but
which wasn't higher than shoplifting, either. There were
four of them, all older than I expected—early fifties, in
one case, and less lean than your basic storm trooper.
They didn't knock me around. They didn't look particularly tense. They just didn't think I would run any more.
And they were right.

The older guy patted me down and, having satisfied
himself that I was unarmed, signaled that I should stand
right where I was. Two of the others got back in their
aerostat and lifted it off. It was powered by hot, smelly
air and it barely made a whisper.

"Macho spirit alabama?" the older guy said to me.

"I don't speak your language," I said, which caused
him to raise an eyebrow and shoot a look at his compan-
ion, a short, round man with a neat beard. The other one

carried a weapon of some sort which hadn't been well cared for. I was almost as relieved to see an honest-to-God piece of machinery as I was nervous about facing it. Then I noticed that it had rust on it. For that matter, the cop uniforms were unimpressive; they wouldn't have passed an inspection even in today's low-pressure Air Force. The khaki fabric was threadbare in places. Neither had much in the way of rank insignia, though there were a few more colored gizmos on the older guy's togs than on the deputy's. I wasn't going to underestimate these guys, but I couldn't help thinking of them as Sheriff Andy and Deputy Barney.

"Luggage left envelope," Barney said, gesturing with the pistol.

"Telephone pole," Andy told him, which seemed to shut him up. I'd have to remember that magic phrase.

We waited there in the brush for about fifteen minutes until a military meat truck drove up. It was bigger than Hissam's pet and had a passenger compartment where the stake bed was. It reminded me of an armored personnel carrier. The two drivers looked more like regular Army than Andy and Barney did, and acted accordingly, "assisting" me into the back and sitting me down where they could all keep an eye on me.

Then we were off on close to half an hour of hot and stuffy jolting across the countryside. Presently we leveled out, having found a paved road, and soon the flap was being opened.

I stepped out to find myself greeted by several more R.A. types, and one man in an American gray business suit, who said, and I quote, *"Come with me, Lieutenant, and don't try anything. You're in a lot of trouble."*

11

I was so surprised to hear English that I almost didn't see the kind of strange place to which I'd been taken. We were up in the mountains in a valley so small that the lengthening shadows from the mountains to the west reached all the way to the east wall. The ground was grassy and well tended. In the distance, between the buildings, I could see rows and rows of electric vine. I was in either a military installation or a prison. Not that it made much difference one way or the other.

The buildings themselves were clearly cousins of those at the shopping mall—one- or two-story shapes that seemed to have grown out of the ground like mushrooms. Houseshrooms. These were rounder and, to judge from the chunks of whatever was lying around each base, older. In fact, the more I looked at it, the less strange it seemed: it was just like a prairie dog village, only bigger.

That was the last thing I saw before I was injected into the nearest houseshroom.

I guess I expected the interior to be dark, wet, and squishy, but it was at least as nice as the place I lived in on Guam. Drier, anyway. The floor was pretty substantial, dark and smooth like slate. The walls were pale gray beneath their covering of colored paper and announcements. Light came from panels in the "ceiling." Maybe if I'd pried one off I'd have found a giant lightning bug in a cage, but I wasn't given the opportunity. My new pals kept me moving along. Somewhere deep in the bowels—well, that's the word that occurred to me at the time—of the mound, we came up against a slit membrane.

"You'll be staying in here," English Speaker said. And I was pushed through into a cell of some kind, furnished with a built-in, or grown-in, desk and bed. A wicker chair completed the ensemble. There was a window covered by a thin yellow membrane and a bucket-like protuberance in the far corner which was just what I was afraid it was.

All in all, getting captured by Sheriff Andy and English Speaker wasn't the worst thing that had happened to me in the last week—but only by comparison. The beginning of my "captivity" was benign enough. I had barely stretched out on my cot, which had a rough woven blanket for covering, when the good sheriff returned with food, a big bowl full of some kind of pleasant-smelling stew. I was reminded of bacon, oddly enough. The utensil provided for my use was a dull wooden spoon.

I ate; I used the bucket; then I passed out.

At one point in the night I woke up to find that some thoughtful soul had dropped a uniform coat over my shoulders. Bless him, whoever he was: the temperature must have dropped into the low fifties.

Far-off rumblings roused me out of sleep toward dawn, meaning I had slept, undisturbed, for eleven or twelve hours. I felt a bit crusty, but rested and fed, and had I not been dreaming about Gus and Maia, I would have felt fine.

101

I was locked in, but the "cell" was substantially more comfortable than your average municipal holding tank. Maybe it was because it was organic, not made out of concrete and steel. The locked—but unbarred—window afforded a view that was only seventy-five-percent wall.

For the longest time I stared out the window at that patch of sky, saw it grow steadily lighter, tried and ultimately failed to recognize Mercury, which should have risen moments before the sun, which I could see. (It struck me that this was one of the reasons I was better suited to doing weather forecasts than to navigating thirty-million-dollar airplanes full of nuclear-capable cruise missiles.) Then I heard the knock on the membrane. I half expected a voice to say, "Room service."

"Come in," I said.

It was my close personal friend, the man with the English. This morning he was dressed differently, in black pants and long-sleeved pullover shirt. The only splash of color came from a purple sash of some kind that stretched diagonally across his chest. It was an improvement over the $1.98 FBI-style suit I'd first seen him in. I took this to be his native garb.

"Good morning. Sleep well?"

"Yes, thank you."

"You weren't disturbed in any way? I left very strict orders that you were to be left alone." He sounded serious.

"I have no complaints," I said. "You people really know how to treat a prisoner . . . if that's what I am."

"Oh, you are. More or less."

"That's an interesting phrase. More or less. Is *any* of this ever going to be explained to me?"

I caught him with a half-smile on his face, which cut about ten years off his apparent age of forty-five. He was one of those stolid, heavyset guys who either teach Slavic Languages at a university or, in frustration, become building contractors. The kind of guy who likes to work with his hands. But clean, blond, like a movie Nazi. He even had a shaving cut near his mouth.

"I suppose," he said, "that that's why I'm here. To explain. Of course, I'll be asking you to explain some things, too."

"Fair enough. I've got nothing to hide."

"Good. By the way, my name is Bext Linn." He didn't extend his hand and neither did I.

"Rick Walsh," I said.

"I know."

We sat down, me on the bed, him on the desk chair.

"So what am I charged with?"

He took out a small notebook and a pen of some kind and began to write as he answered. "At this point unlawful entry is our charge of choice." He looked up. "What you tell me this morning will determine whether we add kidnapping and murder to the list."

"So that's what you meant by 'more or less.'" So far I wasn't particularly worried. These people seemed reasonable, and what do reasonable people do with illegal immigrants? They send them *home*. "Well, if it'll help, I plead guilty to entering your . . . world . . . without authorization. You should understand that it was unintentional."

He merely made some notations. When he didn't ask another question immediately, I decided to: "Where exactly *am* I, anyway?"

Instead of telling me, he said, "Where do you think you are?"

"In an alternate world. Some other universe that exists right next to mine."

"Then you know."

"I'd like to hear it from you. I've only got a theory. You must know the facts. After all, you speak my language . . . and I not only don't speak whatever it is you speak around here, but I have no idea how I *got* here.''

"All the information I have suggests that you walked.''

"Very funny.''

"I don't think I actually can explain it to you,'' Linn said. "It's not my field, for one thing, and I'd almost certainly confuse the issue. I suspect there would also be a language barrier.''

"You're doing well enough. How did you pick it up, anyway?''

"Well, I know how to walk, too.'' There was that half-smile again. "Picture this. Everything in your world is actually made up of microscopic particles. Nevertheless, the vast majority of the 'space' you or an automobile or the city of Tucson occupies is simply that—empty space.

"But it's not empty, if you look at it another way. It's merely occupied by other types of particles, those that on a larger scale make up this building . . . a dragon . . . and, at the moment, you and me.''

"A universe in the, uh, intervals,'' I said. "I'm in another 'interverse.' ''

"That's one theory, yes.''

"How did I get here?''

"The process or event that determines which interverse we inhabit has the properties of a wave, with crests and troughs. At the trough the difference between the two is relatively small. You can cross over. You can be transformed, if you will.

"Is this at all helpful? These are mathematical concepts, of course. To be properly appreciated, my statements should be in notation.''

"No, thanks. I think I'm confused enough for one day.''

He failed to see the humor. "Now,'' he said, and got serious.

We went over everything that had happened to me since I crawled up on the bank of the wash. The farmer, the mall, the dragon. And it didn't take long at all. I thought I was being cute and heroic by keeping Hissam's name out of it, but Linn pounced on that right away. "You're withholding information," he said, and he mumbled some words in another language.

"The man who gave me a ride was named Hissam Varney," I found myself saying. I even tried to pronounce the name the way the farmer had.

Linn merely nodded and wrote this down. As he did, he said quietly, " 'Varney' is a title, not a name. It translates roughly as 'farmer-laborer.' " Then he added, "Farmer Hissam turned himself in immediately after letting you off."

"What's going to happen to him? He was just being kind . . ."

"Farmer Hissam was well aware that he was not to give rides to strangers in a restricted area," Linn said, once again not answering my question. "You may be pleased to know that his story corroborates yours."

"I have no reason to lie to you."

"Let's hope not," he said. "Do you know Maia Chios?"

"Why do you want to know?" Give him a little of his own medicine.

"What was your relationship?"

"We were lovers."

Linn's face was impassive, but his eyebrows knitted together ever so slightly. "When did you see her last?" He clearly didn't approve—but was it my "revelation" or was it just me?

"Eight months ago," I said, and added, "Since you're the one with all the answers, you'll have to do the conversion into your dates."

"Eight months in—your world," he said, "is also eight months here. More or less." He was frowning again. "You haven't seen her in that time?"

"Look, three days ago I walked off an airplane expecting to be met by the girlfriend I had not seen in eight months. What I found instead was a lost wallet and a three-week-old baby who turned out to be my son."

If I'd expected the idea that Maia and I had been lovers to upset Linn, it was logical that the news that there was also a child would really shake him up. But there I was disappointed. He merely stared at his notebook, then at me. Then he got up and said, "Come with me, please."

We went down the hall to another cell like mine, though this was crammed full of medical-type equipment. On the bed, hooked up to some flashy tubes, was a frail, elderly man with wisps of silver hair who wore an outfit much like Linn's, only with a bronze sash and a few other indicators of rank. Obviously this was Linn's boss. He was conscious, but only just. "Tell this man what you just told me," Linn said.

"From the beginning—?"

"Don't be stupid," Linn snapped. "Tell him about your relationship with Maia Chios, and about your *son*."

So I told them both about getting off the plane and not seeing Maia but finding Gus and learning he was my son. As I went through this, Linn translated for his boss, sentence by sentence. I could feel the older man's growing agitation.

I didn't need to finish. The old guy's face flushed red and he just shook his head. He said a few angry words to Linn and I recognized a couple of phrases from Hissam's earlier temper tantrum. Then he pointed at me and gave Linn some orders, and Linn hustled me out.

"What was that all about?" I said.

"I couldn't begin to tell you."

"Okay, let me be selfish for a moment: am I in more trouble now than I was before?"

"This morning our major concern, as you probably

guessed, was in finding Maia Chios. This was a difficult situation, but not especially complicated. Now it appears we must not only find the woman, we must find the child, too—and then decide what must be done with them. This is not only more difficult, it is complicated to such a degree that it takes my breath away.''

I said, ''Is there anything I can do?'' but Linn's attention was already directed elsewhere.

When Linn took me back to my cell he said he didn't know how long he would be gone, but encouraged me to get some air.

The sun was almost straight overhead, as was that same goofy bull's-eye cloud formation. Time might have passed at the same rate in the different worlds, but I was clearly in a different time zone. It had been early evening, Mountain standard time, when I ''crossed over'' and found myself in late morning in the Twilight Zone. If twenty-four hours had indeed passed ''over there,'' I was already in big trouble with the Air Force. Absent Without Leave is still an operative phrase. Add another unusual disappearance for the mysterious Lieutenant Sanchez and his task force. Linn had given me no hint as to when or if I'd be allowed to return.

I had free run of what in the real world I'd have called a parade ground. It was just a grass quad that had not been overmarched. The base itself didn't appear to be too active or too large, either, though I had little in the way of actual evidence of that. It was just the same instinct that allows you to feel the difference between a street in Platteville, Wisconsin, and one in Los Angeles. (Do great numbers of busy people clustered together give off vibrations of some kind? My weather charts don't say so, but they must.) It was quiet. It was pleasantly warm. There was a sweet hint of orange blossom in the air.

I felt as though I were in the square of some small town.

And I couldn't help thinking of Maia, how after we spent that night together I'd become so desperate to be with her . . . so happy in her company . . . drunk on her, if you will, yet was never able to know her. We had spoken dozens of times in the months we were separated, and I knew that she was still working in the library (she had stories about her fussy little boss, Mr. Warshofsky) and how her classes were going and what the weather was . . . but never managed to suspect that she was *pregnant* . . . much less an exchange student from the World Next Door.

If you get the idea that as I walked alone around the square, with only the semi-watchful presence of Barney the Guard for company, I was feeling sorry for myself, you'd be right.

Maybe I would have kept walking until I dropped. Maybe I would have tried to sneak off between a couple of buildings when Barney wasn't looking, but before I slid into a paralyzing self-pity, I heard from somewhere nearby the roar of a dragon. It actually made the ground shake. I looked around for a place to hide, but all I saw was Barney hustling toward me. He wanted me back inside, *now*.

Linn was waiting in my cell. With him was Sheriff Andy and a couple of other uniforms. These new guys carried briefcases. "Please sit down," Linn said.

"You ought to have a sign or something out there about those dragons or you're going to lose your next prisoner—" Fueled by nervous energy, I was starting to babble when I saw the clear signs of tension in Linn and the others.

"Something has happened," Linn said. "We need you to come with us."

"I'm your prisoner. I would imagine you could just pick me up and carry me."

Linn sighed. "It would be best if you came voluntarily. We realize that you have no particular reason to trust us, but we haven't harmed you . . . and this may be your first step in resolving your present . . . difficulties.''

It suddenly struck me that I wasn't entirely at their mercy. Could it be that it mattered to someone not only that I lived but that I be happy? Comforting thought.

One thing they don't teach you at Squadron Officers' School is that you often exercise greatest power by not exercising it at all. "I'll be happy to help out. What can I do?''

They looked relieved. Two of the uniforms got busy opening their briefcases and drawing out what looked like religious vestments (from one) and a book (from the other). Linn slipped into the vestments and thus reminded me of one of those parish priests from a movie about gangsters. He began speaking in a language not known to me. The uniforms handed the book to Sheriff Andy and displayed some well-worn electronic gear whose purpose I couldn't guess.

It looked like an exorcism. Or last rites. But the subject—me—just sat on the bed as if watching a ball game.

Linn kneeled in front of me and made some signs, touching my forehead. Then he said, in English, "This will only take a minute.''

I almost said, "Will it hurt?'' but refrained. They looked so serious!

Then some of that gear was clapped, Walkman-like, over my ears, and shields went over my eyes, and I could hear and see nothing.

I wasn't afraid. My hands were in my lap and my butt was on the bed.

After a moment I began to see a pulsing light. It remained even if I closed my eyes beneath the shields. And I began to hear a voice . . . too low to understand at first, then clearly: ''. . . Five . . . six . . . seven . . . eight . . .''

"Nine, ten,'' I finished. Only that wasn't what I said.

I mean, the *n* sounds and the *t* sound and the vowels didn't come out of my mouth.

The shields came off. I saw that the book in Sheriff Andy's hands was called, in fact, *The Book*. He handed it back to one of the uniforms and said, "Another satisfied customer." He gave me a tight-lipped smile.

Linn was removing his vestments. "This will make it easier for you to get along in the world," he said, only in his own language.

I could read and speak and understand their language. "How did you do that?" I said.

"Science," Linn said, though I immediately heard echoes that said [knowledge] and [magic], too. "You'll have a lot of time to figure it out. We've got to get going."

I wasn't sure that a lifetime would be enough to figure it out, but I was happy to leave the cell. "Where are you taking me?" I asked as we all walked toward an airbag that had landed in the quad.

"To see Maia Chios," Linn said.

12

I was like a blind man given sight. As I was hustled out of the holding cell and into the quad I realized I could read the signs in the halls and outside on the other buildings. Well, not *read* them: the alien letters still maintained their original shapes. I just knew what the signs meant; better yet, in some case I felt "echoes" of alternate words. When I looked back at the building I'd been staying in, I saw that it was called "Griffon's Nest" and/or ["Winged Lion Nest"]. The quad itself was dedicated "In Memory of . . . [a name which didn't translate as anything logical]." There was a title attached to the name that I found interesting, however: "Priest-Warrior." It made me take another look at Linn, who had hold of my arm. Come to think of it, that black garb did look like it belonged to a priest or minister. At least in *my* world.

Thinking "my world" set off a series of echoes—[earth] or [America] or [Arizona]. Here's the tricky part. Saying "this world" aloud gave me the *same echoes*. So where

111

the hell was I? It was like one of those ancient mariners' maps that had blank space around the edges labeled, "Here be dragons." I was with them.

Then I got an idea. Air Force pilots who fly around the Southwest learn that there are places even they do not go without authorization, primarily places in western Nevada. Places where the Air Force equivalent of dragons reside. The pilots call this "Dreamland," as in "If you're caught in Dreamland, you've wrecked your career."

I was in Dreamland. In more ways than one.

As we got strapped into the airbag and lurched creaking into the air, I complimented Linn on his "magic." The words came out in the other language.

"Don't overuse it," he said in English, frowning. "It's one of our most complex and expensive prayers." The last word echoed [spells] and [programs]. "The recoil could lay you out for a week."

Maybe that explained why it made my head hurt to think with it. I found I could switch back to my own language by uttering a few words in plain old English; the "prayer" obviously hadn't erased that ability.

Off to my left, in the hills surrounding the base, a dragon was emerging, probably the same one I'd heard roaring earlier. As we lifted off, it crawled out of the shadows long enough to give me my first good look at the beast.

The dragon wouldn't have been out of place in a Japanese sci-fi movie, in silhouette. It had a gray body the size of a DC-9, a long tail, a long neck, and a pair of wings.

But the details were different. It had more angles to it than your basic big lizard. Flat sides, even edges, as if it had been assembled. The wings and tail were definitely segmented. I did some rough calculations of the stress and weight this baby's backbone would have to carry, and gave myself a headache. Bone wouldn't work at all, but then who said the dragon's skeleton was made of bone? It might be some sort of organically grown composite, like everything else around this place.

The head was boxed and muzzled: there were no huge red eyes turning malevolently toward me, no hot lizard tongue snaking out of its mouth.

Linn saw where I was looking. *"Hammer light,"* he called it, which echoed as not only [dragon] and [serpent] but as [aircraft] and [firestorm].

"Do people fly those things?"

"I do," he said.

That was hard to imagine. From what I could see of the dozen ground-crew men coaxing the beast out of its lair, simply prepping a dragon for flight was quite a job. Even though we were gaining altitude and distance, I could smell the beast. I could just about feel his hot breath.

As I watched, it unfolded its wings and beat them once . . . twice . . . three times. And off its runway perch it went, dropping low toward a valley, then, with gathering strength, rising over the hills. The beast turned enough to let me see that its ugly head was baffled and blindered, and that, yes, there were actually *people* on its back. I think I would rather share a bunk bed with an H-bomb.

The dragon kept turning, casting a shadow on the land below, until it caught up with us, shooting past in silence, leaving our pitiful little airbag awash in its wake.

All I could say was "Wow."

I guess no translation was necessary, since that was exactly what the other passengers said, too.

After a few moments it was clear to me that we were flying into the city of Chios [capital] [castle].

I've flown into cities of all sizes, from Los Angeles down to Davenport, Iowa. Chios would rank in the upper third. From an altitude of three thousand feet I could see that it had a clearly defined "downtown" district of taller structures or growths—nothing over five or six stories—

and what appeared to be satellite clusters of commerce to the northeast and east. In between lay the same kind of urban blight you'd find in any large concentration of humanity. I don't mean it was shabby or run-down; I was too far up to see that. But it was just blocks and blocks of brightly colored single-story and two-story houseshrooms, some parkland, many trees. If it reminded me of any place, it would be Tijuana.

Suddenly we passed over an unusual structure which bordered on the "industrial" area—an open pit of fire perhaps a hundred yards across. It was hard to tell; the rim was packed with machines of some sort, and leading to the machines was a maze of vines or wires. There was bubbling in the pit and it reminded me of film footage I'd seen of active volcanoes. Maybe that's what it was. I hoped it wasn't too active. Not far away there was a second volcano. How many? Is this where "power" for the city came from?

We passed over a river in which I swear I saw a boatfish carrying passengers. There were no freeways, but lots of wide streets full of traffic. It was late afternoon; maybe it was rush hour.

(In Tucson it would be dawn on Thursday, August 28. I'd be an officially missing person by now.)

There was air traffic, too. Other airbags like ours and perhaps even larger. But they kept their distance. No dragons.

Finally we began to descend, and as we did, a structure up ahead caught my eye. I thought for a moment it was a park on a hill—then I realized I was looking at a park atop a massive three-story 'shroom the *size* of a hill. This place was big, sprawling over a couple of city blocks, and old, from the looks of the vines growing up the sides.

Above the hill, on a pedestal taller than the tallest building in Chios, was a golden winged lion. We headed toward the base and landed.

Ten minutes later, after being marched through dark and ancient corridors—corridors without signs, meaning my newfound translating ability was useless—I was shown into a suite that could have been featured on *Lifestyles of the Rich and Famous*. Linn nudged me forward as a guard type opened a door at the other end, and Maia entered.

She looked as though she hadn't slept in a week. She looked wonderful. *"Rick?"* I'd never seen her so surprised.

Then she put her hand over her mouth and ran out of the room.

I tried to follow her, but Linn stopped me. "They didn't tell her you were here," he said, and he wasn't happy about it. "Wait." He took the handlers aside and they had a brief but animated discussion while I looked around the room. The composite walls were white and so was the tile floor. There was a long gray couch along one wall—actually it was more of a raised platform covered with some cushions. An embroidered rug on the floor. The dominant figure, again, was the winged lion. Membrane windows on one side looked out on a courtyard.

It was so well kept that it all looked brand-new and incredibly old at the same time.

Linn was back. He spoke quietly—not whispering, just using a voice that only I could hear. "They only found her two hours ago and brought her straight here," he said. "Since they didn't see any marks on her and she said she'd not been harmed, they assumed she was well. Idiots [infidels] [gentiles]."

Since I'd just gotten used to the idea that Maia was alive, and whole, I was about two laps behind Linn. "Who kidnapped her? Who is she and what's this place?"

"Taking your questions in order, she was taken from your world by Heretics"—strange echoes on that, ultimately resolving as [Atheists] or [Devils]; I took it to be a place name that had the same meaning—"because she is the daughter [granddaughter] [heiress] of the Griffon [leader] [God]. *This* is her home."

Griffon = [God]? There are times when people aren't helping you when they answer your questions. "Can I see her?"

"She's asking for you."

The room Maia had disappeared into was a bedroom. Even though it was larger than the waiting room, somehow it seemed cozier. Maia was sitting on the bed, blowing her nose. An older woman was patting her on the shoulder. "Shall I stay?" she asked Maia.

"Please go." With a look that X-rayed me, the woman left.

Maia was trembling as she faced me.

"I, uh, missed you at the airport," I said.

She started to laugh and cry at the same time. I sat down and put my arm around her, and she leaned into it. "I'm so sorry," she said. "I *wanted* to tell you. It was just . . . just—"

"—It was just too complicated?" I rocked her a little, the way I would have rocked a fretful Baby Gus. "You could have started off small. 'Rick, I haven't been entirely open with you about my past. I'm from the world next door, the one left of zero, north of Tuesday.' I could have handled that."

"You wouldn't have believed it for a minute." It struck me that her accent was gone. Of course! She was speaking in her own language. "You wrinkle your nose when people talk to you about ESP and astrology. I've seen you. I didn't want you wrinkling your nose at me."

"Fair enough," I said, and, though I didn't want to beat her up about this, it just came out, "but you *could* have told me about Gus."

She sat back and stared across the room for a moment, her eyes shining with tears. "That was wrong. I was afraid and I was all alone. And I thought if I told you while you were overseas, you might not come back.''

Well, she had me there. I'd given occasional thought to my theoretical reaction to her hypothetical phone call—maybe Maia was right. Maybe I *wouldn't* have come back.

"Rick, how did you get here? Where is Gus?''

Oh God, she didn't know! "Maia, I don't have him. He was taken. With Jayan.''

She waited for me to go on, so I told her what I could. When I was finished, she merely nodded and took several deep breaths. I had been sitting next to her, hands in my lap. Now I took her hands in mine and forced her to look at me. I've never seen such fear in anyone's eyes. "You're worried and I'm worried. But we can do something. We can find Gus.''

"You don't know," she said.

"Don't know what? How to find them? Who we're up against? Maybe you'd better tell me.''

Once upon a time there was a Chosen People who lived on the plains of a land called . . . well, don't worry about what it was called then, because it's changed. It was *this* land, more or less. Dreamland.

They weren't particularly peaceful; Chosen People rarely are, since they usually aren't the only Chosen People around. This particular group of Chosen People had one advantage over the others—their "God" actually existed. He could be consulted. He could be relied on. He took an active part in what was going on.

And He was a jealous God. He helped His Chosen People to subdue their enemies and build a great society of their own, a society devoted to truth, justice, and the worship of this particular God, whose symbol was the winged lion—the griffon.

Because the Griffon chose to interact with His Chosen

People, He was forced to "assume" human shape . . . meaning that one day, He would die.

The first Griffon, the great one who oversaw the rise of the Chosen People from wanderers to rulers of an empire, dictated rules of succession, which were scrupulously followed over the centuries. The present Griffon was the one hundred and sixty-sixth in the unbroken line. In His human aspect He was a man of perhaps seventy . . . a man who had fathered children and grandchildren, among them Maia.

"Okay. Then who are these Devil People?"

"Disbelievers. Our enemies. We've had problems with them for centuries. That was one of the reasons I was sent over [translated?] to your world."

"Are they the ones who took Gus and Jayan?" She nodded. "I see. The Devils want to capture the princess." I was trying not to be sarcastic, I really was. But I've always had a certain Midwest America scorn for "royalty," either the classic kind or the Kennedy kind—and now here I was, involved with a "princess." It didn't make me particularly happy.

"How many of you 'royals' are there? There must be dozens."

"The Griffon isn't some horny old king from *your* world, Rick. He's God. He's above most human . . . frailty." Having lived in my world, she knew how this must sound. Yet she was absolutely sincere. "My father was killed fighting the [Devils] when I was a little girl. There is only my mother and me."

"Can't you or Jayan succeed Him . . . ?" I didn't need to finish the question. "I get it—the successor can only be male."

"And that's why it's so important that we find Gus. Not only for you and me—for everyone."

We were never entirely alone during our conversation. Nannies wandered in and out. The guards could be heard conversing outside the door. But as darkness fell and lights went on, food and drink appeared unbidden. We ate and we talked, and realized we were finally alone.

Gus's absence was a nagging ache to both of us, but it was an ache that couldn't completely immobilize us because we could do nothing about it . . . not yet.

"Explain this to me," I said. "If you have God on your side, how can you even *have* enemies like the Devils?"

"For everything holy, there is something unholy," she said, as if that explained it all. This was beginning to sound a lot like good prayers vs. bad prayers. God vs. Satan.

"What good would it do them to grab you?"

"To them I was a symbol, something they could trade for concessions."

"Such as?"

"Disputed territory. They want more of the Noon Lands [untranslatable] than they deserve. They want us to give up our dragons. Things they have been fighting about for centuries."

"Why doesn't the Griffon just put a stop to all of this?"

"Why don't people in your world just be good and stop fighting? It's simple to say but it's hard to do."

"What good does your Griffon do, then?"

"He answers prayers," she said. Somehow we had wound up on the bed together. I was lying on my back and she was kneeling over me.

"Have I changed since you saw me?" she asked.

"Hell, yes," I said. "You've gotten shorter and fatter—"

It took her a second to realize I was joking. "You can never be serious."

"I'm sorry. I don't know how I'm supposed to act any more. I barely got to know you and we were separated. Nothing that has happened since then has made the tiniest amount of sense to me. Should we be doing any of that

119

here?'' I added as she began unbuttoning my shirt. "How are you feeling?"

By way of an answer, she lowered her face to mine. I rolled her over. "How are you feeling?" she asked, teasing.

"Inhibited."

"Gus is all right, for the moment."

"How do you know that?"

By way of an answer, she looked over at the closed door. *"Anchor medieval,"* she said. No echoes. Suddenly the door was open. *"Anchor marshal."* The door disappeared. No: I looked closer. Sealed.

"More magic."

"Dominion," she said. " 'Over the beasts of the field and everything that lives.' You call it magic. Royals have more dominion than anyone. And mine is telling me that at this moment Gus and my mother are alive and well."

Then she whispered more words so quickly that I couldn't catch them. I'm not sure they were in the language I "understood," anyway. And she smiled. And all of a sudden I felt amazingly uninhibited.

Some time later we arose and, wrapped in sheets, drifted over to the window. We had a view of the courtyard, which was actually more of a private garden, and of the night sky, whose stars were surprisingly bright considering that we were in the heart of a city. I hoped they were looking down on a peaceful, sleeping baby boy. And his grandmother.

"I always wondered where you were from," I told her as we stood in the window, my arms cupping her breasts, my face brushing the back of her neck. "This is your room." And kissed an ear. "This is your garden." Her neck. "It's even your sky."

"Don't be silly."

"Maia, I'm not Carl Sagan, but I know the moon when

I see it. Or Venus. Or Orion's Belt. And I've got to tell you that nothing up there looks right to me." And before she could answer: "And don't whisper some little prayer that will make me think so, okay?"

"Okay."

I had begun to wonder just how effective these "prayers" or "spells" were. And had Maia used one of them to attract me to her? I didn't think so. I didn't *want* to think so. But most of all, I didn't want her to use them on me any more. Even when the results were as pleasant as they'd just been . . .

"We're going to catch cold," I said presently.

Reluctantly we turned away. I let Maia walk off with the sheet and began to gather up my clothes—not out of excessive tidiness, mind you: they were the only clothes I had. "You can't sleep here, you know," Maia said.

"Oh?"

She shook her head. "Remember where we are. Come with me."

She led me to an adjoining room that had a layout that was a mirror image of hers—undisturbed, of course. "I see. This is where you kept all your other men . . ."

"This is where my nanny [guardian] slept," she said, primly princess-like.

"What happens tomorrow?"

"We begin to find our son."

13

Sometime during the night my clothes were borrowed and cleaned—by prayer, I suppose. All I know is that when I woke up I found them in substantially improved condition, yet unmolested. My car keys were still in the back right pocket. (My wallet, alas, was still sitting in Maia's Mazda in what I would persist in calling "my" world.) Even the piece of paper I'd picked up in Hissam's meat truck was there. Unfolding it, I realized for the first time what it was: a prayer.

How important was prayer to Maia's people? Important enough so that prayers were what street urchins hustled, I guess. I didn't feel especially enlightened by that realization: I knew what this prayer said and how to say it . . . but I didn't know what it meant. Probably some sure way to pick up women.

The door to Maia's adjoining room had been closed and locked, which I took to be further work of the phantoms of the night. I looked around for a bathroom, but was momentarily distracted by the quite spectacular view out the window. It was dawn, or just after, and dark enough in the west that I should have been able to recognize some stars, but I failed again. In the courtyard below I could see stone walkways between trees and flower beds which looked muddy enough to suggest that rain had fallen during the night.

That struck me as odd: after years of tennis and masturbation I have a slightly arthritic elbow which is as good an indicator of changing barometric pressure as any instrument. It usually stiffens to the point where I can hardly bend it, yet it hadn't bothered me at all. There hadn't been enough breeze to ruffle your hair, much less bring in a front and take it out again. Yet there wasn't a cloud in the sky and the day was likely to be clear and warm. Was Chios the city close to some major body of water? If so, it would have to be something the size of one of the Great Lakes. These little differences between the two worlds were starting to accumulate.

On the other hand, the bathroom appeared to be a good argument for parallel human thinking. I suppose when you get down to the level where the act involved is the lifting of a toilet lid, you don't need prayer. The operation of the tub stumped me briefly, though: there was a faucet, but no other fixtures. Where there should have been fixtures there were words . . . they sounded like nonsense when I read them aloud, but damned if I didn't hear some clanking and whistling from inside the walls. Then hot and cold water started to spill out of the faucet, enough to fill the tub. I climbed in, though I confess I didn't linger. As soon as I was finished, I read the second sequence of words on the wall, and a drain opened.

The brief dip made me feel better. Made me feel that I was in charge of things, that I was adjusting well to my interdimensional travels.

Then I noticed something strange as the water drained

out of the tub. It didn't go round and round. I must have knelt there, naked, staring at it for a good five minutes, until long after all the water was gone. I was so curious that I even plugged up the drain with my hand to stop and start the process a couple of times.

There was no Coriolis effect in Dreamland.

Where I came from, in the northern hemisphere, water ran down drains with a clockwise spin; south of the equator it was the other way around. Fifth-grade science.

But, then, where I came from, the winds blew, too. Air circulated as the world turned. It's where we got weather.

What Dreamland had was climate. Ring-like cloud structures formed by temperature and driven across the sky by the sun. As far as I knew, it only rained at night. That could be caused by heat exchange, again, not by prevailing winds or cold fronts or anything I might recognize. Maybe this world didn't *turn*. Maybe it wasn't even *spherical*. Maybe its "sun" was nothing more than a fire chariot and the stars were just lights in the sky.

I fought the urge to throw on my clothes and go charging out the door. For one thing, the only door was locked. I concluded it was just as well. I had had my mind stretched enough for one morning. There are, indeed, some things *this* man was not meant to know.

I managed to remain in this Zen-like state of acceptance for fifteen minutes or so. Then I began to resent being left alone and locked in. I tugged on the door and pushed on it, and even tried kicking it, just like a TV detective, failing miserably.

Then I remembered Maia's demonstration of the night before. *"Anchor medieval,"* I pronounced.

The door opened.

I didn't expect to find Maia in her room, and she wasn't. It hd been picked up, however; all evidence of our previous night's gymnastics had been removed. And her door wasn't locked.

I half expected to find a pair of guards outside, but I was alone. Trying to retrace my steps, if that's the word, from the day before, I went down a hallway. I hoped to find a stairway, since I knew I was on an upper floor. An elevator, if such a thing existed, wouldn't do me much good, seeing as how it would either have an attendant or require me to know how to start it. Toilets had "directions" written on them—did everything else? I didn't want to wind up back at the base of the Griffon statue . . . not that I was trying to escape or anything. Let's just say I was curious.

I found a ramp that led down to the next floor, then another, then a third. At the second level I'd heard voices, but had kept going. There was no fourth ramp: I guessed that I had reached the ground floor.

I kept expecting to find dripping walls and torches—you know, the usual accent points of your basic castle—but no one would do the least thing to conform to my preconceptions. The walls were finished, painted, even paneled. There were lights in the ceilings. The floors were carpets or rugs or something so much like parquet that I half expected to hear the dribble of a basketball.

Finally I emerged into the courtyard. And I was not alone. People were hurrying from my left to my right. The men wore uniforms or suits that wouldn't have earned a second glance in downtown Tucson (no ties, though). I only saw a couple of women; they wore long dresses and veils, but I assumed they were either servants or members of religious orders. My outfit wasn't entirely out of place. At least, no one was crude enough to make a comment. I merely joined the herd.

Which headed into a tunnel that opened on a domed arena the size of a convention center. On his best day, Bruce Springsteen might have had trouble selling out this place. But somebody better was playing this morning: the seats were filling up.

Michael Cassutt

I squeezed myself out of the flow of traffic and loitered by the door. I wasn't all that anxious to sit down, but I didn't have many other options.

A young man in a coat of many colors approached me. "May I be of assistance?" he said in the language of Dreamland.

"No, thank you." I smiled in what I hoped was a perfectly legitimate way.

"You should probably be seated. The service is about to begin."

I headed toward the last row of seats, but the usher tapped me on the shoulder. "Pardon me, but you'll be happier in the men's section." He nodded toward the front. The back was filling up with women and children.

"Of course." I got away from him before I did anything else silly.

The front of the arena was clearly better: where the women and children's section consisted of rows of medieval pews, the men had individual chairs and kneelers. Padded, too.

Hoping that I wasn't taking someone's assigned place, I knelt down and took a look around. Rising before me was an altar and, below that, three pulpits. There was a giant TV screen above the altar, and, as you moved from the altar toward the main entrance, where I was kneeling, smaller screens at regular intervals. Shafts of colored sunlight poked down from a stained-glass roof. I could smell incense.

What was most interesting, however, was the people that were coming in. Here were men with leathery faces, bruised hands, and worn clothing. Manual laborers and quite a lot of them. More men in suits. The suits took pews toward the front, behind the soldiers. The suits tended to be chubby. The longshoremen or whatever were uniformly thin. They looked, in fact, like men who occasionally went hungry.

Further back there were women, too, all of them in long dresses of one kind or another, from the very plain to those that could have been made of embroidered silk. All of the women had something on their heads, either a hat or a scarf.

The children looked like children anywhere, I suspect. Fairly bored.

I realized that not only did the churchgoers divide themselves along sex lines, but they were subdivided into suits and everyone else.

In front of everybody, just short of the altar and the pulpits, was a single pew standing alone. As I watched, as the church filled almost to capacity, Maia and a man of about thirty-five whom I didn't know walked in and knelt down.

Then the service began.

My religious upbringing was, at best, informal. During Mom's post-divorce fling with Presbyterianism I was a regular, if skeptical, attendee. In college I would drift into the odd service depending on whom I was dating. And my ex-girlfriend in Omaha was ostensibly Jewish, meaning I'd gone through one Seder. And, of course, I'd seen snatches of Oral Roberts or one of those guys.

This service had a little bit of all of them. The basic message was that the Griffon had been very good to us, and we owed Him everything. That there was no difference between what the Griffon wanted and what our leaders wanted. Hard work and thrift, therefore, were not only good but holy. All right-thinking men knew their place, and kept it, unless chosen by the Griffon for special service or sacrifice. All right-thinking women knew their place, too.

We learned this—I should say, we reaffirmed this—in a series of "questions" from the "priest" and "answers" from the rest of us, broken up with a couple of songs from the choir. I joined right in. For one thing, they made it easy for you: the screens all over the church lit up with various slogans and directions and text so quickly that at times it looked like a Chinese music video, but you could read it. And everyone around me was, with great and heartfelt enthusiasm, adding his and her voice to the throng. I would have been quite conspicuous by my silence. Conspicuous was the last thing I wanted to be in that place.

About halfway through the service, a little crippled girl was carried in from the wings. As those around me, suits and longshoremen, passed colored pieces of paper and coins embossed with the Griffon's logo to collectors who appeared suddenly, the priest-priest in charge of things begged the Griffon to make the little girl walk again.

I guess we weren't generous enough. The first time she tried to stand up, she fell. More money made its way to the collectors. More praying and singing. Finally the little girl took several steps. Displayed on the screen, her face showed utter surprise and joy. As if she had really been cured.

But they saved the best for last. Everyone knelt—even the priest. The Chinese video garbage went away . . . and the sign of the Griffon appeared on the screen. The choir sang, then shut up. The Griffon logo went to black, and was replaced by the face of a thin old man.

He sent us greetings on this fine day—this holy day. He congratulated us all on our work, on our families, on our continuing struggles. He went on to say that one who was lost had now been returned to us, prompting a stir of whispers around me, and that punishment must now be meted out to those who had caused her to suffer. "Destroy our enemies," he said. "For too long they have fouled our world with their lies and sins. The final battle approaches. Let us prepare. Let us be strong. Let us begin—today." He rattled off a prayer that seemed to fill us all with power and energy. We had heard the Word of God.

And, as the screen went dark, the people stood, shouting a word that translated only as "Amen!" "Amen!" "Amen!"

I was exhilarated. It was impossible not to be caught up in this. The Griffon hadn't identified the enemy, but even *I* knew we were going after the Devils.

That was the highlight of the service. Once it was over, there was a mad rush to the exits. I tried to swim upstream against the crowd, but not fast enough. Maia kept getting further and further away. She never did look my direction.

But the man who was with her did, glaring at me with a mixture of curiosity and loathing. Or so it seemed. When I realized that Maia was out of reach, I decided to get out of there.

He followed me.

It wasn't exactly a chase. Neither of us was able to make much progress, given the crush of people. But he knew how to slide through a Dreamland crowd—probably using some special prayer—and he caught me before I could get to the door. (What did I think I was going to do outside? Call a cop?)

Close up he was shorter than I'd thought—no taller than I am, and I have to lie to make five ten—but no less intimidating. He was dark-haired and hawk-nosed, and kind of stout. Good-looking, I suppose, and wearing what passed for a business suit here in Dreamland. I turned to face him and he sized me up, too.

"Nice show," I told him, wondering how it would be translated.

"We try not to think of our service as a 'show' [farce]," he said, which sort of made me feel like a heathen. "You and I need to talk."

"I don't even know who you are."

"My name is Stenn Kolbett." The name echoed too faintly to be understood, but names do, I guess.

129

"I don't need to tell you mine."

"No. I've heard a lot about you. Come with me."

We left through a side exit. The last of the worshippers had dispersed. Waiting for us was a type of car creature that I hadn't seen before. A meat truck was blocky but this was sleek, like a panther or a cheetah, only bigger. A Dreamland sports car.

"I don't know if this is true around here," I told Mr. Kolbett, "but my mother told me never to accept rides from strangers. I know your name, but I don't know anything else."

Stenn looked down at the ground for a moment. When he raised his eyes it was hard to tell if he was furious or vastly amused. "Very well. I'll assume my job is not of interest to you. You want to know the source of our . . . connection."

"Yes."

"I am betrothed to Maia Chios," he said.

"Oh." Oh my God. I wanted to run.

But he was *enjoying* this. "Are you happier now, Mr. Walsh?"

"I suppose that depends. Are you going to kill me?"

He waited long enough to answer. "Possibly." Then he climbed aboard his sport beast and gestured for me to do likewise. "Let's have breakfast first and think about it."

14

Ten minutes later the catmobile stopped in front of a walled villa in the shadow of the Griffon's statue. It had been a fascinating ten minutes: the catmobile had two speeds, fast and faster, and seemed to be steered by Stenn's thoughts alone. We had avoided at least three collisions in the crowded, narrow streets.

Perhaps this was how Stenn intended to kill me. If so, he damn near succeeded. It's amazing how much second-guessing you can do in just a few minutes. Had I really gone with him just because I was pissed off? Smart, Rick.

His villa had a Spanish or Mediterranean feel to it and wouldn't have been out of place in one of the older, richer parts of Tucson. We penetrated the outer wall, then crossed a small courtyard before entering the house proper. If someone had told me the place was as old as the Griffon's mansion, I'd have believed it: the walls were crusted and peeled, like bark. Membrane windows had been patched. I got the feeling that a good, strong wind would scatter it across the hillside. But they didn't seem to have strong winds in Dreamland.

Stenn had not spoken since we left the temple, though I always had the feeling he was watching me, expecting me to try something. Curiously, though I wasn't sure I should have come, it never occurred to me to make a break for it.

We were met by a pair of servants, a boy of perhaps fourteen and a man in his thirties who was either a much older brother or his father, both of them wearing the same faded livery as they attempted to repair a household appliance. "Moroch, Hemel," Stenn said, "this is the [infidel] Walsh." (Well, that's how it echoed.)

They both stopped what they were doing and moved apart. Apparently everyone was expecting me to act like a wild beast. "No," Stenn told them. "I don't think that will be necessary." He blinked. He was a man with a lot on his mind. "Hemel," he told the father, "bring us breakfast in the [chapel]."

The [chapel] was what I would have called a library. It had a desk and floor-to-ceiling shelves covered with scrolls and tchotchkes and books. On one wall was a special niche reserved for the Book. On the opposite wall was a foil-like membrane of sorts that reminded me of a big-screen TV.

Stenn motioned me to a chair, then settled behind his desk. "I was surprised to find you at the service," he said. "Maia's people are very nervous these days. You should have been completely swallowed [locked up]."

"I was swallowed, but I got out."

"You realize, then, that if anything happens to you, it's your fault. According to the Book."

"I'm operating on the assumption that *everything* that happens is my fault, Book or no Book."

For a moment he was confused. Then he allowed himself a ghost of a smile. "Oh! You were being ironic. A bit of advice: irony and sarcasm don't share [translate] well.''

He looked around his chapel—everywhere but at me. "It would be pointless for me to envy you, yet I do." I thought he was referring to me and Maia. "I've always wanted to see your 'other world.' ''

"Frankly I'm surprised you haven't. Everyone else I've met here seems to have been a visitor at one time or another."

"What do you expect? There's been traffic between us for almost fifty years."

"Oh, really?"

He had gotten up and gone over to the special niche. Now, carrying the Book, he returned to his desk. "Yes. It's quite an interesting story. We thought we were being attacked. There were unexplained explosions that wrecked thousands of [acres] in the [Noon] Lands. Fires broke out. This went on for several years, until people were found—dazed, dirty, unable to speak the Language, unfamiliar with the Book, ignorant of the Power. Much like you.

"Eventually we were able to map the points of congruence between the two worlds and construct formulas that allowed passage between them."

Fifty years ago, call it 1940. What could have caused Dreamland to feel attacked? Well, World War II was starting, which eventually led to atomic bombs. If a few well-chosen words could move you from one world to another, a nuclear blast could easily have relocated the entire state of New Mexico.

(I remembered that UFOs became quite popular a few years later—Dreamland's gift to my world, perhaps?)

"That's amazing. Frightening, too."

"Why do you say that? Surely we're no threat to you."

"I wasn't thinking about any threat. It's just frightening to learn that things you believed aren't true."

"Then you are a religious man."

"Not quite."

"Well, then, how can you have beliefs?"

"You can believe in the structure of the atom or the fact that water flows downhill without being a religious man."

"I'm not so sure about that."

I would have given him an argument, but breakfast was brought in at this point. The condiments and settings were, like the house, classic but worn. The two-tined copper fork had gone green from use. The meal itself consisted of a hot, bready cereal and what could easily have been stewed apples. There was tea, too. I'm afraid I was so hungry I made a pig of myself—there were spots of "apple" on my shirt within moments—but Stenn was too busy mumbling his way through his Book to notice. I hoped.

Then I realized that he wasn't eating at all. Figuring I'd made yet another serious error in etiquette, I stopped shoveling food into my mouth and said, "I'm sorry."

He looked up. "Why?"

I gestured toward his untouched breakfast.

"Oh, would you like mine?" he asked.

I tried to explain, and saw Stenn laugh for the first time. "No, no. Please eat. It would be a sin for me to test you while you were hungry. And do take mine."

I'm not proud; I took his plate. Between bites I said, "Why am I being tested?"

"To prove your worthiness, of course."

I resisted the urge to be sarcastic. "Should I be thinking about getting away from you?"

He sighed. "I'm sure you realize it wouldn't do you any good."

"That's what I thought." I chewed some more. "What happens if I fail?"

"You die. How's your breakfast?"

It had been fine until two seconds ago. "This isn't poison, is it?"

Stenn got that tight little smile on his face, then picked

134

up a fork, stabbed one of the few remaining bites, and popped it into his mouth. "Hemel's cooking has its limitations, but he wouldn't poison you. Not deliberately, anyway." He helped himself to a second bite. "Your test will be brief. Think of it as an interview." He made one last prayer, then, apparently finished with his preliminaries, closed the Book and touched a button on his desk.

"Are you some kind of priest? Is this official Griffon business?"

"[Heavens, no!] I'm a lawyer. And if the Family knew what I was doing, they would test *me*."

A *lawyer*? "Excuse me for asking a purely personal question here, but why are you doing this?"

He actually took a few moments to think about it. "For love," he said.

I guess it wasn't necessary for him to elaborate. He didn't get the chance, because at that point the door opened and a woman entered.

Stenn clearly wasn't expecting her. He was out of his chair so fast I thought he would shove her through the door. "[What are you doing here?]" he snarled at her. Then, to the world at large: *"Hemel!"*

A shamefaced Hemel stood in the open door. With him was a truly wretched-looking little man, wide-eyed with fear. "I'm sorry," Hemel stammered. "She wouldn't listen—"

Stenn stared at Hemel and his captive for a moment, then roared, "Go!" before slamming the door.

In the space of a single breath, he had regained control. "It was your decision," he said to the woman.

"[I wanted to see the visitor]," she told him, almost pleading. She was a dishwater blonde perhaps thirty years old who would have been extremely good-looking but for the fact that she was so thin. She wore a short jean skirt and T-shirt, and I was just thinking she would have looked right at home in Tucson when she turned to me and offered her hand. "I guess I have to introduce myself. I'm Sharon Loder."

Sharon Marie Loder, Amphi High School class of '79. Part-time student at Pima Community College, part-time exotic dancer, until seven years ago, when she found God—and just as quickly found herself in Dreamland. "I was with Kerry Standke one Saturday and we were giving out prayer booklets downtown. It got late and we missed our bus, so we decided to walk.

"This van pulled up. I mean, I was twenty-one and I'd seen a few things. I thought I could tell which guys were weirdos. This was just a college kid, all by himself, and he offered us a ride. We had a long way to walk, and it was getting dark, and it was actually a bit cold. Our chances of catching a bus were zero. So we got in.

"For the first few minutes, things were fine. You know, chitchat, what's your major? That kind of stuff. Kerry was real nervous. She was kind of heavy and shy, so I had to do the talking.

"We headed up Stone toward Speedway, but when we got to the intersection, instead of turning right this guy turned left.

"Right then I knew we were in trouble, although I probably didn't do what I should have, which was scream my goddamn head off, because there was only this one guy.

"Anyway, he told us to shut up and drove under the freeway—not very far, not even out of town—and pulled off. It was dark by now and I had my hand on the door, ready to make a break for it.

"But he grabbed Kerry and started to hurt her. I couldn't just run away, so I tried to help. Of course, that was just what he wanted: he slugged Kerry so hard he knocked her out, and threw me against the inside of the van. He was pulling at my shirt, and I just started to pray. And then I woke up here." She laughed. "At first I *thought* it was heaven." She gave Stenn a look.

He had sat silent throughout the entire ten-minute monologue, simply staring out the window. His precious Book, which had been so important to him all morning, no longer concerned him.

"Do you want to go back?" I asked. You might consider that a rude question under the circumstances, but, then, these were rude circumstances.

Sharon glanced at Stenn in a way that would have made me nervous. Part of it was love, I think. Part of it was . . . hunger, maybe. But he was oblivious. "Let's put it this way: I never asked to go back."

I was getting tired of this, so I stood up. "Thanks for the breakfast and the test. If that's all, I think I'll be going."

Now Sharon looked at me, and there was no mistaking her expression. She thought I was some kind of idiot. "You can't just leave like that."

"Why not?"

"He isn't finished."

I looked at Stenn while addressing my words to Sharon. "Well, why doesn't he say something?"

Instead of replying, Stenn suddenly began reading aloud from his Book. Actually he was chanting words he knew by heart. But he kept his eyes on the Book, and off us.

Sharon squirmed on her chair. "Has it started?" I asked. I felt compelled to whisper.

"Yes. You better sit down."

I wanted to walk out the door. I distinctly remember turning toward it, even taking a step. But I found myself sitting down. I started to protest, and found that my ability to speak had been taken along with my will to leave. Sharon told me quietly, "This is a very powerful prayer. Its recoil can be fatal. You can't disturb him."

Stenn suddenly looked up from the Book. "It's time,"

he said. He focused on me. "I must ask you some questions."

My voice had returned. "Isn't that what you've been doing all morning?"

He ignored that. "What are you going to do about Maia?"

"I didn't know she was engaged."

Sharon laughed. I decided I didn't like her. Stenn frowned. "Are you blaming her for what has happened?"

"No. I guess I'm pleading ignorance. Of her origin, of her past, of the consequences."

"I don't believe this." That came from Sharon.

"Is there some reason why we're having this conversation in front of this woman?" I asked Stenn.

"Yes," he said, visibly agitated. Without elaborating, he tried to go on: "Would the consequences have been any different had you impregnated a woman from your own world?"

"Maybe not. They would have been more comprehensible to me. I would have known what to do."

"But what will you do now? I believe that's what I asked. It's very important."

I had had about enough. I felt as though I'd been abducted and interrogated once too often. But the question reminded me about what was important. Forget about Stenn or Sharon or catmobiles. What *did* I want?

"I want to find Gus," I said finally. "And I want to marry Maia." It just came out.

Sharon laughed again. "He's got to be kidding." But Stenn was mumbling something to himself. Presently he looked at her. "He's telling the truth," he said, referring to me. I was relieved, partly because telling the truth struck me as the best way to pass the test, and partly because I needed to be sure of my feelings about Maia and Gus.

If the Power said I loved them, I must love them, right?

Now Sharon got agitated. "But what about the recoil?"

"Why do you think I wanted you to stay out? What did you think the [bum] was for?"

I wasn't at all sure I understood what the problem was between these two. But suddenly Sharon stood up as if she was going to make a run for it. "Sit *down*," Stenn ordered. And by God, she sat. To me he said, "Since you have passed the test, I have no choice but to let you live. Maia would be very angry with me if I killed the father of her child."

"If I'd known you were serious, I'd have stayed at the temple."

"You didn't have any choice." There was a moment when nobody spoke. I cleared my throat and was about to utter some inanity when Stenn exploded: "Do you have any understanding of the pain you have caused? Not only in abandoning her when she was pregnant, and then losing the child. But to her family? And to me?"

"All I can do is apologize, and try to do better. I told Maia—I didn't know she was pregnant until four days ago."

"You were intimate with her!"

I was about to slip into irony again—"Haven't you ever heard of birth control?"—when I realized that Stenn had possibly not, in fact, heard of birth control. And might find it quite against the Book. "I was irresponsible," I said, "I have no excuse."

He glanced past me, toward his library, toward Sharon. "Maia and I were brought together. Our relationship was arranged. Yet I loved her. She abandoned me years ago, but I still love her, for what she was. And now I will kill for her."

I felt as if both Stenn and Sharon were expecting me to make the next move. Or maybe they were just postponing it.

"Well, you don't have to kill any more. I passed, right? I forgive you."

"You don't understand anything," Sharon hissed. "Now someone *else* has to die."

I didn't have to ask who, either. To look at the emptiness in Sharon's eyes, you'd think she was already dead. So that was what this recoil business was all about: if you said the prayer, if you invoked the magic, you had to see it through.

A death prayer meant someone was going to die.

"Look," I said to Stenn, "this is really crazy. Why don't you just call it off? Forget it."

Sharon didn't look at me. "You *can't* call it off." I'd never heard so much contempt packed into five words.

Stenn stood up. "It's time for you to go." He walked around the desk and took Sharon's hand. She was so frightened she was shaking.

"Wait a minute—" I said.

"Can't you just go?" Sharon said. "This is private! I knew the rules. I took the chance. I deserve it. Okay?"

Stenn was already speaking in a language that didn't echo. Sharon fell to her knees in a faint. I could feel a chill in the room.

I backed out the door and let it close. I wanted to run like hell, and probably would have. But at the bottom of the stairs stood Moroch and Hemel, and they were trying real hard to keep out a pair of Maia's guards. The guards looked angry. They'd probably been looking for me all morning.

The frying pan had to be better than the fire. I opened the chapel door. But what I saw there made me wish the guards had me:

It wasn't Sharon who was on the floor, but *Stenn*.

When Sharon saw me she threw herself at me, and not in search of comfort. I think she genuinely wanted to kill me.

I hadn't been in a fight since tenth grade. And that had just been a five-minute shoving match between me and Bobby Timmerman. This was war. I covered up to save my eyes while slamming backward into the bookshelves. Sharon stumbled and I was able to grab her hands, hard, and pin her to the floor. "Stop it!" I said.

Suddenly I was no longer the enemy. Sharon just let go and began to sob silently. I helped her sit up. "He took it himself," she said. "It was meant for me." She looked at me as if I were supposed to provide her with some answers.

"The guards are here," I said.

Sharon forgot about her anger and her sorrow. "You have to get out of here."

"Look, let's make it easier. I'll turn myself in—"

"Aren't you in enough trouble?"

She had a point. "I don't know what to do," I said, realizing that the longer I waited, the fewer options I had.

Sharon wrung her hands together and tried not to look at Stenn. "Meet me in the Devil's Quarter, a place called Six and Nine. I'll try to get there before dark."

"Where's the Devil's Quarter?"

Having just wrestled her to the ground, I knew how strong she was. Still, I was a little surprised that she could drag me to the window. "Out there."

"Out there" was a balcony overlooking a roof. There were voices at the door. Moroch and Hemel's last stand. I took one last look at Stenn. He was sprawled on the floor, his eyes open and staring. What had killed him? I wondered. A heart attack? Aneurysm?

"Wait a minute!" I hissed. "What am I supposed to do?"

"Christ." She closed her eyes for about a second and a half. "There's a place in the Devil's Quarter called Six and Nine. Go there. Wait."

Then I jumped or got pushed.

15

Even as I skinned my shins on the tile roof in my haste to get away, I wondered just what I thought I was going to prove. The worst the guards were likely to do was return me to Maia. She wouldn't let them do anything awful . . . would she?

If they were her guards.

If they didn't blame me for what had happened to Stenn.

All in all, these were questions I didn't feel like answering. What I wanted at that particular moment was to be alone and to be in charge. If I managed to hook up with Sharon later, so much the better. If not, I would at least have had a few hours in which to think.

I scuttled and slid across the roof, relieved that it had only a gentle pitch to it, and reached the edge. There was a garden below me, so I grabbed hold of the overhanging tiles and dropped down.

I came within three inches of landing on a cactus-like shrub which would have made an already-questionable day substantially less enjoyable. Some pretty blue flowers were never going to be the same, but they died so that my ankles would remain unbroken. In moments I was moving under the shade of some leafy trees. Down a grassy slope and between two buildings I found a side street. No one else was about, so I felt conspicuous. I assumed the guards were more or less behind me, but given that there were apparently no straight streets in Chios, that wouldn't necessarily remain true.

The neighborhood seemed nice, what I could see of it. The walled-villa look predominated. As I walked along, purposefully but not *too* fast, I caught glimpses of gardens and alleys, and very little else. No people, no catmobiles, no children, no pets.

Yet I could feel that there was traffic nearby. I could hear the buzz of music and voices and footsteps coming from somewhere down the Hill. Turning once at each intersection, I let myself float there.

I don't know how long I floated. At some point I realized there were other people on the street. A couple of meat trucks passed. Then I came to a pretty substantial boulevard with a grass median. There were no villas beyond it, just blockier multifamily dwellings and shops.

It would have made me feel safer to have crossed it with a crowd, but no one would accommodate me. Most of the people, in fact, were on the other side. Looking left and right, I could find no more secluded spot for a crossing. All my careful zigzagging had gone to waste: here I was, the only man in an entire world wearing a U.S. Air Force uniform, crossing an open street alone. I thought seriously about simply sitting down when I reached the median to wait for the guards.

Well, why make it easy for them? I sprinted across, kept moving right past the initial clusters of people and shops, and didn't resume normal locomotion until I was three blocks into the "poorer" section. Some people looked my way as I passed them, but whether they were trained by experience to ignore strange people emerging from the Hill area, or just unusually reserved, they had no other reaction.

In some ways, it was as if I had crossed the border between Mexico and the United States. The streets were narrower, unpaved, yet somehow more colorful. I was overwhelmed by the smell of spices, flowers, and wagon shit—and became a bit more careful about where I walked. This was trickier than it should have been because the wagon shit and the street were much alike when it came to texture and color. And the fact that the day grew hotter meant that *everything* began to smell like wagon shit.

Was this the Devil's Quarter? And who was this Devil, anyway?

People were definitely in business. Some stood in front of shops and made their pitches directly to potential customers. Others did the ancient thing, sitting on mats wherever they were able to find or make space. Many of these sang or played music.

Yet there weren't many transactions—at least, not that I could see. And from what I saw of the goods for sale, no wonder: pots and pans, bottles with stuff in them, comic books, raggedy clothing. You would have had to be rich and a tourist, or poor and destitute, to consider acquiring any of this. And a lot of it was food . . . yellow, blighted vegetables, worm-eaten bread, greenish meat. I could be wrong: maybe this was good stuff in Dreamland. But no one was dying to buy. They just seemed to be *outside* because it was better than being *inside*.

It was the eyes that told the story. People looked right through each other. Collisions were frequent, even though the streets weren't that crowded—certainly not compared to Nogales on a Saturday afternoon, much less, say, Calcutta. There was some weird ritual that took place every time somebody bumped, too: there would be a quick exchange of words, and the one who couldn't keep up would back off. Probably everything in a Dreamlander's life was like that: the prayers you knew and how well you knew them determined everything. If you couldn't keep up, tough.

It wasn't all Calcutta. In one place I saw a young woman pour a skin of water over a soapy, naked little boy. They were standing in the muddy street, yet they seemed happy. The boy, anyway. He was waving a toy dragon around.

I stopped to watch. The mother, quickly aware of unwanted interest, put herself between the boy and me. "Do you know a place called Six and Nine?" I asked, hoping the translation program was still working.

I think she was relieved I wasn't interested in some more perverse transaction. "On the square," she said, nodding down the street.

The square turned out to be another mile away. It was a lopsided open space dominated by a pigeon-spattered statue of the Griffon, and a torn viewing screen displaying another in a series of prayer services to the indifference of everyone except old men and women huddled on the benches.

I found an empty place and sat down. I'd been walking for at least a couple of hours and had managed to put maybe three or four miles between myself and the Hill. I examined the establishments facing the square, and there was Six and Nine.

Chapter Six, Verse Nine, actually. Where you would expect to find the name there was a faded reading from what I took to be the Book: "And in His sorrow the Griffon drank."

All right, the place was a bar, and not an upscale bar, either. I should have expected that: Sharon had suggested it, and she did not strike me as upwardly mobile in Chios terms.

I sat down to wait. I didn't have the option of going

inside, since one constant of human nature across the many universes is, I'm sure, that bartenders don't like deadbeats, and my assets at the moment didn't include cash.

There wasn't much to occupy my mind in the square. I felt at home to about the same degree I had in Japan, if you allow for the fact that all Japanese are always going places together while nobody in Dreamland went anywhere. There was enough visual stimulus from the moundlike buildings and "natural" walkways. The utter lack of symmetry in design, both in dwellings and in the startling variety of wheeled creatures that passed through the square, was starting to annoy me.

I had reached the point where I was homesick for the sight of a straight line.

Sharon surprised me by arriving before dark, maybe three hours later, driving (or riding) Stenn's catmobile. She parked it within sight of Six and Nine and walked over.

"I don't like it down here," she said.

"Then why are we meeting here?"

"Well, I tried to book the Hill, but they were busy tonight. Don't be an idiot."

I followed her inside. "I should warn you right now: I'm broke."

She didn't seem to care. We found a table close enough to the front membrane that we could see the catmobile in addition to the big-screen TV over the bar. (These people really liked their church services.) I was relieved to see that the table and chairs were basically just that. At least they didn't make noise when we sat on them.

"Don't drink anything but the egg [wine]," she said. "Unless you enjoy vomiting."

"Thanks," I said, "I'm trying to quit." I tend to have a fraternity boy's use for liquor—I drink only to be more fun at parties—but at the moment the idea of a little comfort in a bottle did not depress me.

A dour-looking waiter delivered a bottle and two glasses. Sharon poured, picked up her glass, and promptly downed most of the egg while I was still debating the idea of proposing a toast to the memory of Stenn. I decided to skip it.

"Thanks for meeting me," I said finally.

"It's okay."

"How'd you manage to get away?"

She shrugged. "I just walked out. Why?"

"The guards didn't give you a hard time?"

"No harder than usual. I was right: it was Stenn they were after. They can tell when someone tries a death prayer. It's against the law."

"I can see why. Still. I thought you'd be in jail or answering questions."

"Why?"

"Because Stenn was killed." I was already pretty sure I had missed some vital bit of information.

"They don't care about that. I mean, they care that he's dead. But what I would have to say about it doesn't matter to them at all."

"Them?"

"The guards. The priests. Your girlfriend's family. I have no legal existence in this world, not that women have much status of any kind, so they refuse to let me take part in anything."

"So you can't go to the funeral?"

She blinked. "What funeral?"

"Stenn's funeral—"

"There's not going to be a funeral."

"How much deader does he have to be—?"

She started laughing at me. "They're going to try and bring him *back*."

"Back to life?"

147

"Yes." I could tell I was making her even more tired.

"What about the death prayer and the recoil and all that?"

"What about it?"

"I thought he was being so brave, giving up his life—"

"Oh, he gave up his life. Count on it. They can bring you back, but it's not easy and it's not pretty. He really died. He will really be born again. You know, six months from now he'll be well, but he won't ever be quite the same person."

How could she be so casual about this? We were talking about death and resurrection with no more energy than you'd use in discussing teeth cleaning. "Then why do it?"

"He's special. If you or I had taken the recoil, forget it. But someone up there likes Stenn."

"Who? The Griffon?"

"Ask your girlfriend." I realized Sharon had polished off most of the egg by herself. Now she seemed anxious to leave. "Look, you can do what you want. No one's after you for being accessory to a murder or anything. Go home."

"I can't."

"Can't or won't?"

"My son is missing."

"That's too bad. It really is. But you don't know this place like I do. *I* don't even know it. Go home." She slid out of her chair. I caught her hand.

"Sharon, why don't *you* go home?"

I saw something ugly in her eyes. Fear and loathing, and hunger, too. She knew she had opened up to me, as if I had caught her naked by accident. "Because I'm hooked. And I'm not the only one."

Then she shook off my hand and walked out.

There were dregs in the bottle and I tried to figure out how long I could sit there ostensibly nursing my drink until I was given the thumb. Not that I found the Six and Nine so appealing. I just didn't know where to go or what to do. I might have sat there for the rest of my natural life, except that at that moment the screen chose to erupt with some kind of attention-getting music.

It certainly got my attention, and that of a majority of the other patrons. The parson on the wall screen disappeared and was replaced by the sign of the Griffon. That dissolved into the face of a handsome man with silver hair who said, "Good day. Let us pray." He bowed his head and recited some words about "truth is the tree [spine] of which the knowledge is the fruit [flesh]." Or something like that. Every word echoed; "truth" and "knowledge" didn't translate with notable clarity, which is why I remember few of the actual prayers I heard.

That done, our viewpoint changed to that of someone sitting in the audience. "On Griffonsday last the Heiress [Princess] Maia was taken captive by Devil forces in a criminal attempt to exchange her for prisoners properly held in Reeducation Complex Five. Acting with great heroism and under the guidance of the Griffon Himself, elements of the Civil Guards determined where the Heiress was being held and restored her to freedom.

"Those responsible for this outrageous act have been sent down [excommunicated] [executed]."

Then he was replaced by rather more interesting footage. Three huge dragons were taking off from a mountain. They looked mean.

"In retaliation," our spokesman continued, "three Autonomous Strike Units of the Griffon's Nest Squadron were sortied against enemy strongholds at the border of the Noon Lands."

The "stronghold" looked like a poor village clinging to a mountainside. Our point of view was from one of the dragons, so it wobbled as the driver junked from side to side. One of the wobbles brought the wing dragon into view. Almost leisurely, it toppled into a dive, opening its ugly mouth as it did.

Suddenly the mountainside erupted in flame. In a way, it was perfect that this was on TV, since the whole business reminded me of something I'd seen on TV when I was about nine years old . . . a napalm strike in Vietnam. My cheerful bartender came to life long enough to mutter, "[Get them!]"

I could see a dark patch, sprinkled with flames, on the slope beneath the village. Obviously the dragon strike had missed. The lead dragon banked in a wide turn, tilting the horizon at a thirty-degree angle, bringing us back on a heading that would take us right over the village. But we dropped lower and lower, until we were level just above the treetops. I waited for another eruption of flame, but it didn't come. Instead a black, fish-like shape dropped from under the left wing.

The fish spewed flame and shot toward the village. At that moment the dragon roared and pulled up, heading for those bull's-eye clouds. Suddenly the clouds went yellow. An instant later, an explosion rocked the dragon so sharply that I thought it was lost. Then it leveled out again and turned.

The village was gone. For that matter, so was the mountainside.

"That action took place this afternoon," the spokesman said. Had he been talking all along? I couldn't remember. "Our heroic units have returned safely to their base."

All around me people were nodding in approval. I was the one who stood up and shook his head.

Maybe. I suppose I shouldn't have been surprised that the Dreamlanders had missiles, even missiles with tactical nuclear warheads—or explosives strong enough that it didn't matter.

But I could have sworn that in the brief moment when that missile hung in the air below the dragon . . . as its motor fired . . . I could see the letters "USAF" on its side.

A *little* two-way traffic?

I hadn't even decided how outraged I should be when there was another shock.

Maia was on the screen.

I hadn't gotten a good look at her during the service, since there must have been a hundred rows of seats between us, but that wasn't the case now. She was wearing some simple white dress and had a scarf over her head. Her only jewelry was a necklace that looked like black pearls. Yet I'd never seen her so beautiful. It made me ache.

"Let me just say," she told the audience, smiling, "how happy I am to be here with you . . . to be home with my family . . . by the grace of the Griffon." She cleared her throat. "I can't speak for long today, but I can tell you that I'm fine, that I haven't been harmed, that we can all be proud of the men of our Civil Guards. Without their skills, I don't know what would have happened to me.

"As most of you know, I've been in seclusion for the past year while I complete my studies. It was while in transit from Green Mountain to Chios that I was abducted. But now I'm home, among you, and free. Thank you all for your prayers."

Maia waved to our point of view, then we were back to the spokesman, who said, "Griffon's blessings to you all. Good day."

Good day, my ass. It was pretty obvious to me, having grown up in the Nixon years, that the spokesman was lying—and so much for the myth that Dreamlanders couldn't lie to each other—but it really pissed me off that Maia was part of it.

I began to see that she was a hell of an actress.

But what bothered me even more was that she hadn't

mentioned Gus. Not once. Was she trying to pretend he didn't exist? *Somebody* was.

I took to the streets again. The bartender never seemed to care that he was losing the turnover on my table, but I had been noticed there in the Six and Nine. I saw one guy pointing me out to his friend, who slipped away, probably to call the guards. (If the Griffon truly were God, He would have to have eyes and ears everywhere. Being a snitch was probably a holy chore . . .) In fact, what I really wanted was just to get away. If possible, I would walk back to the river and scream random syllables until the ''door'' opened. I couldn't do anything for Gus. I obviously didn't know shit about Maia. It was time to look out for myself.

Maybe the egg had done its work, because I was depressed and angry.

I hadn't gone two blocks in what I thought was the way out of town when I found my way blocked by the massive walls of the Hill. I backtracked to the square, to the front door of the Six and Nine, and went off in another direction.

Five blocks this time. There was the Hill again.

The egg had done its job too well. I couldn't even *walk*.

I turned around and headed back to the next cross street, went to my left down an alley—

—And came out in front of the Hill.

I could take a hint. All roads seemed to lead to the Hill.

16

I walked right up to the front door of the temple at the Hill and, surprisingly, found it open. It was dark inside except for a couple of lights glowing dimly on the altar, but I could see well enough to make my way down the center aisle.

Now that I was here, I suppose I could have expected some answers. In my world I wouldn't have bothered, but in Dreamland the Griffon listens. Even if, most of the time, He says no.

I didn't really expect the Griffon to do the answering. There were other, handier candidates—like Maia. Until that stupid broadcast I had begun to think I knew her.

Which made twice in the last three days that I'd had to radically reassess my view of her. How much more of this could I stand?

I was well into a series of heated imaginary dialogues with her when I realized I was not alone in the temple. Someone was approaching from the shadows to my right.

I didn't consider running away; it might just be a late worshipper. Or, what the hell, even somebody else from my world looking for guidance.

Actually, it was both. It was Maia.

She knelt down next to me. I realized I had been on my knees for over an hour. No wonder I was getting irritable.

She had shed her professional Heiress uniform for something more practical, what looked like riding clothes. In fact, there were streaks of dirt on her face. She'd been busy. I prepared myself for a bit of frostiness, and I wasn't disappointed. "I'm sorry being here is so difficult for you."

There you had it, as good a conversational first strike as you'll ever get. "I missed you, too."

"Where in the Griffon's name have you been?"

"I was visiting a friend of yours," I said, unleashing an attack of my own. "A guy named Stenn. I was with him when he was killed."

I hit home. Maia sighed. "I was afraid of that."

"Look," I said, "what you did before we met is none of my business. But Stenn gave me the distinct impression that you two were still engaged. Or was he mistaken?"

"No. He was telling the truth, but only in a very technical sense. The betrothal had not been formally terminated, but it would have been. I had breached the agreement by going away in the first place." We were silent for a moment, neither of us looking at the other. Finally Maia said, "How was he?"

"Before or after he died?"

It was childish of me, but I wanted to shake her up, and I did. She turned and looked at me as if I were a stranger. Then she got up and walked away.

I wondered whether I should follow—whether I *could* follow—because Maia quickly went around to one side of the altar, pushed aside a curtain, and disappeared into a chamber beyond.

How do you knock on a curtain? I settled for thumping the composite wall a couple of times. From inside I heard a muffled "Go away."

"Maia! I'm not going away!"

The curtain was suddenly pulled open. Maia stood there, furious, but something she saw behind me kept her from speaking. I turned, and saw that people were entering the temple. More lights were coming on. Some kind of service was about to start.

"Come in here. I don't have much time."

The chamber off the altar was a changing room of sorts. Maia calmly stripped off her activewear, washed her face, and began to don the Heiress uniform again. "I suppose you have a right to be angry. I know what it's like to have to deal with the customs of another world, and I had more preparation than you've had.

"But, Rick, you're never going to understand me and you're never going to understand your son, until you accept the truth that here the Griffon is God. Dominion actually works. Our lives are governed by something more than our desires. Hold this, please." She handed me a veil. "If you would open your mind you might begin to understand that everything that occurs has a purpose, even suffering. The biggest difference between us is that I'm part of a plan, and I believe in it, while you're part of it, and you don't. Thank you." She took the veil.

There was something beautiful about her certainty. It wasn't the smug and annoying righteousness that you find in recent converts to Catholicism or Scientology . . . this was more pure, like the trust a child puts in her parents. And God damn you if you destroy it.

"Look, I'm sorry," I said. "I'm worried about Gus and I got angry when I saw you on TV and you lied about him."

"I'm worried about Gus, too," she said quietly. "I've been out all day searching for him." Then she added: "Whatever gave you the idea that I have freedom of speech, especially when I'm wearing this uniform?"

"Why does the Griffon worry about what the peasants think? He's got all this power—why doesn't He just cloud their minds?"

"The recoil from a prayer that strong would probably kill even Him."

"Well, maybe my problem is that I can't understand how the existence of my world can be such a big secret when you have your dragons firing U.S. Air Force missiles at the enemy. You don't pick those things up at Sears, you know." As I said this I peeked out through the curtain. "Nice of the Griffon to show up in person." I was referring to the beefy star of this morning's service. Dressed in his vestments, he had appeared at one of the entrances leading in from the Hill itself. A priest-warrior was with him.

"Where?" Maia demanded. She got quite agitated, so I showed her. "You scared me," she said. "That's not the Griffon."

"Well, who is he?"

"Even when He is well, which He hasn't been for years, the Griffon never appears in public. That man is a priest known as the Face of God. He carries the Griffon's message to the faithful. He kisses the babies."

"No wonder you were scared." I nodded at a heavily retouched portrait that hung in the chamber. "This must be the Griffon, then."

"Why do you say that?"

"Come on, Maia, who else would have His picture in the temple? Besides, I've seen Him."

For some reason that surprised her. "You have?"

"Sure. He was in the cell next to me at Linn's camp. No wonder He doesn't go out. He looked sick—"

"Rick, you're not joking about this, are you? You really saw that man?" She pointed toward the picture.

"Absolutely. He was thinner and older, but it was definitely the same guy—"

"And He was with Linn?"

"He wasn't really with anybody. He was very ill."

"But Linn was attending to Him?"

"Yes. Maia, what's this all about?"

She was peering out the curtains again. "And there he is. The bastard." She meant Linn, who was standing with the Face and looking indecently cheerful.

"I have to go out there," she said. "You can stay here."

I looked around. It was a weird little place. "No, thanks. Why don't I wait out there with you?"

Now she was uncertain. "You won't understand this . . ."

"I'll try. I promise."

"All right. But whatever you do, don't go near Linn. And come with me as soon as the ceremony's over."

"Maia, are you okay?"

"I'm fine."

It didn't matter what she said, she looked nervous, even frightened. "Is it something about this resurrection? Stenn coming back? Because I'll try to help you work things out, really—"

"That's sweet, Rick. I want Stenn to live again for exactly the same reasons I'd want anyone to live again. Nothing more. I told you, it's over."

"I love you."

"I love you, too. That's the whole problem."

I wasn't handling this well. The fact that most people wouldn't have handled it any better wasn't much consolation. So I did what I should have done earlier:

I kissed her. She drew back at first, not resisting, but not helping. Then she relaxed and let me hold her. "No one tells the Heiress much in the best of times, and these aren't the best. I didn't know what had happened to you.

157

So I prayed all afternoon that you would meet me here tonight.''

"I'm sorry I'm being such an idiot," I said. "I'm a scientist, remember? And so far I haven't seen anything that couldn't be explained by science or coincidence."

She frowned. "Well, then, step outside. And remember what I told you."

I took a place among the arriving worshippers while Maia went forward to her place in the royal pew.

I wanted to ask what, exactly, was going on, when I saw a coffin being wheeled down the center aisle. It wasn't quite a coffin as I remembered them, but, then, my experience with funerals was limited. It was less of a box and more of a sac or pouch . . . squared off in the Dreamland fashion, which is to say, not much, and still organic. Recently alive, like its contents.

Oh yes: the lid was a life-sized death mask. I would have known Stenn anywhere.

Three priest-warriors took their places upon the altar. One of them was my old friend Linn. If he noticed or cared that I was in the audience, he hid it. Somber music played somewhere above us.

Another object was wheeled up the aisle: a gurney bearing the white-sheeted form of a very old woman. I suddenly remembered the frightened-looking little man Hemel had brought to Stenn's library door . . . the intended victim of this morning's sacrifice . . .

Maia had been right: I wasn't going to understand this.

The ceremony had its own tragic pomp. Acolytes of one kind and another scurried back and forth across the altar, tending to the victim, dousing the coffin with spices and incense. The music was beautiful. All around me people seemed to be engaged in an important if magical process. It was a celebration, not a funeral. The priest-warriors chanted and those in the temple responded. I actually felt

158

left out. Which was stupid: I wanted to be left out. I wanted them to stop.

The victim started to moan. She was an old woman, eighty-five at best, but she sounded like a beast of the fields. That voice couldn't have belonged to her—

Then the coffin moaned in answer. Soon they were doing a duet. The music got louder. The voices of the priest-warriors became more insistent.

I felt a chill on my neck. On the altar, Maia covered her face with her hands. The moaning turned to one long scream. The victim sat up on her gurney and raised her arms—

—Then fell back. The music and chanting stopped.

Stenn was on the gurney.

And the death mask on the coffin was that of the victim.

"She asked to be a partner in the ceremony," Maia said. This was perhaps ten minutes after its conclusion. In the general joy and grief, Maia slipped down from the altar, linked her arm in mine, and led me out of the temple and into the Hill.

"I didn't ask you to justify it," I said. "I only wondered who she was."

"She was related to Stenn and she was very ill."

I accepted that. I imagined that the Griffon was very merciful toward those who made such a sacrifice. Was that ceremony any worse than things that occurred in my world?

"Maia, what is wrong?" She was in a hell of a hurry.

"We need to find someplace we can talk."

"What about your room?"

"I don't think it's safe."

On my best day I couldn't have told you how long we walked, or where. Down, down into the bowels of the Hill is the best I can do for a description. We didn't run, though both of us felt like running. Clearly we were making a strategic retreat, but a stately one. Maia would pause here and there. At first I thought she was checking for signs of some kind, but then I realized she was getting reacquainted with the place that had been, until Tucson, the only home she'd ever known.

We even ducked through a secret passage, emerging into an entire floor of the palace that I had not suspected. The place was almost totally dark except for starlight coming through distant, membrane-covered windows.

"This is where the Griffon lived," Maia said.

It was obvious that He hadn't lived there recently. The floor was littered with huge, humped shapes—covered furniture, I hoped. The air was full of dust and mold. I sneezed.

Maia seemed right at home. She glided from one hump to another, running her hands across them, in search of something. "I used to hide here when I was little," she said, "whenever Jayan wanted to punish me. They never found me. I don't think they knew I'd found the way in."

She pulled back one of the skin coverings, revealing a plain desk. On the desk was a Book so old that pages fell out when Maia opened it. "I'd sit by the window and read the prophecies. My favorite was the one about the Heiress who was exiled to another land far, far away, and fell in love with an infidel."

"The Heiress finds a mate from outside the immediate family. Typical biological imperative."

"If you say so. I've always believed that I was the Heiress in the prophecy. It was just a little girl's fantasy until I found out that our priests could [walk] between worlds. From that day on I tried to convince my mother to let me try it."

"Where was your father while all this was going on?"

"He was killed fighting the Devils when I was three. I don't really remember him." For some reason that struck

me as terribly sad. For the father, I mean. Not to be remembered by his daughter.

"I'm sorry. So Jayan finally broke down and said yes?"

"Not Jayan. She never budged. But I dug around in this
Book some more and found another prophecy about a re-
deemer who will come from a place 'beyond this world'
to renew us all. I made sure that the Griffon Himself heard
about that one, and my request, in that order."

"So that's what all this is? Fulfillment of some . . .
prophecy?" I'd almost said "idiot" prophecy.

"You know me well enough to answer that." Which,
of course, was no answer at all. "Rick, I'm really scared
of Linn."

"I thought he was a priest-warrior. One of your good
guys."

"A priest-warrior doesn't turn the Griffon into a prisoner."

"How do you know He's a prisoner?"

"He's been ill for years. Some of my family even
thought He was dead. From your own description, He was
in no condition to be ordering attacks on the Devils, or
giving orders of any kind. Yet He is. Well, somebody is."

"Somebody like Linn."

"That's what I'm afraid of." She sighed. "I wasn't always alone in Tucson, you know."

"No, I don't know."

"I had guards. Not always, but from time to time. It
would have been difficult for them to actually live there
the way I did—too many questions. So they checked in
with me. We had signals. As long as I sent them, they
pretty much left me alone."

I wasn't really surprised by the news, and I was long
past being upset by surprise itself. "Then how the hell did
someone manage to kidnap you?"

"I don't know. I was waiting there at the gate. The
plane was late and both of us were getting tired and fret-

ful, and Gus had just spit up. I had a handful of dirty, smelly napkins, and I asked the ticket agent—''

"Was she an older woman?" I asked, thinking of Hazel. Maia nodded.

"I asked her to watch him for a second while I walked twenty feet to a garbage can.

"I . . . saw them. I don't mean I recognized them. But you know how you can sense when a person is disoriented? These three had that look. It was probably the same look I wore the first few hours or days I was in your world. And they were heading for me.

"I didn't think. I just started to walk away. I hoped that they wouldn't follow me, but they did. It was so quick I didn't even have time to scream."

"They just grabbed you in the middle of a crowded airport, dragged you out the front door, and no one noticed?"

"No." Her eyes narrowed. "They walked me back to this world. It couldn't have taken more than a second."

"I thought you had to be in some special location. A 'wavicle' in the surface of space-time or whatever."

"You do, but there are lots of wavicles, especially around Tucson. That's why I was there."

Just when I thought I was growing accustomed to this place—"You're telling me *Tucson* is some kind of border town for the Twilight Zone?" I laughed, but as I did I realized it made a certain amount of twisted sense. After all, the valley in which the city sat was one of the oldest inhabited regions in all of North America. It was home to the Aerial Phenomenon Research Organization—APRO for short, UFO Central to the rest of us. I seemed to recall that the space colony society was founded there. The eco-terrorists, the Monkey Wrench Gang, hung out in the neighborhood. And there was the whole Sanctuary movement . . . I guess we just didn't realize how far, trans-dimensionally speaking, all these illegal immigrants had to travel . . . the future and the distant past, side by side . . .

If you really wanted to get weird, you could think about Mount Baboquivari, the Papago sacred mountain a few miles outside of town. It was supposedly home to the gods, and the point about which the whole universe turned. Right.

"Rick, are you about through?"

"Sorry."

"All I know about Tucson is that it's one place where the barrier between the worlds is so thin it's almost non-existent. It's sort of a nexus, and rips or tears or wavicles spread out from it like the spokes of a wheel. The further you get from the center, the stronger and less penetrable the barrier is."

That sounded like a twisted version of the inverse-square law. Since even twisted physical laws didn't seem to apply in anything else I'd seen in this bozo world so far, I didn't get too excited. "It doesn't matter," I said. "What's important is that these guys grabbed you, but missed Gus. What I still want to know is . . . *who got Gus and Jayan?*"

"I thought it was the Devils. But now I'm not so sure."

"Well," I said, thinking about it, "let's think about it. You said you had guards. Did *they* know about Gus?"

"Rick, I hadn't even told my mother."

This was just beginning to confuse me more, not that that took a great deal of effort. "All I know is, if your Civil Guards thought that the Devils or agents of Untruth had taken Gus and Jayan, they'd have been very stupid to nuke one of their villages. They aren't stupid people. So they must either *know* where Gus and Jayan *are* . . . or *they* are the kidnappers."

I'd never seen Maia shocked before. Surprised, yes. You'd think I'd just proved to her there was no Griffon looking after her. Maybe I had.

"Well . . . Linn *was* the one who insisted on resurrecting Stenn."

"Okay, consider that. Now, why?"

"That's just it. I don't know. I'm willing to believe that some of the guards might be corrupt, but not Linn himself. Please."

I wasn't going to get more out of her. It was as if I'd let the air out of her. What I'd seen before was shock. This was despair. "You know," I said, "I'm not going to tell you things if you keep reacting like that."

Suddenly we heard a thumping noise.

"Someone's here!" Maia whispered.

There was light beyond the walls nearest us. We could see it through the cracks.

"Guards?"

Maia took my hand and nodded. "Come on."

We left through an exit I hadn't noticed. I believe it was a hole in the wall.

We emerged from the Griffon's quarters on the other side of the Hill, then hustled down to the basement, where Maia simply grabbed the nearest meat car. A quick prayer and we were off.

Twenty minutes later we were on the outskirts of Chios in a car and heading west. Unfortunately, we weren't alone. It may have been a coincidence, but another meat car—and only one—was going our way. It was hard to see from a distance: meat cars had orbs on the front that glowed like fireflies in the dark, but not well. This didn't prevent Maia from driving like a maniac. Well, I suppose I had to expect that; she'd learned in my world.

"Where are we going?"

"To hide you."

"Great. What about you?"

"They're going to find me no matter what I do. The Power, you know."

"If you say so. What about Gus and Jayan?"

She just stared at the road. "I'll keep trying."

We headed up into the hills on a little-used two-lane road, passing some of the poorest-looking places I've ever seen in my life. The brighter stars were past zenith now, meaning it was almost midnight. As we approached a turnout, Maia pulled off the road and got out. So did I.

"This is as far as I can go. The road ends soon. I'd like to lead them away from this place before I'm caught."

I looked around at the bare hillside, strangely bright in the starlight. "Am I supposed to hide here?" She answered by walking away. "Maia, why don't we fight them?"

She shaded her eyes and pointed to a peak in the distance. "There's the center of the world," she said.

"It's just a mountain."

"Maybe." Then she turned and hugged me.

"I don't know what I'm supposed to do," I said.

"You'll think of something. You always do. Now, say these words for me," she whispered.

"Why?"

"You'll need them! Please!"

"Okay."

And she said, "*Arsenic railway—*"

"*Arsenic railway.*" We were using her language, but it didn't echo. Is this the case with "true names"? Did Maia's people use the "true" language?

"*—Liquid dominate apollo—*"

She was clinging to me harder now. "*Liquid dominate apollo . . .*"

"*—Assonance light tree mare.*"

I got as far as "*Assonance*" when she kissed me. And, as I finished, pushed me. "*. . . Light tree mare.*"

Then I dropped into real darkness.

17

I had that strange worried-all-over feeling I'd suffered the first time I'd been "walked" between worlds—I mean, I had no doubt that that was what was happening to me. Even as I dropped I could see the stars disappearing somewhere above me. As if someone had closed a door in the sky.

I was thinking in double time, of course, the way you do when you're in a car accident. I remember wondering how long the crack remained open during that *first* transition . . . and realized I couldn't have been more than a few steps behind Gus and Jayan's kidnappers. Then I hit and rolled.

I didn't fall more than a few feet, and my landing, to use the term loosely, was cushioned by a good-sized cottonwood bush that definitely came out second best in the collision. It was almost completely crushed . . . and I got off with nothing more than a scratch. Well, I had had the laws of motion on my side (God only knew what kind of weird velocities these interversal transitions gave a body), but the whole thing reminded me too much of those tornado stories. You know, ''Piece of Straw Driven Through 2×4!'' Your head knows it can happen, but your heart says, ''No way.''

But there I was. Standing in an open field in the dark. Sunrise was approaching, however; there was enough light in the east that the mountains around me had shape while the stars had already begun to fade. Nothing moved except a cool desert breeze, which meant that I was no longer in Maia's windless home. Which, unfortunately, *didn't* necessarily mean I was in mine.

I heard a birdcall, faintly, which made me realize that my ears were ringing. Well, if anyone else around there had an excuse to be hypertense at that time of the morning, it was me. As I began walking toward the sunrise, it cleared up.

You could take the position, I suppose, that Maia had tricked me, and as I stumbled through the brush giving off odd flashes of rogue fury, I would have agreed. But I tried to look at it from her point of view. If our last conversation was any indication, she was in a terrible situation. And given my skill at maneuvering in her world—an objective observer would class it as negligible—I was nothing but a burden to her . . . in Dreamland. In Tucson I had a chance to do something. All I had to do was figure out what. I planned to get to that right after I figured out where I was.

It didn't take long. One moment I was walking on dirt and the next I was on a concrete platform. At first I thought it was a helipad—it was about that size. But there was nothing around the pad but scrub, and that didn't make sense.

Then I stumbled in a crack, and in the growing light saw that I was actually standing atop a giant concrete *door*. Who builds giant concrete doors in the ground?

My employers. I was standing over a missile launch silo.

At one time there were over a dozen sites around Tucson, each one concealing its very own Titan II equipped with the latest in multiple-targetable warheads. Nuclear annihilation in your backyard. The last one had been de-activated a couple of years ago, or else I'd have been flat on my face dodging bullets. Instead I sort of chuckled to myself as I looked for the perimeter fence—rusty now, but still in place—that led me to the access road.

Just as well. Military police and missile crew commanders aren't the sort of people you can explain trans-dimensional travel to.

By the time the sun peeked over the mountains I had learned two things: I was north and west of Tucson, and a guy driving a battered truck at five-thirty in the morning will pick up a grungy-looking boy in uniform.

My benefactor was a minister-slash-disc jockey on his way to sign on a station in South Tucson for his Sunday morning broadcast. *Sunday* morning? Okay, that would mean it was August 31, Labor Day weekend. I was lucky to find anyone on the streets. We jumped on I-10 not far from the road where he'd found me thumbing, and when he got off at 22d Street I had to choose between heading to the apartment, which was about four miles away, and trying to find the car, which was more like eight.

Well, I really hate not having wheels. And assuming I knew who to call—Tanque Verde Apartments was small and the landlord lived elsewhere—to let me in at 6:00 A.M. on a Sunday, I'd *still* have to find some way to retrieve the Mazda. So I hiked over to Grande and did more thumbing. And by seven o'clock I was unlocking the door on the driver's side. The Mazda was dusty and had held several days' heat, but it hadn't been touched. My wallet was still wedged between the front seats.

The engine started and I didn't even have to say a prayer. I was in business.

There was a yellow police-line sticker on the front door of the apartment. I wadded it up as I let myself in.

The rescue people who'd come for Hazel had picked her up and nothing else. The debris was still lying where I'd found it Wednesday night or whenever. The cruel thing about late summer in Tucson is that a few days' neglect can look like years. Since the windows were still open, there was a thin film of dust on all this debris. And it was cool enough—the overnight lows take place about four in the morning—that I thought I was in a tomb. Did wonders for my attitude, believe me.

I had a mental list of fifteen things I needed to do, which included:

   3) Hazel?
   6) Call Alquist at D-M and find out if I was still
      employed.
  12) Get a decent shave.

I had them in standard USAF priority order, but things being what they were, I got to them more or less at random. The D-M locator wasn't working on Sunday, of course, and the duty officer at Base Ops said Alquist was off for the day, so #6 could wait. I got the decent shave about third, if you have a loose interpretation of the word "decent."

What on earth was I going to do about Hazel? I thought about calling hospitals, then about calling TWA—but assuming I would actually get personal information over the phone, who would I find there on a Sunday? Only then did I remember that I *had* her goddamn address and phone! Which made me feel so stupid and tired that I tore up my

mental list and gave myself a good couple of hours' sleep
with the air-conditioning on.

It was restful. The bedroom still smelled of Gus.

The phone rang once, twice, three times. "Hello?" It
was a woman's voice.

"Hazel?" I said. "It's Rick Walsh."

Without an instant's hesitation, she said, "I need to talk
to you right now. Can you come over?"

No "Where have you been?" or "What is going on?"
None of the questions I desperately wanted to ask of everyone in sight. "Sure."

She gave me directions and hung up.

It was a place in the foothills, or in the foothills of the
foothills, north of River Road in a condo development.
There was some sort of nonsense going on at the U of A,
so I got caught in traffic going north on Campbell. It gave
me time to screw up my respiratory system by overusing
the air-conditioning, and to listen to the radio. I was looking for music but wound up with news.

You'd think a person in my line of work would pay some
attention to current affairs, but long ago I concluded that
news is all the same four stories. President meets with
world leader. Terrorists hijack Kuwaiti airliner. Dollar
lower against the yen. And the Special Olympics. Okay,
Special Olympics is a seasonal story: in the winter it's
replaced by "Fire Ruins Christmas for Poor Family."

I'm not proud of this and it isn't that I haven't made
efforts: I do catch CNN when I'm in the country, and on
Guam I had a subscription to *U.S. News & World Report*.
This is just a way of explaining how I could not know that
for the past few weeks the current scandal was over short-
falls in armaments inventories at several U.S. military in-
stallations. It wouldn't have penetrated my awareness at
all if I hadn't seen—or *thought* I'd seen—U.S. markings
on a weapon in Dreamland. But it was apparently this

week's biggest deal, with the Secret Service and FBI investigating, and several arrests expected momentarily.

In the past week I had been confused, infuriated, humiliated, shocked, and rotated into a few spaces for which I had no words . . . but I had yet to be thoroughly frightened. That's what that news did to me. It hit me right in the chest. It made me weak.

Because I knew now that there *was* some sort of regular two-way traffic between my world and Maia's world. And inevitably it was one of those soul-wrecking systems like the heroin trade in which every transaction takes place at 3:00 A.M. according to rules that are more complicated than a Form 1040, where the players are men—they're always men—who make you feel like a seven-year-old reading the Marquis de Sade. Not only should you not be reading this, every sentence contains a word or idea beyond your comprehension.

Maia and Gus and Hazel and I had about as much chance of changing this as a leaf has of redirecting the wind. It made me feel old.

Hazel was waiting out in front of her condo. She wore a bathrobe and looked frail. After I'd parked and come closer, I saw that she was horribly bruised, too. "Hazel, what are you doing outside?"

She glanced up and down the street. "I'm being careful, for once. I should have taken it up weeks ago. Come in!"

It must have been tough for her to make that trip outside because she all but collapsed on the couch as soon as I closed her door. She had a pleasant town house decorated with the usual pictures of children and grandchildren and the late Colonel Swensen, bric-a-brac from a good number of foreign countries, a bookcase full of paperbacks and some *Reader's Digest* Condensed Books, several crosses (not crucifixes) on the walls, and, strangely, some Tinkertoy aircraft models.

"Good God, Hazel, I hope you feel better than you look."

"I guess I don't take a punch as well as I used to," she said. "You look as though you've had a few rough nights, too."

I got her a glass of iced tea and asked her to tell me about it.

She had just put Gus down for a nap and was already out in front of the apartment unlocking her car door when she realized she hadn't left Jayan the airport number where she could be reached. When she opened the apartment door, there were strange men in the apartment. They had hold of Jayan, who was struggling, and one of them had Gus. "I wondered why I hadn't heard any noise—they'd broken through the back door—but that air conditioner was running. If *I* had one like that I'd worry about missing the Last Trump."

It was apparently all over in a couple of minutes. Hazel managed to count three men (which tallied with my count: one of the four I'd seen was probably waiting in the car). One of Jayan's two captors took off after Hazel, who screamed, to no effect. When he turned away to slam the front door, Hazel managed to belt his partner—who was still holding Jayan—with her car keys. She drew blood, but she knew she wasn't a match for even one of these guys, much less three of them.

Jayan and Gus were hustled out. The man she'd wounded came after her, cornering her in the bathroom. As if it was the most natural thing in the world, he'd simply walloped her. She fell, slamming her face against the toilet. When she awoke she was in the hospital.

I asked her to describe the thugs, if she could. I'd never gotten a very good look at them; she, at least, had seen their faces. "I went through this with the police," she said, "and I'm afraid I disappointed them. All I know is that there were three of them—two thin, one very solid, like a linebacker. That was the man I managed to cut.''

Like a linebacker. "Where was this cut?"

She smudged her face just to the right of her mouth. "Right there."

Like a linebacker, with a cut on his face. "Did this guy have blond hair, cut short?"

"Yes . . ."

I'd been right. *Linn* took Jayan and Gus.

"Rick, are you all *right*?"

I nodded.

"Heavens, you went pale, then got all red in the face."

"I know who hit you."

That seemed to perk her up a bit. "Oh, really? Are you going to tell me? Or do you want to call your friend Lieutenant Sanchez?"

"Hazel, I don't think that would do any good. I don't think this guy and his friends are . . . extraditable."

"Well," she said, smiling too sweetly, "maybe I'll hunt them down myself."

"I believe you would, and you'd probably get them, too, but it won't do any good."

I'm sure my frustration showed. "There's something you're not telling me, Rick. If you'd rather not, that's your business. But I am involved and I am on your side. I want Gus back where he belongs, too."

I took a breath and glanced around the room, my eyes eventually targeting the airplane models. "Isn't that a B-36? And a B-29?"

"Yes. My husband commanded a squadron of one and a wing of the other. I suppose it's kind of silly for me to still have them around, but he loved them so. And don't change the subject."

"Sorry. How's your ability to suspend disbelief?"

She gestured at the crosses on the wall. "I believe in

angels and heaven, dear. What could you have to tell me that could possibly be more fantastic?"

It took me an hour, and in the entire time she never moved. The ice in her iced tea melted; water stained the surface of her antique wooden coffee table, and she never moved.

"And here you are."

"And here I am."

Then she got up and went to her bookcase, pulling out a well-worn Bible in its soft leather jacket. She flexed it, but didn't open it as she sat back down on the couch. "Don't worry," she said. "I'm not going to start preaching at you." She examined the closed book. "It's just a . . . security blanket." She laughed, but not happily. "I was raised to believe that the answers to everything in life were in that one book. Part of me still does." She shook her head. "I can't imagine a . . . a whole other world in which God has human form."

"And human frailties."

"Well, I suppose that's part of the package."

"You're not having much trouble with this concept at all."

"I'm having quite a lot of trouble with it, but I have more trouble with the other possibility, which is that you just got high and wandered off into the desert somewhere . . . I'd rather rearrange my theology than admit that I can't judge people."

"Thank you."

"What on earth are you going to do?"

"Well, I can't just leave them there, can I? If Linn is the person who did what he did to you and took Gus and Jayan, they aren't safe with him. And if there's really some war going on concerning the Griffon, Maia's in trouble, too. I've got to go back."

"*Can* you?"

"Maia taught me some words. I think if I find the right place—the right wavicle or whatever—I could do it. Go back, I mean. What I do once I'm back, I just don't know. I need about a gross of answers first."

"I wish I could help."

I thought for a moment, then said, "You can."

"Okay . . ."

"I need a gun—"

She was shaking her head before I finished the sentence. "I don't have anything like that, Rick—"

"I need you to help me *buy* a gun."

"Oh."

I'd upset her. Well, I'd upset myself. But people who snatch children and beat up old ladies have other unpleasant habits. I'd never fired a gun in my life except for basic training, but I wanted to have one now . . . just in case.

After all, this was the Old West I was living in, wasn't it?

"I can't just walk into a hardware store and buy one," I said. "I've got the money and I can't imagine anyone around here makes a big deal out of it, but I don't even have a local residence—they might make me wait, and I can't wait."

Hazel sighed. "I'm sorry, Rick, but I will not help you buy a gun."

I stood up. "I understand."

"Wait," she said. "I didn't say I wouldn't help you *get* one." I stood there with a stupid look on my face. "Let me get dressed and make a phone call."

"This is a forty-five-caliber, blue-steel Colt Combat Marauder," Vic Roelke said.

We were in the garage of his place on the south side of town, close enough to the concrete at D-M that we could hear the landing gear locking into place on the jets that were coming in. Hazel had left us alone and was having lemonade with Mrs. Roelke in the kitchen.

In addition to some intriguing poster art which looked as though it had been purchased at a car wash, Roelke had quite an arsenal. Several handguns, three or four hunting rifles, and an honest-to-God submachine gun.

"Lot of kick with that one," I said, slipping into that white guy's automatic response mode. It happens whenever I'm around cars, guns, or sports. "No shit" is the all-purpose answer, but I had a few special ones.

"It's a powerful piece of machinery." His eyes gleamed as he put the Colt back in its case, not closing the lid. "Now," he said, getting down to business, "Hazel said you needed a gun."

This was my invitation to either come out with the truth or tell him a convincing story. "I've got to get requalified on the range Tuesday, and I've been such a pussy lately I haven't fired a shot in months. It's real important to get qualified—my next assignment depends on it—but I'd like to do some quiet practicing on my own. I'm afraid that if I go to a range right now I'm likely to run into one of the guys who'll be qualifying me. You know how it is."

By the time I was done, he was nodding. He pulled the Colt out of the case and aimed at the wall. " 'Course! And there are lots of places around here to do a little shooting. Pick up a six-pack, drink it—" He "fired." "Plug it." He handed me the piece. "I was afraid you wanted to *buy* something."

I hefted the Colt. "Is that a problem?"

"Well . . . you know it *could* be." He laughed. "If you shot someone by accident. My gun and all."

"I just want to borrow it. I'll have it back in a couple of days."

"Keep it all week, if you need it."

"Thanks. Maybe I will." I was serious about that, too.

I closed up the case and was ready to make a clean get-away when Vic suddenly turned toward me.

"Oh, Rick, one other thing . . ." For just a moment there I thought I was in trouble. This guy was a cop, after all. Then he said, "How are you fixed for bullets?"

I dropped Hazel back at her condo and she insisted on making lunch for me. Either she had been telling the truth about feeling better than she looked, or she had reserves of strength that kicked in whenever she had to fetch for a fairly helpless male.

When we were finished, I said, "This is the first normal meal I've eaten in a week." And suddenly realized that it really *had* been just seven days since I got off the plane in Tucson. "Thank you."

"You need your strength," she said, "for whatever it is you're going to do."

"I've got some ideas."

"I'll be praying for you."

"That's exactly what I need you to do." And I wasn't kidding. "May I use your phone?"

18

In my rearview mirror I saw red sky and mountain shadows. It was Sunday sunset, well past the middle of the Labor Day weekend, and all over the city students were getting ready for the start of classes at the university, families were having barbecues or huddling in air-conditioned comfort, people were sitting in bars watching the start of the NFL season.

And here I was, setting an ambush.

Heading south on the roller-coaster ride that was Houghton Road, I passed Old Spanish Trail and found the new and unmarked road within sight of a Circle K. I turned west and, at a likely-looking spot, plunged south into the scrub that bordered the new development. It was one of those rare holidays—it had to be related to football—when crews didn't work; their huge graders and Caterpillars sat alone. No one had bothered to throw up a fence—why, when the construction would be completed so quickly?—so I doubted that I'd find a security guard. I stashed the

Mazda behind a grader and got out, tucking the Colt into my jeans in the small of my back . . . just like they do it in the movies.

The dust was settling from my detour into the development—I hoped it wouldn't be noticeable—as I headed toward the nearby wash. I glanced at my watch: 5:25. The paper had said sunset would be 6:13, which was probably accurate. In downtown, with the Tucson Mountains looming to the west, shadows would begin to fall at six. But here on the east side of town, in the flat belly of the valley, I could count on having that blinding light for at least fifteen minutes beyond six.

And six was when I'd told Sanchez to meet me.

I wasn't going to position myself due west of him. I had to assume he was professional enough to expect that. All I wanted was to have him *look* in that direction for just a moment . . .

At five to six an unmarked car turned off Houghton onto the new road, pebbles rattling against its underside. Sanchez must have thought he was going to be late. He skidded to a stop, and I risked a peek from my position. It was always possible someone was in the trunk, or crouched down in the back, but he appeared to be alone.

Well, that was the deal.

Glancing casually left and right, he hurried toward the wash. I froze as he passed me not twenty feet away. He stumbled once. "Shit." He was wearing shorts and a Hawaiian shirt. I must have interrupted his weekend. When he reached the wash, he yelled, "Walsh!"

I tossed a pebble to my left. He turned toward it, right into the blinding sunset, as I jumped up. He was still shading his eyes when I poked the muzzle of the Colt into his back and said, "Hold it."

Had this been a movie, he would have raised his hands. Instead he just shook his head. "Walsh, are you out of your fucking mind? You're holding a gun on a federal officer.''

"What happened to 'Call me anytime, anywhere'?''

"That was before you disappeared. Where the hell have you been, anyway?''

"This is where I say, 'I'll ask the questions.' ''

"So ask. You've already screwed up my dinner.''

I told him to sit down on the fallen tree, facing me, out of reach. He didn't argue. I suppose he really didn't think I'd shoot him—for that matter, neither did I—but he knew that I was pretty pissed off. In his position *I'd* have been cautious and cooperative.

"So who, exactly, are you?''

"You didn't bring me all the way out here to ask me that.''

"You just said I was holding a gun on a federal officer, but last week you told me you worked for the Tucson P.D. Call me curious.''

He sighed. "Don't be an asshole, Walsh. You're in a little *bit* of trouble right now. You definitely do not want to get in bigger trouble with me.''

"Okay,'' I said, gesturing with the Colt, "empty out the pockets.''

Sanchez stood up and without really thinking about it I clicked back the hammer. He stopped right where he was and calmly began to remove items from his pockets. Some change. A handkerchief, still folded. A wallet.

"Kick the wallet over here,'' I said. He did it without even leaving his frozen crouch. "You can sit down,'' I told him.

I kept the pistol in my right hand and, with the left, set the wallet on the log in front of me where I could see the contents without taking my eyes off Sanchez. Since I had to use the left to pry out credit cards and whatnot, the results were predictably slow. I found a Visa from First Interstate Bank of Arizona, a driver's license—suitably worn—and a few other cards. Video rental, HMO, even a goddamn library card. He had his Tucson P.D. clip-on badge stuck in the pouch where you keep the bills.

It didn't look promising, but I guess I wanted to be thorough. I pushed out the badge, taking some of the bills with it, and something struck me as odd. Most of the bills were fives and ones—I think Sanchez had thirty bucks in there—but one of them was folded double and printed in red ink. Mexican money? I thought, unfolding it. Then I saw a familiar symbol.

A winged lion. The Griffon.

I looked at Sanchez. I had the Dreamland money in my hand, and he knew I recognized it.

"So that's where you've been," he said. He stood up. He was like another person entirely. When I didn't respond, he said, "Walsh, do something. Either get off your ass and come along, or shoot me. Because I'm leaving."

So I went along.

We wound up at a storefront on Broadway a few blocks east of downtown. Both of us drove and both of us parked in front. There was a Bob's Big Boy a couple of doors to the north which seemed to be doing good business, but nothing else moved.

The sign said this was the Scholz Artificial Limb Supply, Inc., but inside there were no arms and legs to be seen, just a collection of General Services Administration–style gray desks, personal computers, and phones. I recognized the stuff; I'd used the same things at Offutt and Guam.

"'Welcome to the palatial headquarters of the Special Task Group," Sanchez said. "Excuse me." He picked up a phone and called his wife—at least that's what it sounded like—telling her something had come up and he wouldn't be home for a while.

I looked around, hoping, I suppose, to find helpful information on the walls. Maps of Dreamland, perhaps. Charts of wavicle fields. But I was disappointed. The only thing posted on the wall that I could read was a reminder from some office that employees of the STG were not to expect service from the local branch of the Government Employees Federal Credit Union. There were other notices stuck on a bulletin board further away, but I would have had to get up from my chair and turn on more lights to see them. A bit too obvious.

I did confirm that this was where the "7736" number rang. It was on the phones.

"Okay," Sanchez said. "I'm not from the Tucson Police."

"Then you must be FBI."

"Not quite."

"Please don't make me guess any more."

"Sorry. I'm a consultant for the Bureau right now, but I've done that for CIA in the past, too. Technically I work for the Treasury Department. Bureau of Alcohol, Tobacco and Firearms. We liaise with all the law enforcement and intelligence agencies there are. I guess you could say I'm a general-purpose troubleshooter."

"Sounds like an interesting job. What trouble are you shooting?"

"Speaking of shooting . . ." He gestured toward my belt and the Colt.

"I think I'll just hold on to this for the time being," I said.

"Have it your way. Just don't shoot your dick off inside this building or I'll be filling out paperwork into the next century."

"You were saying?"

"Our particular trouble?" He latched on to a coffee maker and, as he talked, began filling it up. "It has to do with the arms business. Stealing them. Selling them. Using them. All by the wrong people."

I dropped his Griffon bill on the desk. I'd given him his wallet back, but kept that. "These people?"

"Those are *some* of the wrong people. You probably know more about them than I do."

"Well, I've been there."

He shook his head. "Amazing." He switched on the coffee maker and picked up the bill. "We found this on one of the few people we've managed to bust so far—"

"One of *them*?"

"No. Only some of the people involved are from . . . the other side. This guy was a Colombian. If there's something he hasn't tried to smuggle, it can't be smuggled. It probably doesn't even exist.

"He had a few of these things on him when we caught him. I mean, he wasn't going to spend them, he probably just wanted souvenirs." He held the bill up to the light. "We ran this through the lab at Fort Detrick and, Christ, you'd think we'd given them the fucking Shroud of Turin. They'd never seen anything like it. It's paper all right, but the pollens don't exist on this planet. Even the ink is funny." He laughed and tossed it back on the desk.

"So what's going on? What was this Colombian guy doing?"

Sanchez's coffee was ready. He poured a cup and offered me one. I declined. He sat down. "Some people on this side—including some people in our very own military-industrial complex, to use a term from my youth—have made deals with the other side, to give them missiles and other high-tech weaponry."

"How much?"

"We don't know. We only became vaguely aware of it in the past four or five months. There's a lot of this stuff out there. Bombs, nuclear warheads, CBW, missiles. And what's making it very convenient for the bad guys is that we've got a few new treaties that call for the destruction of items like this. What better way to get rid of them than to make them fucking disappear?''

"Wouldn't the Russians be able to verify that these weapons are disappearing and not necessarily being destroyed?''

"Sure, eventually. That's one of the reasons the people I work for are shitting bricks.'' He used a mocking voice. " 'Suppose the Russians find out?' ''

"What do we get? The bad guys on our side, I mean? What's in it for them?''

"I wish I knew. Gold. Drugs. Maybe women.''

"The disappearances?''

"That's what we've thought, from time to time. I'll be honest with you, I really don't know.'' He stared at his now-empty coffee cup. "Are you satisfied now? Are you going to sleep better tonight knowing that this is going on?''

I didn't answer. I was like a nine-year-old playing with a puzzle that I was sure had one missing piece . . . and I'd just found six.

"You've got a dangerous look on your face, man,'' Sanchez said. "Take some advice from an expert: don't.''

"Don't what?''

"Just don't. It may look like the Wild West around here, but it isn't. You don't solve problems by pulling that cowboy shit. I'm going to do you a favor and forget that you sandbagged me—this time. I don't want to have to do it again. I really think you should put your 'rod' away and let those of us who've spent two years on this case do the work.

"Doesn't the Air Force need you to do *something*?''

19

The brace shop/task force headquarters was only a few blocks from Maia's apartment, so I went home and changed into my blues.

I've always hated Sunday nights, even Sunday nights on three-day weekends. Mom and Dad are tired and there's nothing but garbage on TV. You've had all the fun you're going to have. If school doesn't start the next day, it starts the day after that. Even if I hadn't engaged in the quest from hell, I couldn't have stayed home that night.

My fresh parking sticker and a crisp salute got me past the Craycroft gate at D-M even though it was almost seven o'clock. There were a few other cars making the same trip. Air Force bases don't shut down for the holidays.

Base Ops was as quiet as you'll ever see it, however. Unless there's an ongoing exercise, pilots aren't usually in the sky at night. So I pretty much had the place to myself . . . which was the whole idea.

What was I looking for? I was still bothered by Alquist's

connection with Sanchez. I hadn't raised it at the brace shop because I still wasn't sure who Sanchez was working for. Anyone can buy some government desks, dummy up paperwork, and tell a story. I had a clearance, I had access to some files. I was sure something would turn up.

Well, nothing did. I staked out a desk and grabbed the Ops logs and whatnot, setting things out so I'd look busy, in case anyone came in. With a clipboard in hand, I began snooping through the other desks, eventually working my way to Alquist's . . . which had been completely sanitized.

There were three four-drawer gray filing cabinets in Ops, too, all of them locked, though the key wasn't hard to find. I skimmed them and realized quickly that I was facing a potential purloined-letter-style operation: there was enough mind-numbing chaff in those files that you could have left the nuclear enabling codes in them and they'd never be found, except by accident. I couldn't afford to wait for an accident.

If there was anything of value in Ops at all, it would be in the safes, and unlike the files, getting the keys and combinations would be a bit more challenging. Since Ops was technically "down," I'd have to find the duty officer and give him some good excuse to open things up for me. Well, I'd bullshitted my way past a couple of people already today . . . one more wouldn't hurt.

Until I got to the duty desk, that is, and found Ming the Merciless. "Well," he said pleasantly, "if it isn't Lieutenant Wuss." Wuss as in puss, short for pussy. I told you he was clever.

"You know, Escobar, one of these days you're going to have to stop calling me that." I didn't want to have even a moment's unpleasant chat with this guy, but there was always the chance he would go off duty. Or die of a heart attack.

"Oh, I'm sorry. Are you going to bring me up on

charges? Uniform Code of Military Justice, let's shoot the Indian for insubordination.''

"No," I said, looming over his desk as best I could. "Because one of these days I'm going to be . . . *Captain Wuss*." Before he could answer, I said, "When is Captain Alquist due back?''

I think he was disappointed that I didn't want to fight because he just mumbled to himself and said, "Not till oh-five-hundred . . . sir—''

"Thank you, Sergeant." It was the sort of question a lazy officer would ask of the duty desk, and God knows Ming thought I was lazy. I thought that was the end of it, time to go home, get some sleep, and regroup when, as I turned to leave, Ming said, "—just in time for the test."

The test.

"You know, I've been away for a couple of days," I said, improvising. "Is that, ah, test going to be at the range, Sergeant?''

He sort of sniffed. "They're going out to the Alamo site," he said.

"Oh. I should have remembered." What the hell was the Alamo site?

Sometimes it's helpful if people think you're an idiot.

Alamo was a settlement of about nine hundred people thirty miles out of Tucson, just off the freeway between Tucson and Phoenix. In contrast to the desert around it, it was a relatively green place. I knew it for ranches, and for an airfield that once served as headquarters for one of the CIA's secret air forces. One of the few pieces of actual Det 13 paperwork I'd managed to absorb noted that we provided weather service to Alamo Air Park, ostensibly because some Army helicopter pilots from Fort Huachuca were always in and out of there. Okay. If I were doing some aircraft test work that I wanted to keep fairly quiet,

I'd certainly think about using a site like that. And on a long holiday weekend, too.

I had no idea how big this operation would be. Ming certainly knew about it, but he was especially nosy. A full-scale test program would have perimeter patrols and helicopters with night scopes—a lot of unpleasantness. Even though the test was probably ten hours away, the area would be locked up.

But only if it was a big operation. A big, legitimate operation. Alquist was assigned to Project Puff and had gone out of his way to tell me that it was in hiatus. So either that was smoke and bullshit, or this test was for another program altogether, one that I hadn't heard of, meaning it had to be completely and impossibly secret— or very small.

It was after ten when I got off the freeway at Alamo and landed in a Sunday-night nightmare—the place was closed. There was a Chevron station right at the exit, but it was dark tonight. Good thing I didn't have a flat tire. I think I drove a mile before I found a light, and that was on a tavern.

As I sat there in the Mazda listening to the jukebox roaring from inside the bar, I debated whether I should go in or not. It was a small place, one of perhaps a thousand Dew Drop Inns nationwide (are they franchised?). Everyone in there would know everyone else; I would be a Stranger.

On the other hand, was that such a bad idea? Alamo had seen its share of spooks over the years. I was willing to bet that the bartender at the Dew Drop had served a few in his day—or knew someone who had had a chance encounter with some boys from "the Company."

My blue shirt with the badge and bars was folded in the backseat . . . just in case I wanted to be able to pass as RAF. At the moment I was wearing a white T-shirt with blue uniform slacks. Anyone who noticed would link me with strange goings-on at the airport, which was fine. I went in.

The most interesting thing in the place was a TV tuned to ESPN and showing some soccer game which had the full attention of exactly none of the eight or ten patrons. A couple of them were kids—guys in their early twenties— howling around the pool table. The rest were weathered men in their forties wearing dozer caps and drinking beer. One of them was with his wife or girlfriend. Each of them gave me a glance lasting from one to five seconds, then ignored me as I sat down at the bar and ordered a Coors.

The bartender was a guy closer in age to the pool play- ers. When he brought me the beer he said, with a knowing smile, "Just visiting?"

"Yeah," I said. I just glanced around. Everyone was trying, successfully, not to pay attention. "I'm supposed to meet some people at an airport around here, but I think I got the directions wrong . . ."

He laughed and leaned closer. "You want the air park. It's about two miles on the other side of the freeway. You'll come to Water Road, go left, can't miss it. If you see the school you've gone too far."

"I guess I'm not the first guy to come in here looking for directions."

"Well," he said, "let's just say you're the first one to- night."

I took a good slug of the beer, dropped a couple of bucks on the bar, and got up. "Thanks."

I found the entrance to the air park with no problem. It was a collection of buildings out in the scrub surrounded by a chain link fence. There was a sawhorse across the entrance and a sign that said, "Closed." I hadn't planned on waltzing in the front way, anyway. I didn't stop or even slow down, but kept driving off into the darkness.

A couple of miles past the park, the pavement ended,

but the road didn't. From what I could see, it just continued on into the desert. I searched for a trail of some kind that ran at right angles to it, hoping I could use that to get around to the back side of the air park, but found nothing, so I turned off and simply *created* a trail.

Maia's Mazda had not been designed for off-roading, even the fairly benign off-roading you can do in Arizona. I was trying to be careful, but let her take a couple of major slams on the undercarriage before realizing that I'd seriously misjudged the terrain. It was easy to do with the headlights off.

I stopped right where I was, at least a mile from the "runway." With the engine off I could hear desert sounds and the distant, comforting roar of trucks on the interstate. I was angry at myself. I had wanted to get the car into the air park because in the morning that would make it easier for me to pretend I belonged there. Scratch that. My best option now was to set my watch alarm for four and try to catch some sleep.

Wrapped in my sweater and curled up in the backseat, that's what I did.

As I drifted off, I remember thinking that it had become harder for me to picture Gus, to remember what it had been like to hold him. I wondered who was holding him at this moment—wherever he was—then hoped that somebody was. He was only a month old. The thought of him dying . . . his whole life would have been like a door opening and closing . . . a burst of light, then darkness again. It wasn't going to happen.

I wasn't going to let it happen.

I guess I slept, though when my alarm beeped I felt more like I'd been thrown from a moving car. It was still dark; only the movement of the stars across the clear night sky proved to me that time had passed.

Before leaving Base Ops I'd glanced at the SATRAN

sheet for Labor Day. SATRAN comes from the Navy and NORAD. It lists projected overhead passes by Soviet and European spy satellites, though not ours. Ideally you want test flights to take place when there aren't prying eyes and ears overhead, and there was a clear window from 0645 to 0750, and another one in late morning. So I knew that there wouldn't be any hardware in the sky until 7:00 A.M. Allow two hours for setup and the no-doubt-endless computer integrations, and you see why I woke up at four. By 4:30 I was dressed in blues, shaven, nourished by an apple and a Diet Coke (which I'd had the foresight to stash in the car), and was approaching the entrance to Alamo Air Park from the back.

I'd hustled through the scrub and down the west side of the runway fairly quickly. On the other side of the runway, at the south end of the warehouse cluster, I could see two parked, unmarked semi trailers. One of them was clearly a generator truck; it roared to life at 0445. I noticed that guys in blue were wandering around down there, too. They'd either slept on-site or come in early. This gave me an idea.

I'd been right to avoid the main entrance: a jeep and two M.P.'s had been posted beyond the sawhorse with the Closed sign . . . just in case you didn't get the message. I took up a position between two of the warehouse-like hangar buildings and waited . . . Sure enough, right on the dot at 5:00 A.M., just as it says in the book, a second jeep drove up to relieve them. Thank God for military discipline.

Once the change had been made I took a stroll to introduce myself to the new boys, one of whom was a woman. Both were sergeants. When I said, "Good morning!" from behind them, they whirled, braced, and saluted.

"Have either of you seen Captain Alquist this morning?"

"No, sir," the woman said. "We just came on duty."

I snapped my fingers and pointed at her clipboard. She handed it to me.

It was a dot-matrix computer printout for "PROGRAM 980," what you and I call Puff, "TEST 2B." The list of cleared personnel was damned small—a dozen names—which confirmed my suspicions about the size of this operation. Near the top was "CPT ALQUIST," checked off. "He's already here," I said. "Must have missed him." I smiled and handed back the clipboard as if I had every reason in the world to be here. "Either of you got a cigarette?"

She glanced at her partner, who shook his head. "No, sir."

"Thanks, anyway." And I walked off. I don't smoke; all I wanted was to keep their minds off the fact that my badge didn't match any of the names on their list.

The sun was rising as I moved between the buildings. Since Alquist was here, I had to be careful. Bluffing my way past a pair of child M.P.'s was one thing; explaining my presence to Alquist would be a problem.

One of the hangar doors was unlocked. I guess airplane theft isn't a concern in Alamo. I slid it open far enough to gain entry, then closed it. Edging past someone's prize Bellanca, I went over to the grimy windows that looked out on the "test headquarters," feeling confident that if I stayed back in the shadows I could see without being seen. Better yet, one of the windows was cracked; I could *hear*, too.

It was the usual techno-babble, three or four missile guys who were wondering about fuel and control logic. Other people were worried about cameras, and, sure enough, there was that familiar voice talking about the weather between here and "the Ranch," whatever that was.

Then I heard two other people talking, and what they

were saying were things like, *"Macho apollo redress?"* *"Crier knife!"* ["When do we start?"] ["It's too cold here!"]

Not only were these two guys speaking Dreamland, I could understand them.

I backed away. I wanted to eavesdrop, but I also wanted to run and hide. For a moment I wished I had brought Maia's video camera, but the value of an item like that in a situation like this was nil. I was better off with the Colt; I imagined my waving it at the assemblage, ordering them to stop what they were doing, and dismissed it. Fortunately I didn't have to make a choice. The two Dreamlanders moved off into the control truck. It looked like show time, so I sneaked out of the hangar and found a spot where I could see the runway. I waited there and wondered what these guys were doing at a secret U.S. Air Force test site and why my "translation program" was still working.

Then six-thirty rolled around and things really started to happen. A black, delta-shaped thing—I hesitate to call it an aircraft—appeared out of nowhere and buzzed the airstrip at an altitude of about a hundred feet. I hadn't seen it; I hadn't heard it. But I felt the passage. The blow-by knocked me on my ass at the same moment I heard a twanging sound that quickly dopplered down to a drone.

For a moment I thought I'd been singed by a dragon.

When I looked up I could see a razor blade flying toward the sun. It made a sharp right bank and a swing to the south. As soon as my eyes adjusted I got a better look—which was still not a great look, but what do you expect when you're looking at a ghost? (What else do you call something which doesn't exist?) I'd been hearing for years that a new high-altitude reconnaissance/strike plane called Aurora was in development, but apparently missed the news that it actually existed. I suppose that was the idea. But here it was—black, plastic, quiet, and not only tough to find on radar but just plain hard to *see*. And lining up to launch a Puff cruise missile.

The Aurora orbited the field for a good ten minutes, probably to allow final checks . . . and to wait for *Cosmos-3000*, or whatever the Soviets had in orbit, to drop below the horizon. It lined up from the east and headed toward us. Eclipsing the sun with my hands, I saw Puff drop free. The plane peeled away, returning to its lair in Nevada, while the missile whooshed right down the center line of the runway.

It was a nasty-looking little thing, like a black bullet with teeth. I looked at it and had little trouble remembering that in the right circumstances it could turn most of Tucson into green glaze. And it was so small and traveled so close to the ground that you'd never see it coming.

The Puff shot out into the desert, made a turn that would have killed a pilot, and shot back toward the runway. As it came toward us, out of the west, a light appeared, as if someone had torn the sky, but it was between the missile and me.

The missile flew right into it and disappeared.

I suddenly knew what the bad guys in my world were getting from the bad guys in the Twilight Zone . . .

"Who's that?" someone yelled. "Hey, you there!"

I didn't look back. I walked toward that tear in the sky which still rippled, blindingly. When the voice said, "Halt!" I started to run.

When I heard the *crack!* of the first shot, I dived into the light.

20

And fell facedown in a field.

I didn't raise my head for the better part of a minute because I could still hear the roar of Puff's motor. If it blew up, I didn't want to be a shrapnel catcher. But the missile flew off into the distance. It might even have rippled back into my world, I don't know. I never actually saw where it went.

As I got up, I realized that I was still in one piece. They say that nothing focuses the concentration quite like being shot at, but I found it annoying and distracting. Of course, normally when someone shoots at you, you aren't flung into Dreamland. Maybe that made a difference.

And I was back in Maia's world. It was early afternoon and the sun had those telltale ring clouds. I didn't appear to be anywhere near Chios, however. The city was surrounded by mountains, much like Tucson, and Tucson's mountains could be seen from Alamo. If I were in the Dreamland equivalent of Alamo, I certainly should have seen them here. But I was in a meadow, a place with a smaller sky. It reminded me of southern Wisconsin or Nebraska.

Well, no one promised me that there was any symmetry between the geometry of the two worlds. (How big *was* this world, anyway?) I could be hundreds of miles from Chios. I made a 360-degree scan and concluded that I was at least several miles from anywhere at all.

I brushed myself off and started walking south—just because that was one direction I hadn't tried lately.

What I'd seen at Alamo, combined with what I'd learned on my own and from Sanchez, had given me a theory about the business relationship between the bad guys of the two worlds. The Dreamlanders had a clear need, it seemed, for high-tech weaponry—perhaps one should call that "other tech," since their own tech was high enough in its fashion. They wanted weapons against which the Demons had no defense, perhaps because they would not know their true names.

Sanchez knew most of this. What puzzled him was the quid pro quo—what did our bad guys get out of this?

I had a good idea by now. They got a first-strike capability.

I'm not saying that some madman in the Pentagon wanted to blast the Russians (or, more likely, annoying parties in the Middle East) with nukes at the first opportunity. But any military person looks for an edge. At one time or another the edge has been the bomber-delivered A-bomb . . . then the H-bomb . . . then the ICBM . . . the missile submarine . . . the cruise missile . . . Stealth bombers and missiles (if you can't see them, maybe you can't stop them) . . . all of them vulnerable to some kind of countermeasures, because you've either got to hide them right in the enemy's backyard or move them vast distances through space or air or water, hoping they still function when they arrive . . . hoping, in fact, that they arrive on target at all.

What if you took a shortcut? What if you could send your bombers or missiles to their targets without exposing them to attack? By going through *another world*? Puff would be absolutely undetectable—the ultimate stealthed machine.

I didn't go to the Academy and I'll never see the inside of the Air War College. I come from a long line of reluctant draftees and enlisted men. I'm not a warrior, I'm a manager. But even *I* could picture a cruise missile rippling out of the sky over Tucson, disappearing from our world completely, only to ripple back in—over Baghdad.

Sooner or later, someone was going to prove it could be done . . . and once it became known, my world would be a more dangerous place.

And it could destroy Maia's world.

So I sustained myself on my long hike with the knowledge that I was not only saving the world—I was saving two worlds. In my spare time I would rescue my child *and* the fair princess . . .

All I had to do was overcome being lost, alone, and totally dependent on my overtired wit and a weapon left over from some Clint Eastwood movie.

I had long since left the grassland behind and moved into low hills spotted with clumps of trees when I heard voices. I fused myself to the nearest trunk and waited.

I had yet to find roads or fences, but didn't assume that meant I was in the wilderness. The rolling meadow had the feel of rangeland—for all I knew, in the proper season I might find a herd of . . . well, of dragons . . . roaming it, with dragon-herders whipping them along.

It also occurred to me that I might be in a no-man's-land between Dreamland and Devil territory. I had tried to imagine where I would test a missile, had I been a

Dreamland bad guy, but abandoned it as an unproductive use of thinking time.

But now I'd found somebody. Or somebody had found me.

I hauled out the Colt and checked the clip, though I left the safety on. The voices were loud enough to seem close by, yet indistinct enough that I couldn't tell what was being said. It was just noise coming from somewhere in the trees.

Keeping low, I moved toward it. There was a lot of undergrowth. It kept me from seeing more than ten yards in any direction. I hoped it would keep others from seeing me.

I closed in on the voices. They were louder, but still unintelligible.

There, in a clearing, something moved. I froze. But whoever was out there didn't know I was around, or, more ominously, didn't care. Well, by this time I was a bit tired of being pushed around. If I was going to fail, it would be while attacking. I slipped off the safety and, holding the Colt with two hands, scampered toward the voices.

I had a bad moment when I saw a person, wearing a green uniform topped by a helmet, back toward me. "Stop right there!" I screamed. I startled the figure so badly that it fell down. I pointed the gun in its face.

It was a boy. I think he might have been all of twelve.

He said something to me in another language. I'm pretty sure it was "Please don't shoot."

I looked around and saw that he wasn't alone. There were two other kids, a girl of ten and another boy about six. The girl was worried, but I think the little guy was too busy sucking on a piece of candy.

They were playing soldier.

I eased the safety on and put the Colt away before I hurt somebody. "Get up," I said to the older boy, gesturing with my hands. As he did the girl hurried over to him.

When the three of them were clumped together, the family resemblance was clear. Three towheaded kids playing soldier in the woods. Fifteen years ago, allowing for certain dimensional relocations, I would have been one of them.

"Don't worry," I said. "I'm not going to hurt you. I'm . . . lost." I didn't want to frighten them further. My parents used to worry about strangers offering candy—here I was, a stranger with a gun. I wanted to dig a hole and jump in.

The girl looked at the bigger boy, then at me. "Are you from the South [Dreamland]?" she said. Everything echoed and it took me a moment to realize that she had spoken in what was, for her, a second language.

"No," I said. "Though I speak the language."

She gave the bigger boy an I-told-you-so smile. He clearly wanted to smack her, and would, I was sure . . . the moment they were safely away from me.

"Do you speak [Southern]?" I asked the girl.

Before she could answer, big brother said, "She's only had two years. But I can speak it."

"Tell me where I am."

"You're in the woods . . ." His expression didn't give away a thing, but he was testing me. At what point had I ceased to be in charge?

"I can see that. What are these woods called?" I pointed to the "south." "What's over there?"

"Over there is the enemy," he said. "They call this the Griffon's Woods"—he almost spat the name—"but we call it *White Guys*." Well, that's what it sounded like. But "*White Guys*" set up familiar echoes, and I knew that this had been my introduction to the famous agents of Untruth . . . the Devils . . . the enemies of Maia's people.

The kids were named Willek (big brother), Shahr (the girl), and Dymoch (the little guy), and, following introductions, it was agreed that I could accompany them home

. . . at which time their parents would do something with me.

It wasn't much of a walk, for an adult, but Dymoch must have felt he was on a day-long adventure. When I was his age we lived on the edge of town—Dad, for some reason, kept moving to a new development as soon as the old one sprouted neighbors—meaning my sister and I had easy access to fields and to a pine forest. Even to a muddy pool of water someone had dubbed the Frog Pond. A trip to the Frog Pond or the pine forest could consume an entire afternoon. It was at least three-quarters of a mile away.

The sight of these kids shuffling along both cheered me and depressed me. It was reassuring because Dreamland couldn't be as weird as it had seemed if kids could still play soldier in the woods. It was depressing because looking at little Dymoch reminded me that so far Gus had had no chance at a normal life. He would never play soldier or anything else, unless I managed to do something.

Whatever it was I would do.

The kids might have taken me home the back way, but I never saw anything approaching an evolved road, which is the term that was coming to mind to describe these Dreamland roads. No meat wagons, either. And, as we moved away from the meadow into the forest, the trees had a stunted, twisted look.

Finally we emerged into a clearing, and I got another in a series of surprises. These houses looked more like those in my world than any I'd seen in Dreamland. They were built out of logs and boards! Most of them, that is. As we moved between them an occasional sod hut could be seen. But such structures were clearly in the minority. They were older. The future, here in the boondocks, at least, belonged to the hammer and saw.

Some of them even had crude power lines strung to them.

For all their familiarity, the houses were unimpressive: they had that permanently unfinished look that comes from building with available materials. House paint was a concept to which these people could still look forward. Some windows were made of cloudy glass; others were paper or fabric or nothing at all. The roofs were shingles or wood chips.

All of these places would have been condemned in Appalachia, I think. Yet this village was the closest thing to home I'd seen in a while. It felt familiar. Little kids played in the streets with mothers watching. Several men were working on their houses.

The kids' place was about average for the village—definitely a new model as opposed to a prairie mound, but nothing special. Willek told me to wait outside, which was what I had in mind. Ever since we'd entered the village I had been aware that a dozen pairs of eyes were trained on me.

I wasn't looking for trouble, I just needed some guidance. So I immediately did something that, in retrospect, I should have done days ago:

I fainted.

I had never fainted before. I had never been unconscious before, unless you count the time back in high school when I drank six cranberry juice "screwdrivers" in the back of a car, and even then I got sick, then sleepy, without really passing out. I had played football and taken a couple of shots to the head. Woozy, but never out.

So it kind of sneaked up on me. One minute I was standing there in the sunshine, the next I was looking up at an unfinished ceiling in a room lit by a single-bulb lamp. There was a blanket over me. My shoes and belt had been taken off. I found them neatly stacked within reach along with the Colt. (I was so disoriented that I'd momentarily forgotten I was carrying a weapon.)

Well, I'd hardly eaten anything since yesterday, strictly speaking. The donuts and Diet Coke had probably done some strange things to my body chemistry, too. Not to mention the fact that I'd made three "transitions" in the last few days. (If living next to power lines or walking around Tucson in the summer without sunscreen isn't good for you, turning your body's atoms inside out can't be too helpful, either.) My mental state was questionable.

All right, I was a mess.

When I came to, Shahr was in the room, keeping watch. She scurried out and returned with a plump, dark-haired woman about my age. "This is my mother, Kessi," Shahr told me.

Kessi felt my forehead. "How are you?" she asked. She, too, spoke Southern.

"Better now," I said.

"You're probably hungry." She nodded to Shahr, who brought me some soup and bread, which I inhaled. When I had thumbed the last crumb into my mouth, I thanked them. "Not so fast," Kessi said.

"Don't worry, I feel great," I said.

Then I threw up.

It was that sort of evening. I was a terrible burden to those poor people. Had I been able to walk out the door and free them from caring for me, I would have, but every time I raised my head I got dizzy. I even thought about crawling out of that house. Rolling out. I would simply die off in the woods like my caveman ancestors, thank you. That's how bad I felt.

Kessi's husband, Gref, came home somewhere during this process. I wasn't able to focus on him for quite some time. When I did, I saw a wiry, calloused man of perhaps thirty—a hard thirty. I wondered what he did for a living— he might have been a farmer, though my old friend Hissam had spent more time in the sun—and concluded he was a factory worker. Blue-collar.

Gref didn't speak a word of Southern that I could tell. And he really didn't like the disruption I brought to the house. Whenever he hove into view, I made sure I appeared to be unconscious.

It didn't do much good. Later that night he and Kessi had an argument, and out he went. From the kids' reaction, which bordered on indifference, I got the impression this was not an unusual occurrence. But it still made me feel bad—for Kessi, who was kind enough to take in this sick stranger, and for these kids. Any kids who have to watch their parents fight.

According to my watch it was almost four-thirty, and since it was dark outside I took that to be four-thirty in the morning, when I realized I could not only sit up, I could stand up. And I got out of bed.

It wasn't a big house. I realized I had the master bed, which might have accounted for the husband's fury. Kessi was asleep on the couch. The kids were in the other room. The light was out. The place was quiet.

I went to the window, which was shuttered, and opened it a crack. The stars were high and bright, their light spilling down on the silent village. The scene was so peaceful it made me want to cry. I couldn't help but feel that just by coming here I'd introduced some deadly contagion, and for all the right reasons, too.

I knew it was silly. Probably five people even knew I was here. I guess I was just consoling myself with the idea that if I couldn't be effective, I could, at least, be visible.

"Is something wrong?" Kessi had awakened and whispered to me.

"I'm just feeling better," I said. "I'm sorry I woke you."

She got off the couch and came over. She didn't bother

203

to wrap herself in anything in spite of the fact that her nightgown was so worn it basically put her on display. I guess that was how she dressed around the house. I certainly didn't get the idea it was for my benefit. It was just a strange moment—the first time in my life I've found myself in close company with a younger woman who nevertheless made me feel like a child. "I wasn't sleeping too well, anyway."

"Why don't you take the bed? I'm awake."

"It wouldn't make any difference. I won't sleep right until Gref comes home."

"I'm sorry I got him so angry."

"It happens every now and then. If it hadn't been you, it would have been because of the kids, or his work."

"What does he do?"

"What everybody out here does. He makes prayers."

"How do you do that?"

Kessi was amused by my ignorance. "The kids were right: you aren't from around here." She turned on the stove, such as it was, and put on a pot of water. "The priests keep prayers to themselves. You can't really learn them unless you become one of them.

"But people want these things, and every now and then one of these prayers gets out. Gref and the others make copies and sell them." I remembered the street urchin I'd seen on my first day in Dreamland. Obviously he was the distribution end of this particular marketing chain.

"Don't the Civil Guards give you a hard time?"

"They sure do. But they usually don't come out this far, especially with the war."

I learned that the Griffon's Woods were basically a demilitarized zone—an occupied territory—between Chios and its suburbs, and the harsh land of the Devils. Kessi told me that before she was born the Griffon had total control over the area, but that all that had changed in the last few years. She was a bit vague on the history prior to that, which is fair: I still find myself visualizing "history" as a long movie that opens with a lot of colorful Roman stuff (including Jesus) followed by knights and castles, at which time everything becomes black-and-white still pictures all the way through World War II. The fifties and sixties are color movies going blue. Only the last twenty years exist in full color with Dolby sound.

I didn't need additional details. Kessi's people were moonshiners or peasant farmers growing opium. They *had* to be associated with the Devils—who else would have the means or need to undermine the Griffon? I felt a bit smug that I had cunningly managed to get myself this close to them, since they were probably my only hope. Kessi brought me some tea, then retired to the bed (where she fell sound asleep, Gref or no Gref), and I wondered how I would go about actually contacting the Devil leadership.

About dawn Gref returned, and with him were two men in work clothes. Not wishing to further disturb the household, I put on my belt, shoes, and gun and went outside to meet them.

In broken Southern one of the men asked who I was. I told him I had important information about the Griffon and that I wanted to see someone in the military.

Oddly enough, that was exactly what they had in mind. When one of them made a move to disarm me, I had to brandish the Colt. "You're not going to arrest me," I said. "You're going to *guide* me."

After a tense moment, it was agreed that this was, indeed, a mutually acceptable fiction, and we set off.

I never did get a chance to thank Kessi and her children.

21

"It would make me more comfortable if you would allow me to hold that weapon," the officer said in perfect Southern, nodding toward the Colt. "Please keep it where it can be seen."

Eight hours and two sets of "guides" later I had traveled at least a hundred miles from the village in the Griffon's Woods into rugged mountain country much like that of the village that had been bombed by dragons. My first set of guides had marched me to a river, where we all caught a ride upstream on an empty, flat-bottomed barge. At landfall I was handed over to a younger, more professional pair, who popped me into a steam-powered car, not a meat truck, for a long drive over increasingly twisting and mountainous semi-evolved or semi-paved roads, until we reached a large, decaying houseshroom on a cliff.

The cliff, it seemed, was on the spine of a small range growing out of the Griffon's Woods and the grasslands. Beyond us a film of haze suggested a larger city, perhaps one the size of Chios. The sky was the same, full of Dreamland circles.

I had managed to hold on to the Colt the whole time. I don't know why it began to be so important to me, but it was. (I really didn't even know if it would work here.)

All in all, this was the least military-looking bunch of soldiers I'd ever seen. There didn't seem to be a uniform as such: the men were dressed in the usual psychedelic orange and yellow pantaloons and blouses—no earth tones for these guys. Some of them were wearing the same type of blue belt, which could have signified rank or unit. Maybe they had developed a whole new way of organizing large numbers of men for the purpose of killing others. It didn't look like it to me, but, then, the Swiss Guards wore some pretty fancy garb for fighting men, and the Viet Cong wouldn't have passed an inspection, either.

My "host" was Baht, a grimy, bearded officer about my age who appeared to have a lot on his mind. He had agreed to speak with me briefly, and we stood in the middle of the road leading up to the house, as other soldiers rushed here and there. Something was about to happen; you could feel it. And I knew quite well that this was the man I would have to sell . . . here and now . . . or I would never see Maia or Gus again. "You said you have information about the Griffon," he said, "but you're not Southern."

"No."

"You're not one of us, either. This is impossible."

"Maybe so, but here I am." I persisted: "Look, we can discuss who I am and where I came from and take up the rest of the day, or we can exchange information that will be of use to both of us. I know that there's a power struggle going on inside that involves the Griffon's family," I said.

"You can hear that on the [broadcasts]," he said tiredly. I had been afraid of that. Where is press censorship when you really need it? "Of course," I said, improvising, "but do you know the players? Do you know that the Griffon Himself is a virtual captive? And that one of His closest advisers, a man named Linn, is the threat to the holy family . . . ?"

He cut me off. "Come with me." I followed him into the house.

He seemed to have forgotten about the Colt.

When I spoke again, I had an audience of four. Baht had been joined by two senior men and a very senior woman. The men were in their late forties or early fifties and would have been right at home as Air Force generals. The woman was even older, but all of these guys deferred to her.

We sat around a bare wooden table in what had probably been a family dining room before this most recent "occupation." I told them what I knew, from the beginning of my relationship with Maia through the resurrection business, and our "escape" from the Hill, right up to pulling a gun on young Willek. I had considered sanitizing the story—playing down the fact that many of these events took place in another dimension—but I assumed that these Devils knew about my world and its charms: they'd damn near been nuked, after all. And I figured that my knowledge of their interworld operations by itself should prove my bona fides. Either my interrogators knew what had happened, or they worked for someone who did.

It took quite a while, and when I was finished, they chattered to each other in their own language. One of the generals, call him Eisenhower, seemed especially skeptical and chided Baht, but Patton suddenly came to his defense. There was more argument. Sitting there was like being courtside at Wimbledon while John McEnroe played and argued at the same time.

Finally Patton turned to me and said, "By the way, your son is at Rec-Five along with the Heiress and her mother."

Maia, Gus, *and* Jayan! I managed to keep calm, but I felt as though I'd just had the air let out of me. "What are they doing there?"

"Apparently they're prisoners of the faction headed by Linn. Maia was arrested two days ago." Yes, I'd already begun to suspect Linn, but I hate having my worst suspicions confirmed. I was furious to realize I'd spent hours in Linn's company—thinking of him as nothing more than a professional doing his job—when all the while he was holding my son. If I could find Gus by finding Linn, great; if I happened to have a chance to kill Linn, so much the better.

Clearly unhappy, the two senior men finally stomped out. Baht stood by uncertainly, only to be dismissed more gently by the woman, who finally turned her attention back to me. She spoke Southern with the ease of a native, I thought.

Her name was Dorana, she said, and she apologized for her colleagues' unpleasantness. "They can never agree on anything."

"So why don't you keep one and get rid of the other?" I don't know why I said that. Given the way Eisenhower and Patton had tippy-toed around her, I should have just kept my mouth shut. But her manner made me feel at ease. And I was preoccupied with worry.

"Singling out would be Griffon-like. Patriarchal. I won't do it."

"Oh, you don't like the Griffon?" (Not only at ease but downright playful.)

"As murdering, oppressive Gods go, He isn't bad. There used to be better ones. You've never heard of the Mother." I shook my head. "They burned her [five hundred years] ago."

" 'They' being the Griffon's men?"

"And the Griffon Himself. It takes a God to kill a God, or so they say."

"Is that what you're trying to do here? Kill a God?"

"That's none of your business."

"Forgive me, but it is my business. My child is in the middle of this. Besides," I said, "who else is there to attack?"

"Military details are patriarchal," she said. "Like you, I would rather think about the people involved. We might be able to rescue your son. Certainly we will not harm him. The best you can do for him is tell me what you know about the rift between the Griffon and Linn, for example. Or why Stenn was resurrected."

"I was told it was because he was important to the Griffon."

"Obviously," she said. "Only friends of the Griffon's have their lives returned at the price of another's. But it would be helpful to know *why* Stenn was important. Do you see?"

I guess I saw, but it wasn't doing me much good. Maybe it was the language problem. Maybe it had more to do with the fact that Dorana and I literally lived in different worlds, and I'm not talking about Dreamland and Tucson. I was failing to communicate. Failing to understand.

"He was originally supposed to marry the Heiress," I said finally.

She pushed her chair back from the table. "Is this true?"

"As far as I know."

"You don't have any idea what this means." That was certainly true, but I waited in vain for her to tell me more. I suspect she was talking for herself. "We have very little time."

"Before what?"

Dorana hesitated. "I think Linn is going to force a marriage between the Heiress and Stenn, which will legitimize the child."

Until that moment the fact that Gus was, literally, a bastard had never occurred to me. I wasn't so sure it was important. "Big deal."

"A very big deal. The child will then be capable of receiving the Griffon's powers. And given the state of the Griffon's health, the child will very soon be God . . . a very young God in need of a powerful adviser."

"Like Linn," I said helpfully.

Dorana said something that echoed as ["Bingo"].

Eventually I was remanded to the custody of Baht, who was more interested in what I knew about the missiles— he called them terror weapons—the Civil Guards had begun to use against his people than about personality clashes and whatnot. For all of Dorana's good wishes, I had the feeling I was being shunted off to a corner with the unlucky Baht as my baby-sitter. I didn't like it one bit, but saw no easy way to get them to make me part of their assault.

"Explain something to me," I asked Baht, after about an hour of chat about cruise missile kill radii and throwweight and other patriarchal details. "I thought this war was about good prayer and bad prayer. Why are you so interested in these mechanical devices? Shouldn't you be coming up with better prayers?"

"Look," he said, "the Griffon and His priests control the prayers. To do anything truly . . . beneficial . . . you have to become one of *them*. And there are very few priests.

"This oppression is what we're fighting! The people of the South admit no change, nothing but what the Griffon wills—or will allow. I'm from a poor family. In the Griffon's world, my fate would have been determined at birth.

I would have been a laborer *if* I'd managed to survive to adulthood.

"Not that there's anything wrong with being a laborer, any more than there's something inherently evil in being a priest. But it is wrong, I believe, to have no choice in how you will use your life." He turned up his hands. "Even the strongest beliefs can change. Like living things, they grow or die. And when the beliefs change, so does the world, don't you think? Someone, somewhere, had the courage to question the Griffon." Baht smiled. He reminded me more of a college professor than a revolutionary. "It would please me more than I could say to learn that the first crack in the Griffon's armor occurred when *His own forces began to use weapons from your world.* But whatever it was, that single act caused His power to diminish . . . making it possible for others to question, too."

"That's great," I said. "How the hell do you think you and your ideals are going to do against the Civil Guards in a battle?"

Baht tried not to look at me. "We'll lose."

"No doubt about it." I think he had wanted me to disagree with him, but I just let him fume for a moment. Then I said, "Unless you get some outside help. The kind the guards have."

"And where would we get it?" Stenn was wrong; sarcasm did travel. "Are you carrying a secret weapon?"

"You bet." I tapped my head. "Right up here."

He was hesitating. I was too far down the road to turn back now. "Do you have a map of this Reeducation Complex and Chios?"

"Why?"

"So I can show you how to attack it."

I still hadn't sold him. Well, Eisenhower had given him a pretty good chewing. "Listen, we can do this either way: let me have five minutes with Dorana and the other guys, and I'll take the consequences good or bad. Or you

212

can help me out . . . make sure that what I have is what you need . . . and take the credit. I just want to be on the first dragon.''

"We don't have dragons." I wanted to hit him. But he found a map.

"Tomorrow you begin to change this world."

I'd briefed generals before, on Guam and at Offutt. You have to tell them what you're going to tell them before you tell them.

We were back in the meeting room, Eisenhower and Patton in their respective corners, Dorana at the back. I could feel waves of disapproval from her general direction. I didn't want to disappoint her, but I also wanted to find Gus. Baht was lurking by the door, ready, if need be, to make a break for it.

On the table in front of me was a crude sketch of my own making, but behind me on the wall was one of the Devils' own topographical maps—an original ink and pencil creation, too, not a reproduction—of an area about the size of southeastern Arizona. I *hoped*.

I hadn't had time to study it in detail, but it was clear that the conflict between the guards and the Devils was far short of global. If sheer distance was any indication, this was more like a dispute between city-states.

(What about the rest of Dreamland? Maybe this was all there was to it.)

I couldn't read the legends, of course, but I could recognize the mountains around Chios, and Chios itself. I pointed to the mountains southwest of the city and to the main road leading through them. "I was first found and captured by the guards on this road. As you can all see, this road is just a short distance from a military installation."

"That installation is Reeducation Complex Five," Eisenhower said.

"Which is, I believe, the headquarters for command and control of dragon-based weapons, and also the place where the guards put important prisoners. Not only Maia, my son, and Jayan but your people.

"It seems to me that you have no good options. A frontal assault would be suicidal. You won't even get close.

"An all-out attack with weapons of mass destruction would, of course, kill the hostages as well.

"An air attack followed by the landing of a team of commandos is obviously the best approach. But, as you say, you don't have dragons. The terrain surrounding Rec-Five is either mountainous or open desert. You would have to cross miles of desert undetected in order to fight a dug-in enemy which holds the high ground."

Eisenhower growled at this point. "Tell us something we don't know! We've been trying to figure out how to attack this place for months."

I took a deep breath, then said, "Suppose I knew of a way you could move a force across this distance and not be detected? Where you could suddenly appear in the mountains at the Rec-Five perimeter?"

Eisenhower muttered something untranslatable, but in the vein of, "Get those damned reindeer off my roof!" I was losing him.

I looked at Baht, who nodded. He helped me place my sketch over the existing topo map. We had used tracing paper, so the darker details beneath would read through. My map showed Tucson and environs. And roads. And places where one person or a whole regiment could move between the worlds.

There was a little discussion, about five hours' worth, but at the end they had a plan. And I had a promise that I could go along. (Well, I sort of forced that on them: I was the only one who knew the right prayers, for one thing. And who else was going to be able to read traffic signs around Tucson?)

They even let me keep the Colt. I don't suppose it would have been easy to take.

Later that night we moved out in a caravan of trucks and jeeps, both meat and steam. It was hardly an impressive sight. The Devil soldiers may have been motivated, but they were ill equipped and ragtag. The weapon of choice seemed to be a shortened blunderbuss.

I wondered how they would stand up to dragons and tactical nukes.

I was surprised to find Dorana among them, having assumed she was an analyst or mother figure, not someone who dirtied her hands. "Ride with me," she said, and I joined her in the cab of a steam truck.

In the rear there were seven or eight soldiers. We had been rolling for an hour or so when I noticed one of the soldiers talking to herself.

She was praying.

Dorana noticed it about the same time. She shrugged. "Some of us still pray. The old-fashioned ones, those who still believe in the Griffon. Every year there are fewer of them. They either realize that the Griffon has taken sides against them . . . or they die."

"Where do you people go when you die? If the Griffon is God."

"There were earlier [Gods] who simply rose above this life and now reside in a place beyond the sky." She laughed. "Maybe they are now in *your* world."

"I doubt that very much."

22

The transition out of Dreamland and into my world took place at midnight, Dreamland time, just after sunset, Mountain Standard. The trip out to the meadow beyond the Griffon's Woods, which roughly corresponded to the Alamo Air Park, was so harrowing I began to have real doubts about what I was trying to do. (Real doubts as opposed to the merely constant, screaming doubts I'd been having all along.) Those stupid steam trucks kept breaking down—that is, whenever they weren't making enough noise to alert several interverses that we were on the way. And we lost a meat truck on some rough ground. They shot the poor thing with one of those harmless-looking blunderbusses. One blast to the head. I revised my estimate of their lethality.

Then, of course, we had the moment of truth, which had me chanting, *"Assonance light tree mare,"* over and over again, so much that I sounded just like Judy Garland in *The Wizard of Oz.*

The sky rippled. So did everything else. And we came out, in the dark, in a date orchard near some railroad tracks about five miles east of the metropolis of Alamo. (I had tried to keep us away from the air park itself, but along a straight line that ran through Alamo to Baboquivari.) Within fifteen minutes we had formed up on the two-lane road that ran next to the orchard. There were some houses nearby, but no pedestrians or autos; anyone peeking out the window would logically assume they were seeing a military convoy from one of the bases. As long as they didn't look too closely.

I was prepared to confront any nosy Alamoites with the news that they were interfering with the production of *Mutant Dungeon Master III,* an Empire Film, so watch out. But I never had the chance to try it out.

We did tear the shit out of some farmer's dates. I felt bad enough about it that I almost began to feel sorry for his insurance company.

It took three hours via Arizona 89, Grant and Silverbell roads to cover a distance that would have taken about a quarter of that if we'd used the freeway. (I didn't think my movie ruse would convince a state trooper; besides, those Dreamland trucks were *slow.*) Eventually I found myself guiding the convoy past "A" Mountain out Ajo Way, right to the turnoff where much of this nonsense had begun.

I had a chilling thought right then: suppose Maia's car was still there? But I suppressed it. Besides, we weren't quite going to retrace my original steps. We needed to be closer to the location of the Rec-Five perimeter, or its equivalent.

The equivalent place turned out to be a trailer park, a big one. Fortunately, by then it was around 11:00 P.M. Only the streetlights were on.

Well, as we rolled through, I saw the face of one young man in a doorway. He had a beer can in his hand, probably part of the Budweiser insomnia cure. I don't know if we helped him or hurt him, but I saw him toss the can far out the door as we drove by.

Our transition back to Dreamland went without incident. I was beginning to feel like an old pro.

I'm not sure exactly where we emerged in relation to Rec-Five, but we were on some treeless steppe and the sky was still dark. Fortunately, we were alone.

We stopped to let everyone rest, except for a few scouts who went for a recon. I was glad; neither world seemed to have developed the area around Rec-Five. There were no real roads, only failed attempts at roads. Even riding in the cab of the truck, where we had some warning that bumps were coming, Dorana and I had been constantly thrown around. The fact that we traveled the entire way without headlights, finding our way by "starlight," had made it even rougher. (When I got out I saw that the truck didn't even *have* headlights.)

Looking pale and shaken, Dorana went off to be a leader, while I caught my breath. Presently the scouts returned and reported in, though not to me. My job was done.

The soldiers split into three groups of perhaps ten each, one unit heading to the north, another to the south. By default I was attached to the third, which included Baht. Our mission was to strike to the heart of Rec-Five and rescue the prisoners. After some last-minute orientation, some switching of weapons (a couple of soldiers wanted crossbows instead of blunderbusses), we all moved out on foot.

"Stay with me," Baht said, as if I'd considered going anywhere.

We went up and over a dark, wooded ridge. I could smell the stink of dragons in the air. Occasionally a light would bob into view through the trees; the garrison at Rec-Five must have been getting careless. Long before I expected it we came to the perimeter vine. I had told the Devils that this was some kind of bioelectric barrier and so they were prepared: one soldier literally cut lengthwise into the perimeter stalk in two places, inserting a piece of long, loose bypass vine as a bridge. Then he sliced the perimeter from top to bottom, and we were inside the base.

It turned out the stealthy precautions were a waste of time. We hadn't gone ten yards when an explosion flared to my right. The southern group going into action. I felt the concussion through my shoes, and the first brief, hot blast of wind I'd encountered in this world.

Then came shouts and the cracks of handguns and God knows what else. There was new rumbling and roaring beneath us: dragons stirring from their sleep, if, in fact, they ever slept.

We lost some of our unit, one by one, not to enemy fire, but to guard our eventual path of escape. Finally there were five of us, including Baht, running between two buildings, down a passage which opened up on a familiar scene . . . the parade ground dedicated to the Unknown Priest-Warrior.

We ran around the perimeter, not across the quad, a smart move that seemed even smarter when a bomb landed on the grass, showering us with dirt and debris. "Ours or theirs?" I asked.

"Theirs," Baht said as we got up. He pointed toward a building at about four o'clock. I recognized it, of course. It was the Griffon's Nest, the place where I'd been held. "That's the place."

We sprinted directly across a corner of the quad. Just as we reached the far perimeter, I finally saw my first enemy soldier. We came up on him from behind. He turned and, looking just like one of the Supremes, raised a hand to stop us. The hand exploded in a shower of blood

219

and bone. He screamed and ceased to worry that we were rushing past him and into the building.

In the first cell we found a familiar face—Stenn. I didn't have time to exchange greetings and I don't think he recognized me. Anyway, one of the other soldiers took charge of him as we moved on.

In the second room we found an old man alone. The Griffon.

He had apparently been under arrest. "How can you lock up a God?" I whispered to Baht.

"Prayer is prayer. It binds the Griffon as thoroughly as it binds any of us. He could undo it, of course, but if He's weak He might not want to risk the recoil."

Weak or not, what he was was pissed off. Apparently confusing the soldier who found Him with those who had imprisoned Him, He began shouting. To my surprise, this tough soldier began to act like a puppy getting smacked. Baht, too, had suddenly grown withdrawn and nervous.

"Hey," I said to the Griffon, "is this how you treat people who just set you free?"

The Griffon sputtered, but shut up. My three remaining companions, however, looked at me with horror. Of course: no matter how much they professed to be Northern Atheistic Anarchists, they'd probably all been raised to honor the Griffon. Childhood training haunted them.

"I hate to be rude," I told them, "but I still have some people to find."

Baht was the first to recover. "Of course." To the Griffon, he said, "Father, we're from the North."

Suddenly we were seeing a different Griffon. The one we'd found on breaking in was a senile old man; this was a God—or as close to one as I expect to come. "My lost children," he said, smiling benevolently. He extended his hands. "Thank you for coming to me."

One of the soldiers went halfway to his knees, then caught himself. "Your . . . welcome pleases us," Baht said, "though our mission is a sad one. You are surrounded by traitors."

The Griffon smiled, untroubled. "For everything holy there is something unholy. For every God there is a Devil."

"Your Devil is named Linn."

Like storm clouds gathering, the Griffon's face darkened. His manner changed again. "He's evil. He's greed incarnate. To get what he wants, he's willing to destroy the whole world."

Baht glanced at me. "That's what we're afraid of," he said. "We need to find him."

"He's here," the Griffon said confidently. "In the darkness where he belongs . . ."

I was turning to Baht to tell him the Griffon might be referring to the dragon caves when the door opened. It was Dorana, smudged face and all. "You," she said to me. "Come on. We've found Maia and her mother."

I ran out.

The sun was rising. Given what I now knew about this world, I guess I meant that literally. And on this early morning the priest-warriors of Rec-Five were gathered in the wreckage of the grassy quad, under guard. They looked stunned and defeated.

Dorana was in a hurry. "We don't know how long we can hold this place. The garrison isn't actually very large. If the guards stage a counterattack, we're in trouble."

I jerked my head toward the prisoners of war. "What happened to their powers?" I said.

"They've still got them, I suppose." Then she nodded toward one of our soldiers and his crossbow. He'd used up half his bolts. "But iron overcomes prayer." Like scissors cuts paper.

There was a small group of tired-looking Devils gathered in front of the entrance to the dragons' lair, a brick wall with barred windows. The huge sliding door was bolted shut.

Dorana had a quick conversation with one of her colleagues, then said to me, "The Heiress Maia and her mother are still in there. They probably have priest-warriors with them."

"Including Linn?"

"No one knows. We can't attack without hurting them. They've refused to come out without hurting us."

"I guess brick stops iron." Well, paper covers rock.

"This is your big chance. Do something."

"Let's see." I stood up, wondering for an uncomfortably long couple of seconds just what horrors a cornered priest-warrior could inflict on me. I walked slowly toward the side door. "Maia! Jayan! It's Rick!" No answer. I was in plain view by now. I was still carrying my pistol, but I'd stuck it in my belt. I surely looked harmless, and the priest-warriors' skills would tell them that I was . . . or so I hoped.

"Maia Chios! It's Rick Walsh—"

The side door opened. A very tired-looking Maia peered out. Priest-warriors be damned: I ran to her.

Wrapped tightly, safely, in my arms, she sobbed. I suppose I did, too. "I knew you'd come back," she said. "I knew you meant what you said."

"It's the best thing about me."

"Rick . . ." She couldn't bring herself to tell me. "He made me *marry* Stenn."

There it was: I felt as though I'd been punched. Too late again. "Well . . . congratulations."

As my eyes adjusted to the darkness, I saw that Jayan was standing nearby. Behind her were a couple of frightened-looking priest-warriors. "Hello, Jayan," I said. She took a step toward me, then paused.

The Devil soldiers had followed me in. Now they slipped past Maia and me and wrapped up the priest-warriors. I think they were a bit rough about it. I gathered up Jayan and Maia and moved them to one side. Jayan was weeping, too. "Don't be sad," I told her stupidly. "It's all over." She didn't seem to hear me. Then I said, "Just tell me where I can find Gus."

Maia raised her head and wiped her eyes. I realized that she wasn't relieved at all: she was as furious as a human can be. "Linn took him," she said.

Something happened to me then. Until now I'd either been reacting to events or trying to get ahead of the game, with varying degrees of failure. But it was a way of thinking that I understood, that I'd experienced before. Even the "assault" on Rec-Five had been akin to playing soldier back in Wisconsin, or night maneuvers in summer ROTC.

About the time that Maia told me that Linn had Gus, I stopped being Rick Walsh. What I *became*, I don't know.

I remember putting the Colt to the head of the nearest priest-warrior and telling him he was going to lead me to Linn.

I remember following this poor son of a bitch down, down, down into the dragon's lair, through tunnels hewn out of rock so long ago that the mold on the walls had hardened and calcified. The air itself was thick, sickening, perhaps never breathed and almost unbreathable. The light came from flickering torches that probably used that same rancid air for fuel.

I didn't question my guide. It didn't occur to me that he would lead me astray. Maybe I had chanced upon some tone of voice or phrasing—some Dominion—that won me his total obedience, I don't know.

After a while—time had ceased to be of any importance—we emerged into a subterranean chamber the size of a gymnasium. Or so it seemed. It was really too dark to tell. I think I lost my guide at that point. He simply slumped against the wall, eyes wide, and I walked past him. I remember looking back and seeing that he was gone.

I walked forward into the chamber, which, in the dimness, seemed to grow and grow, until I saw that it was full of shapes that breathed and stank of fire and shit. Shapes that shuffled heavy feet and flapped enormous wings. I stumbled on a chain that lay—loose—in my path. Each link was two feet across. But I don't remember being afraid . . . not of the dragons, anyway.

"Linn!"

There was no echo. The air was so full of particulate matter that it effectively absorbed sound.

"I want my son!"

The dragon closest to me raised a lid, exposing a bloodshot eye the size of a hubcap. It mesmerized me for a moment until, behind me, Linn said, "Don't get too close. He hasn't eaten this morning. And don't turn around."

I heard some nearby shuffling . . . and Gus, catching his breath as he wound up for a good cry. "I want my son, Linn."

"That's going to be difficult. He's kind of important, as you may have gathered."

"He's a *baby*—"

"He's the Prince. He's the Griffon's Heir. Never forget that. And *don't* turn around."

He'd caught me trying to move. "Look," I said, "I don't really know a lot about what's been going on here, but it seems to me that you're in trouble. Why make it worse?"

"As you said . . . you really *don't* know what's been going on here. You'd be smart to go back where you came from."

"I don't think so." I wanted to turn as much as I've wanted to do anything in my life. But I could hear Gus crying softly behind me, and I was afraid of what Linn would do to him. "I didn't ask to get involved in this mess, but I can't just walk away."

"You didn't *ask* to get involved?" Linn said with sudden energy. "You idiot. This whole situation is *your fault!*"

"What's that supposed to mean?"

"You *got* involved, friend, the moment you thrust yourself into Maia's life. We were watching her every move. That's why we were *in* your world. And it was only when we looked into your background that we came in contact with people who wanted to sell us arms." He was almost laughing, he was so pleased with himself. "We got the whole *idea* from you!"

From *me*? *My* responsibility . . . ? "Bullshit, Linn. My background didn't tell you anything you couldn't have learned from a newspaper. You were looking for an excuse to overthrow the Griffon—"

"No, no, no. We wanted some way to *preserve* His power. And we found it. Weapons from your world to replace prayer [knowledge]. We had found the means to create a postscientific [postmagical] society. And everything was working fine . . . until Maia became pregnant. Suddenly, you see, there was an Heir. It changed *everything.*"

Then he was quiet for a moment. I realized he was talking to himself . . . chanting . . . in a language I didn't recognize. I started to turn; he kept chanting. Finally I was facing him.

He was sitting atop a dragon. Even in the relative darkness I could see that in his arms was Gus.

I began to wonder just what kind of monster Linn was. Could he possibly have a family of his own? Children? Did he love anything at all?

The hell of it is, he probably did.

"This is a very complex prayer," he said suddenly. "I can pause between stanzas, but I *don't* want to start over."

I took a tentative step toward him, wondering, irrationally, what Gus was thinking about all this. "Why don't you give me the baby? Then you can have all the privacy you want."

He ignored me and started to chant again. I took another step.

Other things were starting to happen. I could hear grinding sounds from above and around me. The cave grew lighter. And the dragons began to stir. I could see that there were more of them than I had thought—at least a dozen. One pair shuffled toward an opening at the end of the chamber.

I fired a round from the Colt.

Gus started crying. But I didn't know any other way to get Linn's attention. "That was stupid," he said. "You have no idea how dangerous it is to start over when you're so close to the end."

"Give me the baby!"

"I need him."

Suddenly Linn's dragon reared and opened its eyes. With Gus under one arm, Linn held his place with little apparent effort. I had to back away.

Linn chanted again, loudly, though now his voice was hoarse and ragged. His dragon turned toward the opening and began to shuffle away. I had ceased to concern him. But I still had the Colt in my hands. I cocked it again, aiming this time at the dragon's head. And fired.

I got him in the left eye.

The scream was frightening. The beast reared and belched flame, then began to toss its head from side to side. But it kept moving toward the doorway. I dived at its side.

Its flesh was like leather and had more folds and wattles than a bloodhound's. I dug in and began to climb toward the spine.

It was no worse than standing on the deck of a pitching

boat. I took a couple of steps toward the saddle where Linn and Gus rode, fell on my face, then got up and took more steps.

We were almost at the door. In front of us was a ledge from which the other dragons were launching themselves into the air.

Linn's shouting came to an end, and he turned to me, eyes shining triumphantly. "It's finished."

The dragon was surging beneath me. A few steps more and we'd be airborne—

Linn's breathing was ragged. His face flushed. He looked like a man about to explode.

"I want my son."

"Take him. I'm through."

And though I wasn't more than three feet from him, he threw Gus toward me. I dived and caught him, and began to slide off the dragon.

There was roaring all around us. The dragon was flapping its wings. I tried to hold on. To Gus, to the dragon. Made it halfway.

I landed on my back and shoulder on the cold, hard rock of the dragon's perch. I managed to cradle Gus so that he landed on me. At least, I think so. I wasn't too coherent for a few moments. Not only was I in pain, but my vision was dominated by the black underside of Linn's dragon as it launched itself over the abyss.

The dragon roared and spewed heat, then circled above us and flew off.

I sat up and beheld my son.

I guess rock breaks scissors.

Gus was dead.

23

Somehow, someway, I was able to carry Gus's body back to the entrance to the dragons' lair. With each step I alternated between utter fury and terminal despair. Maia, Jayan, Dorana—no one heard me approach; their backs were to me as they watched the dragons rising into the sky. Jayan was the first to notice, and she knew from the look on my face what was wrong.

Maia was next. "What is it?" she said. All I could do was shake my head. She screamed. Jayan and one of the priest-warriors grabbed her.

All I wanted to do was sit down. I wouldn't let go of Gus. I mean, he was still warm.

"This is bad. This is very bad," Dorana was saying. "The dragons are loose." Apparently we were all in danger, but I wasn't sure why. There was a lot of confusion. It was clear that sooner or later I would have to move. I just couldn't be convinced of the necessity, now or ever.

Finally Jayan sat down next to me. "You did your best,"

she said quietly. She placed her hand on Gus's forehead, brushing back one of the wispy curls. "He goes beyond the sky."

"It should have been me." All I could picture was a door closing forever.

"What happened?"

I told her that I'd come face-to-face with Linn, that he spoke some major prayer which set free the dragons and killed Gus.

"Then he was lost to you the moment Linn took him," she said. "He must have wanted Gus to give him the strength for a death prayer." When I stared at her like an idiot, she went on: "A prayer of such power that its recoil results in the death of the one who speaks it. Linn must have hoped he could channel it through Gus without killing himself."

"But why Gus?"

"He not only had Griffon's blood, but once he was legitimized, he had the Griffon's power. Only a Griffon has the power to control a death prayer of such magnitude."

I struggled to stand up. "We have to go," I said.

"Yes, but—"

"*Now,*" I said. "I have to see the Griffon."

The walk back to the building on the quad seemed to take days. It was like running in a dream. The faster I tried to go, the slower I went. I lost track of my surroundings. I remember staring at Maia, who was walking next to me, unable to take her eyes off poor Gus, and wondering, "Who the hell is this woman?"

I was even having trouble distinguishing between the Devil soldiers and their ostensible prisoners, Linn's priest-warriors and Stenn, too. All of them acted equally dazed, glancing up at the midmorning sky with disbelief, as if awaiting the return of the dragons.

The first to greet us was Baht, who stepped forward before he saw what I was carrying. Words must have died in his throat, because he said nothing as I approached. "Where is the Griffon?" I said.

On his face was a mixture of horror and ultimate fatigue. "In the room where you left him."

I turned to Maia and Jayan. "Wait here." To Stenn I said, "You're coming with me."

He probably thought I was going to kill him. It crossed my mind.

As we hurried down the hall, I said, "What will Linn and the dragons do?"

"They'll destroy our land many times over, if that's possible."

"I'm sorry. Can anything be done to stop it?"

He just shook his head.

"So you're just going to stand there until you die."

"I've already done it once."

"That's what we need to talk about."

A few moments later we were at the Griffon's quarters. "What are you going to do?" Stenn asked.

"Just watch." I shoved the door open with my foot, then closed it, leaving Stenn outside.

The Griffon was seated in the straight-backed chair looking out the window. He seemed to be expecting me—or someone equally disturbed.

I placed Gus's body on the bed.

"I bring you your great-grandson . . . Father."

He made several signs, then slid off the chair and knelt down next to the bed. For a moment He was neither a senile tyrant nor an all-knowing God—just a grieving man.

"This is the first time I've seen him," He said.

"Then you're not really seeing him, are you?" I was as angry as I ever hope to be, and long past hiding it.

"But I suppose a Griffon is used to killing children. It's just part of the job."

"Yes. I suppose I do kill them. I certainly feel their deaths. But I also feel their births, their entire lives. You can't have one without the other, you know."

"Have you ever tried?"

"I expect you know the answer to that."

"You said that for everything holy there is something unholy. Sing a *life* prayer for your grandson."

He sighed with visible weariness. I suppose He was the one person who could accurately be said to have had the weight of a world on His shoulders. "And you should know the reasons why . . . I . . . cannot."

"I don't know much of anything right now."

He let His hand rest on Gus. "I am the Griffon because I can imagine this world. I know its true names. I know its possibilities. If I were to speak the life prayer under these circumstances, I would go beyond the sky. I would no longer be a part of this world, and there would be no one *left* to imagine it."

"Yes, there is," I said. "Right here." And I pointed at Gus. "Imagine this child alive. Give *him* your true names and possibilities."

"There are risks," the Griffon said.

"To you? You're going to die someday, Father. So am I. Can you imagine a better way than giving life to a child?"

I don't know why I said what I did. It's not as though I was a debate champion. I could never pick up women with a few good lines. I'm a lousy salesman.

"The risk is not to me," He said, so tiredly and quietly that I thought I'd lost the battle.

But, no. For once in my life, I had been able to convince someone to do something just by using words. This time *something happened*. The Griffon started to chant— no, He started to *sing*. It was a prayer as gentle and lovely as Linn's had been loud and ugly. Not only did I feel better just hearing His voice, I think the Griffon did, too. Only at the end did His voice break. Then He bent down and kissed Gus on the forehead.

And Gus took a breath. Through my own tears, all I could see was the color returning to his face.

I looked up . . . and where there had been an old man there was a lion with an eagle's head. Its eyes were full of pain, the worst pain imaginable, yet it radiated strength. It breathed once.

I glanced at Gus. When I looked up again, the Griffon was gone.

The most beautiful sound in two worlds is that of a baby crying.

For several selfishly precious moments, I sat on the bed and held Gus, feeling his warmth, his breath, his squirming and almost insubstantial heft. He was upset, too, and understandably so: he had just been born a second time.

Maia was waiting alone inside the front door to the Nest. When she saw me coming down the hall with Gus . . . and heard him . . . she threw herself at us, hitting me so hard I thumped my head on the wall. We remained a blubbering, weeping three-headed creature for some time. As she took Gus from me, Maia managed to ask about the Griffon. I told her that He had gone beyond the sky. She nodded as if she'd known it all along.

I realized that, outside, people were shouting. "What's happening?" I asked. Had this been going on for some time? Maia just shook her head; she was totally absorbed in Gus. So I went to the door.

A dozen people, including Jayan, Dorana, and Stenn, were standing with their backs toward me. They were looking to the east and pointing. I stepped up behind them and took Jayan by the arm. "Gus is alive—" I said, and didn't get a chance to finish the sentence. She ran to find him.

I looked up, like the others. The sky was the color of autumn leaves, a churning burnt orange smeared from due east almost to due north and at least thirty degrees above the horizon. "What the hell is that? The dragons?"

"Yes," Dorana said. "Hundreds of them. Far more than anyone thought. They must have been locked away for centuries, asleep. Now they're everywhere."

"It's more than that," Stenn said, shaking his head. "Linn released the dragons. This is something far worse . . ."

I was about to ask just what could be worse than a squadron of dragons when the mountainside in front of us flared as quickly as a match striking. The air was suddenly hot and full of ash. My eyes stung. Blinking to clear them, I saw the by-now-familiar winged shape of a dragon . . . aflame, falling toward and disappearing behind another mountain.

There was a moment of blessed relief when a wind came up suddenly.

My moment of relief quickly turned to horror. *There was no wind in this place!* Yet here it came, from the west . . . gentle, sporadic gusts that got more intense.

Is this how the wind begins?

I squinted straight up at the sun . . . and saw that the ring clouds were dispersing, stretching into jet streamers. It was like one of those time-lapse weather movies cranked up to an uncomfortable speed. The tequila sunrise had now been stirred clear across the sky, from east to west. I tried to make some sense of this. A huge firestorm—we'd studied the aftermath of nuclear strikes—would suck vast quantities of air into its heart. That could explain the gusts of wind: even though the nuclear-wind models assumed point explosions and mushroom clouds, large-scale instantaneous burning would have the same effect.

But it wouldn't reach the jet stream. And it would die down quickly.

Yet, all around us, the newborn wind began to howl.

I think we were all transfixed by these sights. At first no one tried to run; we only reacted, like passengers in a falling airliner, or cattle awaiting the stockyard hammer.

Then I saw that Maia, Gus, and Jayan had come out of the building. Having lost them so many times before, I forced myself against the wind and reached them just as the roof came off the building.

It missed us and it missed Stenn, but it slammed into Dorana and Baht and one or two of the priest-warriors. Pieces of it, and them, sailed off into the sky.

We hugged the ground, the five of us, while all around us buildings flew apart, exploding from the radical changes in pressure, as they would in a tornado. The difference was, a tornado would blow over in seconds, certainly minutes, while this storm gave no sign it would ever be over.

I rolled over on my back and looked up. It may have been my imagination, it may not have been: the sun was expanding and receding at the same time.

"We've got to get out of here!" I shouted to Maia and Jayan. I didn't wait for an answer or argument. I dragged them up and herded them, as best I could, toward the wreckage of the headquarters building. A corner was still standing and we huddled behind it.

"We've got to find a membrane!" I told Maia.

"I don't know where to find one here—"

"I do," Stenn shouted. He was still clinging to us, in a way. Well, he was Maia's husband. "This way!"

I reminded myself that membranes were more like fault lines than weak points. We shouldn't have to reach the exact spot to get through to another world . . . just some other place on the line.

Assuming, of course, that the growing apocalypse hadn't changed all that.

* * *

We managed to edge around the shattered building and into a ravine of sorts, in which we received shelter from the constant blast of the wind in exchange for bombardment by small rocks and some not so small. All we could do was go and stop, go and stop.

Every few steps I would say the prayer Maia had taught me, *"Arsenic railway liquid dominate apollo—"* to no effect. But we kept going.

Jayan struggled to keep up. It wasn't age; we were all equally battered and slow. She kept looking at the growing chaos around her with what I took to be a perverse pride. *"He* did this," she said once.

"The Griffon?"

"When He reimagined Gus, He also imagined a world without Linn."

"This looks like excessive force to me."

"Linn is fighting it, of course. And for each death spell there is recoil."

I was pretty sick of this whole prayer business by now. "I'm glad I live in a world without Gods."

For the first time I saw Jayan smile. "Are you *absolutely* sure of that?"

We lost the protection of the ravine and emerged into what once had been woods but was now a collection of broken trunks and branches. Maia took up the prayer. Since we could no longer make forward progress against the wind, we began to zigzag, hoping that we'd luck into a membrane.

But we didn't. Nothing was happening. We were feeling earthquakes every few seconds now. The whole place seemed about to blow, and we were going to blow with it.

I had my arm around Maia, and suddenly I knew that I had to save her, that we had to be together. "I love you," I said. "And I mean it."

She looked at me and, as if it were the most natural thing in the world, said, "I love you, too."

I think the mountain behind us was starting to move. The ground rumbled as if a subway were passing beneath us. We prayed in unison as we stumbled forward, clutching Gus. Stenn was two steps ahead. Jayan lagged behind.

". . . *Assonance light tree mare!*"

The sky was completely burned by now. And where the wind had once been hot, it was now cold . . . damp. Maybe that's what happens when a world starts to turn. Things turn upside down and inside out. It scared the hell out of me. At this point even a TV weatherman with his $1.98 satellite photographs would have told you the same thing: get out.

We paused for breath behind a tangle of fallen trees. Stenn raised his head and squinted over them. "We're almost there!" he shouted.

"The prayer's not working!" I said.

He didn't hesitate. "I'll make it work."

And he clawed his way over the trees. I saw him scramble down the other side and stop. He got to his knees. With the roar of the wind I couldn't hear his words, but he was clearly shouting the prayer.

It wasn't enough. Nothing happened.

Then Stenn did a brave thing. He stood up in that wind, which lifted him off the ground and carried him toward me. He shouted the prayer as he flew overhead, disappearing in the storm of dust.

The membrane opened above us, a calm hole in the air out of which a shadow spilled. "Go!" I shouted, lifting Maia and Gus. Maia turned, reaching for Jayan, but I said, "Don't look back!"

And they vanished.

Shielding my eyes—it had suddenly gotten very bright behind us—I reached for Jayan. But she was gone. Just like that.

I stepped up—

—Thunder exploded around me. I had the awful sensation I was crawling out of a well-lit hole into darkness—

—And then, strangely, I was on my knees in a pasture, in the shade of a big juniper tree. I could reach out and touch Maia and Gus. All of us caught our breath as we stared at a pair of massive, smelly creatures before us. Herefords.

Overhead there were contrails. You could hear the sounds of eighteen-wheelers on the highway. We were home.

We walked toward the sunrise, a gentle morning breeze in our faces.

24

If I'd had time to worry about it, I would have been concerned that one of these "transitions" between worlds would land me inside someone's refrigerator, or worse, in the middle of a mountain. When I said as much to Maia, as we carried Gus across that field, being sure to keep out of the way of the cattle, she told me that a membrane couldn't exist near a mass more substantial than air or water. Like the seed thrown on barren ground, it wouldn't grow.

I wasn't just being chatty and ignorant (though I was a *little* curious), I was trying to take Maia's mind off Jayan and Stenn and everything else that had happened. I needn't have worried. All she wanted to do was find some milk for Gus.

Well, we were surrounded by milk in its natural container, I suppose, but I was willing to bet that a full-grown human would be uncomfortably hungry before I figured out how to convince one of these animals to relinquish some. Better yet, unless the point-to-point geographical correspondence between Tucson and Dreamland had been seriously altered, we had to be close to the city proper. So we decided to walk.

I think we managed to get a hundred yards before we came to a fence and a fairly major street. Not far away was a 7-Eleven. Before we reached that we passed a sign telling us that our cow pasture was the Roger Road Experimental Farm of the University of Arizona's Agricultural Research Department.

In the 7-Eleven I came close to causing an unpleasant scene when I reached for my wallet (like an American Express card, I no longer leave my home world without it) and exposed the Colt. Fortunately the clerk—a heavy, bearded guy wearing what used to be called hippie glasses—figured I wasn't likely to bring a woman and infant along when robbing a convenience store. Nor would I be wearing a battered Air Force uniform and name tag. "Sorry," I said. "I should have left that outside."

"It's cool," he said. "I need a jolt of pure adrenaline about this time of the morning."

I had some cash, so we were able to buy a baby bottle and formula and diapers as well as some coffee and donuts. Gus had fallen asleep on the walk, thank God, but he was awake now . . . and not happy. I didn't know when he'd been fed last—and considering what he'd been through, I don't suppose it made much difference.

But you can't just give a baby an unsterilized bottle— even one who's been brought back to life. The clerk helped us out by pouring some water in a plastic pan along with the nipple, and zapping the whole thing in the microwave for a couple of minutes. It was one of those kids-don't-try-this-at-home deals, but it worked.

Somewhat refreshed, we hiked a couple of hundred yards to Campbell Avenue, where we caught a southbound bus to Broadway, about four blocks from Maia's apartment.

We put Gus to bed and while Maia cleaned up and changed, I called Hazel, who insisted on coming over immediately. I didn't dissuade her. I wasn't really worried about anyone else from Dreamland making a visit to the apartment—I couldn't imagine there was *anyone* alive in Dreamland any more—but I didn't want to leave them alone.

Maia was about to collapse. I unfolded the hideaway bed for her and told her Hazel was coming to stay. I think she managed to nod once before falling asleep. Then I went into the bathroom. About halfway through the shower the realization that it was Wednesday, a couple of days after Labor Day, nine days after my arrival from Guam, took hold. If the doorbell hadn't rung, I might have stayed in the shower all day.

Hazel brought her Bible with her. "This is my recreational reading of late," she whispered, "and it's all your fault."

"Bless you."

She shook her finger at me, but she seemed pleased that I was alive.

"Oh," I said, "I almost forgot." I gave her Roelke's Colt. "I only used two bullets."

Hazel frowned. "Rick, you didn't . . . shoot someone."

"No." Well, not unless the dragon counted. I supposed it would have gone better if I'd had a sword, like Conan the Barbarian, but sharp objects make me nervous.

Before I left, I tiptoed into Gus's room and kissed him, for luck. For me.

Hazel let me take her car, which, under the circumstances, was an incredibly brave move. It saved me untold hours of waiting in the hot sun for another ride on Tucson's misnamed rapid-transit system.

I realized I was taking a chance on going back to D-M, but it was either that or become a fugitive from justice. The Air Force technically owned me and would until the day they said they didn't. Besides, I didn't *think* I'd been recognized at Alamo. Even if they found the car, it was registered to Maia; there was no reason to link it with me.

Ming was on duty at Base Ops. By now I was certain that the man never slept, which probably explained his lack of charm. "Good morning, Sergeant," I said.

"We've missed you around here, Lieutenant," he said with unmistakable glee. I had to admit, he was a master: his words were always neutral at worst. You can't court-martial someone for *tone*.

"Thought I'd make a token appearance. You know, a little morale builder for the troops. Captain Alquist around?"

"Not at the moment."

"Thank you, Sergeant."

I drove out to the trailer at AMARC. Steeling myself, I plunged through the door. My worries were premature: there was no one around. So I sat down at my desk, and there was the damned Air Force letter—still unmailed. And today was September 3, the last day it could be mailed.

Did I want to leave the Air Force? It wasn't just a question of what I was going to do with the rest of my life—I had to think about Maia and Gus now, too.

I was still staring at the letter when Alquist finally walked in. He was with another officer, a black lieutenant I didn't know. They were talking about the Phoenix Cardinals—hardly secure, compartmented information—but they broke off when they saw me. "I'll see you later, Scott," Alquist told the lieutenant, who quickly disappeared. To me he said, "Rick, did I do something especially awful to you?"

I knew I deserved some of what was about to land on me, if not exactly all of it. "Nice to see you, too."

"I know I said things were slow around here, but that wasn't your cue to disappear for a fucking week." Shaking his head, he sat down at his desk. "You're on the AWOL list, you know."

Either Alquist really *didn't* know about Dreamland and the weapons traffic, or he was a better actor than several of our former Presidents. "So what do I do?" I said carefully.

"Depends on what your story is." He looked up from his paperwork and gave me a sickly smile. "I realize this is a faint hope, but you aren't going to claim you had a legitimate reason for taking off like that, are you?"

"I guess not," I said. What the hell, let him think I'd spent the week in a whorehouse in Nogales.

"Okay, then. Your girlfriend was missing—use that. People always respond to a tale of personal tragedy." He threw some papers in an Out basket and stood up. "If you're lucky, they'll dock you and toss a minor reprimand in the file. If you're exceptionally lucky, it won't percolate up the chain of command until you're in L.A. By that time they might decide not to waste the airfare it would take to bring you back . . . unless, of course, you fuck up again."

"This was sort of a once-in-a-lifetime event."

"Good." Now, having given me the RAF response, he changed gears and became good old Greg Alquist again. "What really happened to her?"

What *really* happened to all of us? That was the question of the week. "All I should say is that it involved a certain Special Task Group and a holiday outing up at Alamo."

Alquist's face flushed and he damn near stumbled over a chair. "You're kidding."

"Have it your way."

I thought I was going to lose him. I've never seen anyone more surprised. But he was resilient. Finally he said, "Shit, nobody tells me anything any more." He went back to his desk and dug up some forms, which he sorted. Finding the right one, he jammed it in his typewriter. "As your temporary superior, I'm telling the C.O.—his eyes only—that you *weren't* AWOL this past week, you were on a secret special assignment."

"Thanks."

He snorted. " 'Thanks.' Just promise me that someday you'll tell me who's working for who."

"That reminds me," I said.

"What now?"

"I need to check in with STG one last time."

He was only too happy to have me out of there. "By all means, Lieutenant."

"Your problem, Walsh—one of your problems—is that you keep looking for white hats and black hats, and there aren't any. The good guys aren't all good, and even the bad guys aren't completely bad."

Sanchez and I were having patty melts with fries in the Big Boy next to the STG office. He hadn't wanted to talk in there; the phones were ringing louder than a Wall of Voodoo concert and people were running around like someone was giving out free money.

I was tempted to correct this analysis of my "problem"—Sanchez hadn't met Linn—but I stuck to the point. We'd been talking for half an hour as I told Sanchez as much as I could about what had happened, and, frankly, I was getting tired. Finally I'd asked whether Alquist was a good guy or a bad guy.

"Okay," I said, "then tell me how *gray* he was."

"Light gray." He grabbed the check and stood up. As he paid at the register, he said, "He thought he was getting a chance to play James Bond or something. Spy games with no congressional committee sitting on his back. And he just got in over his head."

We walked back to the brace shop. "I was trying to run him as an agent-in-place. You know, 'keep doing what you're supposed to be doing with the missile tests, but let me know what's going on.' He did a pretty good job."

"What happens to him?"

"I haven't decided yet." He looked as tired as I felt. "The Colombians I turn over to Immigration, and they do whatever they do with guys like that. The two from the Twilight Zone disappeared last night. This is not the sort of case I can take to court." I could understand that: most of the evidence and witnesses were in another world and most of the systems involved were classified.

The moment we were back in the headquarters, people began to assault Sanchez with phone message. He motioned me to the chair in front of his desk while he attended to the most urgent.

While I waited I took my Air Force TDY letter out of my pocket and read it again. Whether I was testing myself or what, I don't know, but I signed it on the "accept" line . . . then shoved it back in the pocket. I still wasn't committed; I could always throw it away.

When Sanchez returned a few minutes later, he said, "I want to show you something." He made me come around his desk. Spread out before us were dossiers—missing persons reports—many of them with new yellow Post-its on them. He picked one up. "Laurie Steiner, strange disappearance number one, twelve years ago. Tucson P.D. found her out on Oracle Road last night—unharmed, twelve years older, and unable to say where she'd been.

"In the last twenty-four hours I got three others back, too. Isn't that amazing? And I wouldn't be surprised if *all* of them don't show up, by and by."

I'd asked the Griffon to imagine Gus alive, but He'd obviously gone beyond that. He'd reimagined all of

Dreamland to the point where it became something else entirely. Maybe that included "returning" those who had been "taken." "I hope so."

He closed up the files and sat down, happy. "What do *you* think I should do with Alquist?"

"You mean, after the Air Force transfers him to North Dakota because he lost a test article?" I said. "What he needs is to be sat on. He's probably salvageable."

"Could you do it?"

"What, be his keeper?" Maia, Gus, *and* Alquist? Ten days ago I was responsible for only myself. "You know, I could. But that's just talk; no one's going to send him to L.A. with me."

"That could be arranged."

"Get serious."

"Watch." He picked up the phone and dialed a long-distance number. Into the phone he said, "This is Sanchez at STG-4 in Tucson . . . Who's our point of contact at the Pentagon?" He listened for a moment, writing down a name and number. "Thanks," he said, hanging up and dialing again.

It took about two minutes, but when Sanchez hung up, it was quite clear that within a few weeks, Captain Alquist would be serving *with* Captain Walsh at Space Systems Division, Los Angeles.

But was Captain Walsh going to be there?

"I've got to go," I said.

Sanchez grabbed my hand. "Go with God, man."

There was a mailbox on the corner. I took out the TDY envelope and dropped it in.

Oh yeah: first I said a little prayer.

25

On the news later that day there was a brief story about a fire that broke out on remote Mount Baboquivari. It was astronomers at nearby Kitt Peak who saw the smoke and complained about its effect on their seeing.

Mountain fires are not unheard-of in this region, but when they're not started by arsonists or careless campers (unlikely, given the rugged terrain and extreme isolation of the peak), they're usually started by lightning. With the end of the monsoon season in the past week, meteorologists at the National Weather Service were unable to explain the origin of the fire, which burned several thousand acres.

The different theories provided amusement during a slow news week. Spontaneous combustion was a favorite. An astronomer even speculated that a small meteorite had done the trick.

But I think some horror bled through from Dreamland. I wonder—if I went out there today and explored those slopes, would I find the carcass of a dragon?

* * *

Anyway, Kate, maybe this will help you understand how your brother went from being a carefree bachelor to being married to a widow whose child he had fathered. (Yes, we got married; Alquist and Hazel stood up for us.) All in the space of nine days last September.

Maia and I are getting along well. We have moments, of course. But she's gone back to her part-time schoolwork and part-time job at the library while I finish mine. We made a deal with Hazel to take care of Gus a couple of hours a day, but the rest of the time we handle things. Soon we'll be relocating to California, a process both of us anticipate with equal parts fascination and dread.

Yet, no matter how aggravated we are by the strains of being adults, being parents—Gus has a cold; Gus won't eat; you know all about it—we try to think of his every day as a gift that has been given to us. Whether we deserved it or not.

Someday, of course, we'll have to deal with the question of his origin. We'll have to tell him, whether he believes us or not. Maia and I are sure that the wavicles are gone and that it is no longer possible to walk between the worlds. So what's left of Dreamland is what Maia and I remember. Dorana, Baht, and the Devil soldiers. The palace of Chios. The Griffon's Nest. Stenn, who turned out to be a brave man.

And Jayan, of course. Maia misses her more than she will ever say.

I'm hardly an expert on it, of course: I only got a biopsy of the place. It truly exists, now, only in Maia's memory. She is the Heiress in all ways.

She does sing Gus some pretty Dreamland lullabies. She calls them sleeping prayers, and I'll teach them to you when Molly has a baby brother or sister.

Does he have powers? Is Gus the Griffon's Heir? I don't think so, but it really doesn't matter.

I'm going to enjoy watching him grow up.

FANTASY BESTSELLERS
FROM TOR